CAROL SMITH

Twilight Hour

SPHERE

First published in Great Britain in 2008 by Sphere
This paperback edition published in 2008 by Sphere

A CIP catalogue record for this book is available from the British Library.

ISBN 978-0-7515-4065-9

Typeset in Berkeley Book by Palimpsest Book Production Limited,
Grangemouth, Stirlingshire
Printed and bound in Great Britain by Clays Ltd, St Ives plc

Papers used by Sphere are natural, renewable and recyclable
products made from wood grown in sustainable forests and certified
in accordance with the rules of the Forest Stewardship Council.

Sphere
An imprint of
Little, Brown Book Group
100 Victoria Embankment
London EC4Y 0DY

An Hachette Livre UK Company
www.hachettelivre.co.uk

www.littlebrown.co.uk

Twilight Hour

Prologue

Gale-force winds swept over the moor, buffeting trees and sending the wildlife scurrying into shelter. All was quiet in the village square. The shops were closed and the rain sluiced down, pooling itself on the cobblestones, making walking a hazard. Windows were shuttered against the storm and only the foolhardy ventured outside. The pubs were closed due to lack of custom, the locals knowing when best to stay at home.

Above a small thatched cottage just off the main street the smoke rose merrily from the chimney, dodging the raindrops as though they did not exist. With its thick cob walls and ancient beams it had survived for four hundred years. In the fireplace glowed a wood-burning stove; the room was warm and inviting. A small group was gathered by candle-light, their attention focused upon one woman, middle-aged and of no great distinction, half-reclined on the settee. Though soberly dressed, she exuded power which, despite the odd pallor of her skin, made it appear that she glowed from within, keeping them hypnotised. Her eyes were closed and her breathing sporadic; now and again she emitted a sigh. Between restless fingers she clutched an ivory fan.

A deeper sigh.

'Is there anyone there?' the hostess asked. They all strained to hear. Outside the weather grew steadily worse; casements groaned and the letterbox rattled but no one in this warm cocoon even noticed. Each had come pursuing enlightenment.

'I have lost my fan.' From the medium's throat issued a voice so girlish and light it was hard to comprehend that she could be faking. The entire assembly leaned forward, totally rapt.

'I must have dropped it on the way down.' A note of gaiety entered the voice; a young girl full of the sparkle of youth, tipsy with happiness. 'He danced with me.' She was clearly thrilled. 'He said I had beautiful eyes.'

Silence then as if she were contemplating.

'And then what?' The hostess could scarcely breathe; this was more than her wildest hopes.

'Lady Cunard said they must leave so they did.'

'Where are you, dear?' asked the hostess gently.

'Also what year?' hissed an onlooker, male.

The hostess, finger to lips, shook her head. This was no time for interruptions.

'Here in the manor, of course,' said the voice, with a flirtatious giggle.

'And the occasion?'

'My birthday,' she said. 'Also my coming-out ball, which was why he came. Now they have all gone back to Castle Drogo.'

Recognition; a local name. Appropriate for a prince of the blood. Their concentration grew more intense; even the drowsers snapped awake and one complacent woman laid down her knitting.

A lengthy pause then a sharp exclamation. Something unexpected was happening now. An edge of slight concern had entered her voice.

'I smell smoke,' she said. 'I am not sure where from.'

Sweat now appeared on the medium's brow. She tried to rise but they held her down.

'The fire,' said the man excitedly. 'The manor burnt down in the 1930s.'

The hostess shook her head, demanding silence.

The nervous fingers clutching the fan contracted now in acute alarm. 'I can hear the crackle of flames,' she said. 'There is smoke coming under the door.'

The medium fought but they still held her down. 'Help her, please.' It was painful to watch. What had started off as a bit of a lark verged now on the distasteful.

'Don't worry.' The hostess calmed them all. 'It's happening only in the past. We can't stop now when we are so close to a breakthrough.'

'There are flames.' The medium's voice was shrill. 'And the door is jammed. I cannot get out. Won't somebody help me, please? Or else I shall die!'

Now she was screaming and clutching her throat. The fan slid unnoticed to the floor as her fingers twisted in a horrible spasm.

'Enough!' said the vicar from the shadows where he had stood unseen till now, having entered quietly after the seance began. He pushed his way to the front of the group, making the sign of the cross in the air. The medium's mouth was agape and foaming with spittle.

'I have warned you before.' His face was grave. 'You are dealing with things you do not understand.' It was years since he'd stopped their meetings in the church hall.

'Where am I?' the medium asked feebly now, chalk-white and visibly shaking. The hostess stroked her hand and helped her to rise.

'You are safe,' she said. 'I will fetch you tea.' The vicar made his excuses and left. They had argued over such things before. He did not find it amusing.

The hostess offered drinks all round and was raising the poker to jiggle the stove when a mighty thunderclap overhead rattled the plates on the dresser. At which point the door to the street burst open suddenly.

Petrified, everyone froze on the spot. Did someone just leave or did they come in? All eyes turned to the medium.

Who had fainted.

Summer

1

Aroused from sleep by the sound of guns, Erin rolled from the bed in a reflex action that was already practically second nature. How fast she had become the prey with one ear cocked for impending danger. Her heart went into overdrive until she identified the sound. A summer storm. From between the slats of the wooden blind that concealed the window she could see bright flashes of quivering light from the moor. She slowly released her pent-up breath and raised the blind for a better look. The trees were gusting at furious speed but the rain was now slacking off. She checked the time. It was barely six but she knew she would not drop off again. Too much had happened in too short a time; she was battling to stay calm. It was early June and the night was warm. She went downstairs to make coffee.

Endecott Park. She was on her own. From what she had glimpsed a few hours before as they bundled her furtively into the house, not a single light showed in the complex. Nor were there any cars outside though she'd had little time for a proper look since it was deemed essential she not be seen. The short sharp briefing had been to the point: rigid rules for this enforced exile. She must not lose sight of the fact that her life was in danger. They had smuggled her here in the dead of night to conceal her whereabouts from potential assassins. To her it seemed like overreaction; left to herself, she would not have complied. But the order had come from the very top and could not be countermanded. Not even Rod, her immediate boss, could intervene at this level. As he'd explained in that final meeting, it wasn't only her neck on the line. Because of her journalistic brilliance they were all of them now under threat.

It made little sense when she thought it through. What difference could a single voice make against the vastness of a superpower? But orders were she must go to ground; for no other reason was she here. Abruptly removed from her normal life, she'd been forced to lie to those closest to her about why she was suddenly going away and where to. Something velvety nudged her knee. Perseus, her Burmese cat, was sharing her exile with her. She stooped and gathered him into her arms, breathing into his caramel fur.

'I guess it's just the two of us now,' she said.

*   *   *

In the living room she pulled back the drapes and unlocked the terrace doors. Dawn was breaking; the sky was a luminous pink. It looked like it would be a glorious day. She savoured the purity of the air and was especially struck by the deathly silence. Outside was a flag-stoned patio with a wooden table and matching chairs, topped by a sun umbrella. Whoever had fixed up the house had not stinted on detail. Though to Erin the country could never be home; her real home was the Clerkenwell Road, with the sounds of all-night traffic to reassure her. This territory was quite new to her. Beyond the hedge was a gravelled path and wide stone steps leading down to a croquet lawn. Further on was a verdant thicket of trees, through which she saw flashes of light on water. She should dress before she investigated further.

By the time she had showered and made her bed and unpacked the couple of bags she had brought, the sun had risen above the trees, framed by the backdrop of Dartmoor. She leaned on the windowsill, drinking it in. There was no denying the visual impact. Farmland as far as the eye could see, beyond that the endless moor. Rural England was new to her. She had grown up in Dublin then travelled abroad. Her work had led her all over the world, most recently to the Baltic States and Russia. The Clerkenwell loft was a new acquisition, evidence that she was doing well.

She strongly resented the powers from above who had caused her to make this unscheduled move, hating to think she might be perceived as a coward. Freedom of speech was paramount, the only reason for doing this job at all.

Wearing a T-shirt and nothing else, Erin began by exploring the house which was set on three floors and was airy and light although narrow. Sunlight slanted across wood floorboards. The walls were painted anonymous white. A pleasing space; she could not complain though wondered how long she would be here. Notebook in hand, she made a list. She needed to do a major shop; soap, detergent and cleaning things, coffee, cat food and booze. Faced with it now, it was hard to believe how unprepared she had been.

Erin O'Leary, thirty-six, Campaigning Journalist of the Year, reduced to being a refugee simply through having the courage of her convictions. From what she could see from the map they had left she was quite a few miles from the nearest shops and, worst of all, without wheels. She still hadn't quite got her head round that: the police blockade on the short drive home and the stunning pronouncement that she was over the limit. It made no sense. She liked a drink but, in all her years as a journalist, had never before risked breaking the rules that could affect her career.

A single glass in a Wapping bar with a man whose face remained cloaked in shadow had led to the breakthrough and accolades that had landed her in this mess. That man was now dead. It had happened so fast that not even she had made the connection though upstairs they had and taken immediate action. Her job was suspended indefinitely until they decreed it safe to resume. Too many high-profile journalists had already died for this cause. She was on full pay and the weather was good; she closed her mind to the thought of winter here.

It was time to get going. She had that long walk and serious foraging still to do. She put on jeans, a clean white T-shirt and a pair of comfortable trainers. Outside a van had appeared in the drive and a shorts-clad woman was hosing it down. They swapped a brief passing greeting as Erin set forth.

'She's arrived,' said Jenny, rinsing her sponge and then, in response to his lifted eyebrow, 'her next door.' He was such a pig, forever stuffing his face.

'How does she seem?' He rinsed his plate. She had to admit that he was well trained.

'Hard to tell. Looks pleasant enough. Too nice, I would guess, to be in this mess. Our sort of age with a friendly smile. Fit. She was off for a walk.'

'As well she might. What else should she do? No

point moping around indoors.' He glanced at the clock. 'I must be off too. Don't know when, or if, I'll be back tonight.'

Jenny sighed. She was used to this. Sometimes she went with him just for the ride but today's instructions had grounded her here which was why she was cleaning the van.

'Are you taking the car?'

'I am,' he said. 'I wouldn't dream of interrupting your work.'

The new luxury complex came equipped with individual lock-up garages in addition to a spacious carport. Though they rarely bothered to garage the van, his brand-new Audi was something else. He shot upstairs to shower and shave and came down looking every inch a doctor. Sober suit and a clean white shirt. He had even polished his shoes.

Jenny laughed. 'I'm impressed,' she said. 'You could almost pass as the real McCoy.' She stood in the doorway and watched him drive away. Then she stripped the beds and collected towels; she needed something to fill her time and loved the fragrance of washing dried outside. But first, before she embarked on the chores, she double-checked where she'd put the gun. She had to keep it close at all times. She never knew when she might need it.

*   *   *

The electronic gates were controlled by a zapper which Erin could not figure out how to use. So instead she leapt over the wall, which was not very high. At this point the road was twisty and narrow with high thick hedges on either side that blocked the view and made walking a serious hazard. Unlike town where the traffic flow was controlled by speed cameras and lights, here on Dartmoor it seemed to be anything goes. She knew to face the oncoming traffic and always cross when approaching a bend. All the same, it was pretty hair-raising stuff. But the air was fresh and the sun rode high; she relished the feel of it on her skin. White clouds scudded across the sky like a yacht race. There was open farmland on either side with Castle Drogo perched high on a hill. This Lutyens marvel had been much praised, sometime she'd pay it a visit. Pretty soon she reached the river and paused for a while on a humpback bridge. Despite all she had been through, she still remained calm.

It was almost like being on holiday; she was being paid but had nothing to do. In time she might even start enjoying herself. There were hikers and people walking their dogs through a grassy meadow studded with flowers. Beyond that, woods with trees hanging low over water. She'd have liked to have lingered but hadn't the time. Food and other essentials came first. So on she tramped and, after a while, a right-hand turn signposted the village, still three miles away. How could that be? With a squeal of brakes, a car pulled up and the female driver beckoned her to get in.

'This road is a deathtrap,' she scolded her. 'I am on my way to the village and can drop you.'

The car was an ancient Morris hatchback with a couple of spaniels in the back. The passenger seat and floor were piled high with books.

'Sorry about the mess,' said the driver. 'But I run the library part-time. We don't have the funds any more to pay for a pro.' The eyes behind the lenses were shrewd and not without a flicker of humour. Elfrieda Willcox, she introduced herself. She had lived in the village most of her life, apart from a longish period abroad before taking early retirement. Erin was suddenly at a loss, not quite certain what to say. She didn't want to give too much away nor snub this obliging stranger. She was here on holiday, she explained, a spontaneous break in a house she'd been lent. A new development further back; perhaps Miss Willcox knew it.

Indeed she did. 'The old manor,' she said, with an interest more than just plain good manners. 'I am told they have totally wrecked the place. Before the fire it was quite a historical gem.'

Erin's attention was instantly caught; her nose for news was inherited. All she'd been told about her new digs was that the place was brand new. They had reached the square and were pulling up. Miss Willcox stopped to allow her out.

'The library's over there,' she said. 'Drop in any time you are passing.'

'I certainly will.' Erin beamed and waved.

Just as Miss Willcox was driving away, she stuck her head out of the window and said, 'Remind me sometime to tell you about the fire. And poor Violet's death.'

Erin's first requirement was a sturdy bag in which to carry her purchases home. Being without any transport was a bind. Facing her was an old-fashioned store which, judging from the clutter outside, would seem to sell most things. She wandered in. It was musty and dark, a warren of passages bristling with stuff, every conceivable thing and more than she was ever likely to need. The man directed her through to the back where she found a whole room just of hiking gear including a canvas knapsack, exactly the thing. On impulse she also bought a waxed jacket; she had no idea how long she was likely to be here.

The village was old and picturesque, nestling into the curve of a very steep hill. The buildings were granite, some of them thatched, dating right back to the stannary days when the community thrived from the mining of tin. In the central square was a market house, divided into separate stalls. Erin bought cheese and olive oil and bread still warm from the oven. She ordered wine, which the shop obligingly said they would deliver. The rest would keep; the knapsack was full and she still had to lug it home.

It was already noon. She would stop for lunch before facing up to that walk again though this time she would avoid the road and find her way back through the fields.

The Three Crowns pub was across from the church and dated back to the late Middle Ages, with mullioned windows and an impressive porch. There were tubs of flowering plants outside, perhaps to lighten the granite facade. It would not have been Erin's first choice but she needed to sit.

The dim interior was heavily beamed with polished brass and a massive grate stacked to the rafters with logs. Erin plonked her knapsack down and went to the bar for a glass of wine. A cluster of ancient men were discussing the weather. She looked around and her eye was caught by a striking portrait over the bar that dominated the room with its powerful presence. A moist-lipped girl with a challenging stare and the hint of a breaking smile on her face inclined herself slightly towards the painter, revealing her décolletage.

Black bobbed hair framed an oval face with eyes of a luminous sapphire blue, emphasised by the deeper shade of velvet draped over her chair. In one hand she held an ivory fan. She looked on the brink of divulging a piece of ripe gossip.

Mesmerised, Erin stared back at her, caught by the mockery in those eyes. It was hard to disengage, she was almost alive. The barman came over with crisps and nuts and saw the direction of her gaze.

'Violet Endecott,' he said. 'Commissioned in honour of her eighteenth birthday.'

Endecott. The same name as the park. Erin sensed there might be a story here. 'She certainly looks a handful,' she said. 'I assume she lived in the manor.'

'That she did and she died there too. On the night of her coming-out ball. The Endecotts owned half the county in those days.'

'What's the story?' There must be one. The painting was clearly by an expert hand. She wondered why it was here in the local pub.

They were making noises at the bar. 'Too long to go into now,' he said. 'Come back another time when the place is less busy.'

Before setting out on the long walk home, Erin went over to look at the church. Granite again but cosy inside, it was perched on the crest of the hill with the sweep of Dartmoor behind it as a backdrop. Even today, in the summer heat, a stiff breeze rustled the leaves of the trees; the aged gravestones were all aslant after centuries of bad weather. Many were grouped within family plots, sharing a handful of local names. Her curiosity now aroused, Erin went in search of the Endecotts. There must be a monument for them, surely, because of their local prominence. But, try as she might, she could find no trace of the name. She circuited the graveyard twice and, all of a sudden, there it was, set apart from the other graves, a simple moss-covered slab.

Violet Elizabeth Endecott 1917–1935

Not even 'Rest in Peace', poor soul. Neglected and forgotten.

It seemed so sad. Erin turned away then, impulsively, went back for another look. Far from neglected, the grave was neat, the weeds pulled out and the grass well trimmed. On top of it lay a posy of violets, tied with a velvet ribbon.

2

He laughed when she told him about the ghost. She was growing dottier by the second. Her problem was she had too much time on her hands.

Sylvia, neat in her seersucker robe, paused in the process of warming the pot. 'It is well known in the village,' she said, 'that the house that stood on this site burnt down with the loss of many lives. Some time in the thirties.'

Gerald Brennan merely snorted and retreated into the *Telegraph*. He had heard it all before, it was local hokum. The mysterious figure, occasionally glimpsed on a moonlit night walking through the grounds. In the churchyard, too, at the dead of night, tending an uncared-for grave. This was Dartmoor, such stories were rife. The headless horseman and the hairy hands. It took someone as out of touch as his wife to believe them.

It ought to have worked like magic, he thought, as

he stood in the bathroom lathering his chin. The dream they had shared for the past twenty years of ending their days in the country. His problem was it was premature: he was no way near ready to settle down. Retirement went with advancing years but he was still well under sixty. This country pace was too slow for him; he was already mindlessly bored. He scraped off the stubble and slapped on cologne. Greying, maybe, but he still had his hair, almost as thick as when he was still in his prime. Which was how he felt. The piercing eyes that glared back at him from the shaving mirror vigorously rejected his current position.

The Larches they'd named it because of the trees that blocked the view from the patio doors but formed a formal centrepiece Sylvia liked. She had found a sign-painter near at hand who had etched the name tastefully on to old wood to give it an authentic rustic look. These houses were all identical. Theirs was number seven.

She had loved it when they first moved in, the real-isation of a dream. Not the thatched cottage she might have preferred but simpler to keep clean. She also liked the security of living behind electronic gates in the grounds of a former manor house with strong historic connections. People of note had lived here once, there was evidence in the church records. Endecott Park had a certain ring when she spelled it out to delivery men. She liked to pretend all eighteen acres were theirs.

The reality left much to be desired. She still had her doubts about some of the neighbours and not all the houses were occupied yet, according to Swann Homes. Dreams she had nurtured of upping a grade, of swapping suburbia for Country Life had, sadly, not yet materialised though Gerald urged her to be patient. They had still only been here less than a year; the summer season was only just underway.

It was all very well for him to talk. He had his golf and his drinking pals and still found reasons for regular jaunts up to town. Whereas she was stuck, knowing no one at all, in a village she found sadly lacking.

For a start, there was only one hairdresser, Annie's Place in the village square, where you had to book in advance for an appointment. No dropping in on a bad hair day or when sunlight revealed that your roots were showing. You went when they had a slot and were suitably grateful. Since Annie did practically everyone's hair, she heard all the gossip and spread it around. A session in her salon was like *The Archers* but nobody cared; there was coffee and tea and half the village came in at a time, many just to keep up with the scurrilous chatter. From that vantage point they could watch the square and see all the comings and goings below. They could also see when the Okehampton bus arrived and who got off it.

It was Annie who mentioned the Endecott Ghost on hearing where Sylvia lived. She claimed to have glimpsed it herself one wintry night. 'She was wearing a hooded evening cloak so I can't be certain it was a she, though they say it is poor dead Violet, unable to settle. She walks to the river from Endecott Park – the site, of course, of her family home – then up the hill to the graveyard where she is buried.'

Sylvia shivered. She had to be kidding. No one had mentioned a Ghost when they sold them the house.

'That's what they say. Though it's hard to tell, she's not exactly what I would call chatty. Just hurries past with averted face as though hoping not to be recognised. I suppose she would have a lot of explaining to do.'

Gerald might scoff but Sylvia was shocked. The last thing she needed was something like this, the nights here were dark enough, even in summer. She suspected Annie was sending her up. As soon as she could she left, aware of their laughter. As she stood outside, unlocking her car, she heard the babble of voices raised as at some hilarious joke. She hated it here, they were all so cliquey. Even after a year she didn't fit in.

There was also nowhere that sold decent clothes, another of Sylvia's regular moans, nothing resembling a trendy or stylish boutique. Only dreary fifties-style shops, filled with polyester shirtwaisters and knitwear patterned with sheep. The village remained in a permanent time warp where colours like mustard and rust were the rage and outdoor clothing was fleece-based and weatherproofed. She would just have to pop up to London, she said, an excellent chance to catch up with old friends and absent herself for a while from this horrible place. But Gerald, for once, put down his foot. She had more clothes than she could possibly need but if she was after something new, why not try her hand at making it herself?

She was aghast but he stuck his ground. Their circumstances had changed, he said. He was now retired; they would have to tighten their belts. But he had his cronies while she had none, the main root of her current malaise. In almost a year she had not made a single new friend.

Sylvia was idly preparing lunch. Gerald was out though she didn't know where. He hadn't even bothered to say goodbye. It irked her when he behaved like that; all she had heard was the front door close and the sound of his car moving off. The least he might do was let her know in case there was something she needed brought in. The village was fifteen minutes away, more by the time she had found a parking space.

A cookery book was propped up before her. She was trying a Gordon Ramsay dish. She had the kitchen TV switched to Philip and Fern.

From where she stood, crushing honeycombs, she had a clear view of the empty drive and the central mound that was topped with trees that blocked the view of the road. They had viewed the house first at an early stage when mechanical diggers were still in full swing and the land that had once been a famous old ruin was raw and looked like a war zone. She had not been keen; it had looked too small, not at all what she had been used to in Kent. A wide remove from her fantasy cottage, smack in the middle of a building site. Gerald, however, had been impressed; it was good value for the asking price and if they stuck down a deposit today, they would have their pick of the houses. For once he had over-ruled her qualms and made up his mind on the spot.

'Where do I sign?' he asked the effusive salesman.

Sylvia had problems with the layout. It was semi-basement so the kitchen was dark. The ground rose steeply outside the front door with a flight of stone steps leading up to the drive. All she would see from the sink would be cars and the garages facing the houses.

'If we knocked down that wall,' she had said, 'we could turn it into a family room.' The rear of the house had a splendid view and led straight on to the terrace. She liked the idea of a large open space for when the family came to stay. She would be able to join in the chat, not stuck away in the kitchen like a skivvy. The house in Kent had been built that way with the garden surrounding the whole ground floor but Gerald, who rarely set foot in the kitchen, had other things on his mind. He seemed strangely anxious to sell up fast and move to the country without delay. They had lived there since they'd come up in the world twenty-five years ago. And Gerald was still only fifty-seven, well short of retirement age.

'What's the hurry?' she tried to ask before they set off on this expedition but he was setting the satnav and didn't reply. He was always the same. When the mood took hold he would go at things like a bull at a gate. It was what she had always admired in him: his unswerving determination. This, however, was too important to be resolved without careful thought. It was her life, too, she wanted to say but knew he would never listen. She had gazed despondently at the kitchen, trying to gauge its storage space. With the units still in their boxes, that wasn't easy.

Gerald prevailed as he usually did. They left the site with a verbal promise that they would be the proud owners of number seven. Now all he need do was sell The Firs which, with property prices still on the rise, could be considered a fait accompli. The two men shook hands on the deal.

And that was how it had come about. Within a few weeks they were all packed up and by the beginning of August had taken possession. There wasn't room for all their stuff. Some larger pieces had had to go but, by sifting out, they had compromised and now it was, more or less, perfect. Sylvia liked it, apart from the kitchen, and was even coming to terms with that. Gerald had other things on his mind though she'd no idea what they were.

His car was back. She watched him get out, swiftly checking herself in the glass. One stringent rule with which she'd grown up was never to lower her standards. Even in this new country life she only rarely wore trousers and never jeans. She slid the chocolate mousse into the fridge and hung her apron back on the hook. Gerald was still a handsome man. She tried to keep an eye on him all the time.

The new, young woman at number five was lugging a backpack towards her door. As she stood there, fumbling with her key, Gerald stepped forward to lend a hand.

'Let me take that.' His affable charm was automatic when it came to the fairer sex. The stranger, whose age Sylvia couldn't deduce, smiled up at him and pushed back her hair. Now he moved out of his wife's line of vision; to keep on watching she would have to crane. Furiously gnashing her teeth, she switched off the TV.

*　　*　　*

Gerald, whose day had not been good, perked up when he saw Erin. She was slim and fit, wearing trainers and jeans, a look he especially liked. She had sandyish hair, tied back in a bunch, and a cheerful smile with excellent teeth. He judged her to be in her early thirties and noticed she wore no ring.

'Lord, that's heavy. Did you carry that?'

'All the way from the village,' she said, relieved to have made it home. There had been moments along the way when she hadn't been sure she would get there. This time she'd totally bypassed the road by following the footpath along the river, a peaceful stroll through woods and a field full of cows. She had climbed a stile that led into a lane and passed the door of a friendly pub, resisting the urge to stop for another drink. From there she had walked down a private track and through the farm that abutted their land. Now she stood, triumphant though tired, smiling up at the genial neighbour who was valiantly hefting her bag through her open front door. She wondered whether to ask him in, he was peering past her with interest, but was still too cautious to mingle much with people she didn't yet know. He certainly didn't look much of a threat with his friendly smile and greying hair but until she knew more about him, she had better not chance it.

'I am Erin,' she told him with outstretched hand. 'Probably here for a month or two.'

'Gerald Brennan.' His grip was firm. 'Welcome to Endecott Park.'

Sylvia was waiting inside the door, the familiar edginess etched on her face. Gerald sighed.

'What was that all about?' she asked.

'I simply gave her a hand,' he said, sick of her endless interrogation. Back in Kent she'd had other preoccupations. Petty snobbery, scoring points: the jealousies that made up female friendship, at least where Sylvia was concerned.

'You are late,' she said as he followed her in. 'I wasn't sure you'd be home for lunch.' The kitchen table was laid for two. She had poured herself a sherry.

'You shouldn't have waited.' Gerald was terse. She watched him like a neurotic hawk. He regretted no longer having an office to go to.

He switched on the news to check the markets which still appeared to be volatile. Sylvia prattled and clattered about but, as always, he tuned her out. It was odd how, after so many years, how little in common they actually had. With the children gone and now his career, their life together had shrunk to a vacuum. These little lunches she magicked up were suited more to a bunch of women and barely served to satisfy his masculine appetite. Bread and cheese would have been enough, with perhaps a jacket potato

30

thrown in and a pint of beer instead of a thimble of sherry. But Sylvia cut out recipes and kept them filed in a little tin box. At home she had often met up with friends but here, so far, she had none.

'You ought to get out more,' Gerald said, one ear still cocked to the business news. Even retired, his heart remained in the City.

Sylvia sniffed. She had nowhere to go and nothing to do in this barren wasteland. The views were pretty but very quickly bored her. She could work the shops within half an hour and still come home empty-handed. There was virtually nothing here she was tempted to buy. At home she'd had regular coffee mornings to show off her home to like-minded friends but so far she had met no one here she would want inside her home.

Gerald suggested she join some group, which illustrated how little he knew. Bell ringing, yoga and salsa dancing were not her kind of thing. Nor did she want to learn to ride, though the thought of the hunt did have an appeal. She saw herself graciously serving grog when they rode triumphantly home.

It wasn't enough. She was unfulfilled. She missed her daughters and former friends. The new house, though perfect, was stifling her. She needed some kind of diversion.

3

Lisa, next door at number six, was outside on the patio, weeding. She wore neat clothes and gardening gloves and her hair tied back in a ponytail. They had only been in a week or so and were still busy fixing things up. It was mid-afternoon and very hot. She sat back on her heels to rest, removing one glove to scratch the itch on her nose. Ned had left on the dot of eight for the forty-minute drive to Newton Abbot. He wouldn't return, at the earliest, till six which gave her a lovely clear day. She had more than enough to keep herself occupied.

She knew her neighbour was snooping again, hovering behind her diaphanous drapes, unaware she could be so easily seen. She was always around, with her bleached blonde hair and ultra tan that was obviously fake, and seemed to consider herself a cut above them. Which was ludicrous; their house had a name and a ghastly water-feature thing plonked outside.

Otherwise Lisa loved it here, the first real home she had ever known. Till now she had managed in rented digs, moving around as she changed her job to different parts of the city. Her last address had been Finsbury Park where she had lived for seven grim years till circumstances had thrown her together with Ned whom she'd first met through work. His move to Devon had suited both well; after the shortest conceivable courtship they had come here as man and wife. Which was just in time – she'd be forty soon though was confident that she didn't look it. He was slightly older but they could have been twins which perhaps explained the attraction. Narcissism, she had heard it called when you were drawn to your mirror image. Ned was trim, about five foot nine with a small tight bum and expressive hands with cuticles that were always clean and well tended. He had straight dark hair which he wore brushed back, and silvery eyes behind rimless lenses. A nice-looking man with a sweet, though occasional, smile.

They had most of them fancied Ned at work but she was the one who had married him after a certain amount of strategic planning. There had been a gap. She had left the job to try her hand at different things then, quite by chance, had run into him just when she needed him most. She had been on her uppers and slightly scared, facing a very uncertain future having failed to find any job she really liked. She had tried her hand at all sorts of things: waitressing then working at a stationery shop. Later she'd been an artist's model and sold old plates off a stall in Camden Passage. She was short of cash and the rent was due, it was January and nippy. Both parents were dead; she had no one to whom she could turn.

Until there was Ned, on an underground train, as forlorn and undernourished as her, and she'd hailed him like a long-lost friend, unsure if he'd even remember. He hadn't at first when she'd leapt at him, bolder than her actual nature, but then it clicked, or so he said, and he'd taken her for a beer. From which point things had developed incredibly fast.

Lisa smiled as she shifted her trug and moved across to the opposite bed. Life could do that if you stayed alert and grabbed an opportunity when you saw it. Some might dither; Lisa had not. Things had changed drastically in Ned's life so there had not been any time for prevarication. It was she who had proposed to him. He had come into an inheritance and was thinking of moving out of town which was why she had dared be so bold. They were neither as young as they'd been, she said, and could hardly believe her luck when he didn't reject her.

So here they were now, happy as clams, married six weeks with a house of their own and bright new vistas, certainly for Lisa. They had stopped on a whim to view the house, on their way back to London from Newton Abbot where Ned had just accepted a job in the local town-planning department. He had been off work for a number of years, his health had deteriorated since Lisa last saw him. The diagnosis had been stress; he'd be wise to work away from the city with all its attendant pressures. And then they had seen the sign for the house, almost the last in a smart new complex, and Lisa had liked it so much she had urged him to buy it. She had no savings but he was in funds and, since they would shortly be man and wife, it had taken little persuasion to convince him. It was under an hour from his new place of work, on the edge of Dart-moor, a national park that was one of the most famed beauty spots in the country.

'We'd be mad not to take it,' she had said. It would put the clincher on their union. Then they had not even set a date. Now they would.

So here they were living in marital bliss and Lisa's horizons had brightened a lot. They had moved straight in and were doing it up by degrees. They had already acquired the essentials, Ned was generous about things like that. The fun part would come as they gradually bought the rest. She was happier now than she'd ever been. No one had ever loved her before. Her mother had died when she was four and her father had quickly remarried. Then he'd died too and she'd found herself on her own without a lifeline.

It was more than she'd ever thought possible, the house, the marriage, the man. Even without the other two, the house fulfilled her wildest dreams with its pristine walls and clean-cut lines, the staircase climbing to the room she shared with Ned at the top of the house. Having rented so many dingy flats, she gloried in the amount of space – three bedrooms, two ensuite, and a separate bathroom. Also a study that Ned had purloined where he kept his drawings and draughtsman's tools, which meant he could work at home on the days he couldn't face that long drive. Like her, he was neat which was just as well. They cohabited very serenely.

Since the marriage was new there was still much to learn about sharing space with a virtual stranger, being careful never to cross the line between intimacy and intrusion. Ned had previously lived with his mother who had died very suddenly some years back, during the period they had been out of touch. He had moved into a studio flat on the Edgware Road when they met again. His new prosperity was due to the sale of the family home.

'Why move at all?' Lisa wanted to know when she

saw how cramped his studio was. Just one main room with a sleeping annexe, devoid of character or charm.

'I had to go away for a while. Besides, there was far too much space for just me.' Not to mention the memories; he had lived there most of his life. So he, too, was now alone in the world till he happened, fortuitously, to bump into Lisa. He was forty-three, it was surely time that he thought about settling down.

Lisa had supervised the move though what they both brought was exceedingly sparse: clothes and books, few personal things. Neither was much of a hoarder. Ned had quite a collection of books so the first priority had to be shelves. They had slept on a mattress on the floor while they saved for a decent bed. Most of the money had gone on the house and, in any case, Lisa's needs were modest. She was content just to lie on the floor with the rhythmic breathing of someone beside her, for the first time she could remember no longer alone. But after a while she started to shop, from catalogues and cut-price stores, choosing each piece with the utmost care so as not to exceed their budget. Ned was impressed by what she achieved. She went for an understated look, neutral but with the occasional dash of colour.

'You could really do it professionally,' he told her with genuine admiration. An artist himself, he had very exacting standards.

Carol Smith

He was right. What she needed next was a job. She would take the time to look around and hope for inspiration. She was married now, the pressure was off. He could afford to keep her. She had chopped and changed for most of her life, trying her hand at all manner of things. Once she had wanted to be a dancer but her father had not allowed it. She must learn a trade and support herself; he had new children who now came first. Reluctantly she had learnt to type and worked in jobs that lacked the scope she needed to fulfil her true potential. Or so she believed, having always been very ambitious. At last she'd achieved one major goal by snaring herself a husband before she was forty.

The kitchen was dark but Lisa lit candles which brightened it when they sat down to eat. Her main ambition now was to learn to cook. She started off with simple things: lamb braised slowly with garlic and herbs; local rabbit, freshly shot, bought from the farm shop at Whiddon Down, marinated in wine. Ned seemed indifferent to food, ate without noticing what it was but Lisa determined to be a good wife and make her husband happy. They were still enjoying the honeymoon stage, were thoughtful and courteous towards each other. She always asked him to carve because he was the male. He brought home wine and occasionally flowers and Lisa smiled shyly when he raised a toast. Over meals they discussed what each had done during the day.

Which was not, in Lisa's case, very much though she never seemed to have time on her hands. She still had most of the house to fix up as well as the patio to weed. The house, when they bought it, came fully equipped with a fridge and appliances all built in. The washer/drier was rather slow so she started hanging her sheets outside as she saw her neighbours do. Here on the moor, where the air was so fresh, things dried quickly and smelled really clean when she brought them in, with a lovely fragrance of ozone.

Occasionally, when she was quietly weeding, crouched out of sight on her hands and knees, wild deer would emerge from the nearby woods and venture across the lawn to nibble the hedge. Thyme was the herb to keep them at bay, one of the gardeners told her that and accordingly planted it in tufts round the borders. Lisa, however, liked the deer. She stayed very still when they appeared. They moved in a group of mothers and fawns, with quivering nostrils and soulful eyes, ever on the alert for the slightest sound.

She heard the distant sound of shots which meant huntsmen must be loose on the moor though, thankfully, not allowed within these acres. She saw them occasionally on her walks, striding along with their guns and dogs, macho killers who didn't care, only here for the sport. Lisa, now face to face with it, found it distasteful.

A woman walked past with a dog on a lead, towards the path that led to the woods. Lisa had never seen her before: she must be another new neighbour. She was tall and classy and tastefully dressed, in contrast to the other woman next door. Also she appeared to be younger, closer to Lisa's own age.

4

Auriol Hammond strode grimly by, glad of the company of the dog which at least brought some kind of purpose to her newly restricted life. Stuck in this hellhole against her will, she would shrivel and die without a reason for regular exercise. She loathed the countryside, always had, until the aberration that had brought her here in the first place. Till then her life had been going well with everything she could possibly want, successful career combined with spectacular marriage.

She was tall and blonde and kept herself slim, looking much like the model she had once been before striking gold and becoming rich and successful. It was her idea to develop this land and convert it into her personal space, a place to which she could one day retire and live off her well-deserved earnings. For, despite the proverbial silver spoon, she had worked very hard for all she'd achieved and only missed out on more personal things because of her driving ambition. She had sunk her energies into a dream but fate had dealt her a very poor hand. Her world had crashed around her ears. She was trying to put it back together again.

At least this house was easy to run and she hadn't bothered to bring much with her. The dog had been only an afterthought, she hadn't known what else to do with him. The vet had offered to find him a home but not even she, when it came to the crunch, could do that. Jasper had been her husband's whim, a Labrador puppy with soulful eyes that had grown up into a beautiful, spirited dog. Now two years old, he had quietened a lot and even came to heel when she called his name.

He certainly brightened walks like this, streaking ahead when she let him go, pausing to sniff and cock his leg then trotting back to check she was still behind him. He was rather sweet and helped soften her heart which, goodness knows, had been bleak enough. She had never wanted a pet before, could not see the point. Kids were one thing; she had made that choice and even now, despite everything, didn't regret it. But nevertheless Jasper helped to fill the aching void in her heart.

He was waiting now where the path divided by the

big stone boulder that designated the boundary of their land. To the right was the fork to the Whiddon Down road which led, in its turn, to the motorway. To the left was the path running down through the woods to the farmland that bordered their acres.

'Here, boy!' she shouted and threw him a stick which he caught in his mouth in a neat arabesque, then growled and tossed it around like living prey. He took the edge off her bitterness and lightened her endless misery. At night he sometimes slept on the bed beside her. She turned to the left and he bounded ahead, stick gripped firmly between his jaws, long tongue lolling when he put it down, tail in motion like a conductor's baton. The rhododendrons were past their best but still provided a feast of colour. Beyond them was a clump of bamboo, a throwback to the manor's glory days.

The fire was local history. She had first seen the house in its derelict state and fallen in love with it on the spot, though she wasn't entirely sure why. It had been a ruin since before the war when the owners had suddenly fled abroad. No one knew what became of them, just that they'd never come back to reclaim what was theirs. And now it was hers or, at least, a slice of it. Burning fury ignited her when she thought again about what she had lost. She had to get a firm grip on herself in order not to dissolve.

Only the gatehouse had survived, an elegant struc-
ture of creamy stone with a mantle of wisteria over
the porch. That was the house she had coveted most
though at the time it was not for sale. Privately owned,
she had been told; nobody knew who by. Though
within the confines of Endecott Park, it was separate
from the building site and appeared to be in immaculate
condition. The owner never seemed to be there but
the lawns were mowed and the windows cleaned.
When she asked Swann Homes, who must surely
know, their response had been oblique to the point
of rudeness.

It angered her when they wouldn't play ball since
she had been the original instigator. Not only that
but she'd helped raise the finance; without her input
none of them would be here. Her gloom returned but
the dog was behaving in a slightly peculiar way which
diverted her from her constant brooding obsession.

She snapped her fingers to summon him. He had
backed off suddenly from the path and was now
hunkered down in the bushes, whimpering slightly. It
was not like him to show any fear. She called again
but he still didn't move. She hurried towards him; he
seemed to be petrified. His ears were flattened when
she stroked his head and his eyes rolled frantically,
showing their whites. His gaze was fixed on a sagging
gate, tied up with a piece of old rope. The gate led

into an unused field, beyond the bounds of their territory, overgrown and full of brambles, which seemed a terrible waste of grazing land. She had several times walked along this path and wondered why the field was not used. Even the hedge was overgrown so she couldn't see what lay beyond.

She grabbed Jasper's collar but he still wouldn't budge. She had never known him like this before. Something seemed to have scared him, she didn't know what. A badger, maybe; she had seen their sett and had heard that a male made a formidable foe, especially when guarding a litter of babies. She released the dog and he streaked away, back up the path they had just come down and lay there, whining, beside the stone that marked the exit to the road.

Baffled, Auriol approached the gate, curious to find out what the problem was. She peered through the hedge and scanned the field – no sign of a badger or anything else. Suddenly she was bored by the whole affair. If the dog was going to play silly beggars she would just as soon take him straight home again. They had stretched their legs and he'd emptied his bladder. She had better things to do with her time. Though, as she began retracing her steps, for the moment she couldn't remember what they might be.

*   *   *

She had trained him not to jump over the fence so, once they were home, she removed his lead and released him on to the patio to play, after which she fixed herself a drink. Her licensing hours were flexible, the more so since she had been here on her own. It was not yet eleven but Auriol's hand was already beginning to shake. Solitude was getting to her. She had spoken to virtually nobody in a week. She had a phone but no one who cared; they were all of them busy with their careers. People had been through worse than her and still restructured their lives. She was in her prime, not remotely old despite the way she had started to feel. She needed to get a grip on things and regain control of her future.

She stood in the doorway, sipping her drink and feasting her eyes on the marvellous view. That clump of larches formed a focal point against the stupendous backdrop. Tomorrow, if she were in the mood, she might pay a visit to Exeter and the art shop.

There had been a time in the distant past, before her world had fallen apart – in fact, before it even got going – that Auriol had shown quite an aptitude for painting. With her striking looks and glacial stare, she was cut out to be a catwalk queen but showing off clothes was too vacuous to keep her restless mind occupied for long. She had done it enough to have made her mark then used her social connections to rise. She had worked in a trendy gallery for a while. There she had mixed with the great and the good, among them the movers and shakers of the art world. One thing led to another, of course, and pretty soon she herself was daubing, finding it relaxing as well as fun. She had been encouraged by people who knew enough not to let her waste her time and had even enrolled in an evening class at the Chelsea College of Art.

But Auriol never stayed still for long and filthy lucre had beckoned to her. She was offered a job, which she quickly snapped up, with an upmarket letting agency in Sloane Street. The clientele was very well heeled, mainly derived from the States and the Gulf, and Auriol's queenly manner proved to be an additional asset. They liked it when she talked down to them, felt reassured about signing upfront and were, when it came to clinching a deal, like putty in her hands. The hours were long but the pay was good, especially on a commission basis. Soon she realised she'd found the niche she was designed for.

The art had to go but that was no loss. Sometime, when she was old perhaps, she could watch her grand-children play and do some sketching.

She lugged her packages from the car and spread them out on the living room floor. For one who had largely closed down on life, she'd gone mad in the art supplies shop. Sable brushes and cartridge paper, watercolours and primer. Just feeling the quality cheered her up and strengthened her in her resolve. She mixed herself a strong G and T, opened the doors and stepped outside. Jasper came thundering after her but her mind was on other things. She studied the view through half-closed eyes, figuring out the golden section. That was something she had retained from the coursework she'd done at Chelsea. The larches would be the emphasis of the glorious scenery of the moor, studded perhaps, as a quirky note, with a scattering of match-stick sheep. Auriol grinned; her mood was improving slightly.

Jasper whined and rolled on his back, threshing his legs but to no avail. He had had his outing for today, caged at the back of her car. Auriol pondered and sipped her gin. She felt her synapses tingle and spring back to life. Perhaps, after all, against the odds, she could resurrect something from the wreckage.

She unrolled the paper and flattened it out, weighting the corners with heavy books. Then she drained her glass and replenished it. No need to bother with lunch.

When she woke from a doze it was after four and the light had subtly altered again. She had lost the urge to immortalise the view. She poured more gin to steady her hand then fetched a shawl because she was cold. It might have helped if she'd eaten something but these days she couldn't be bothered. Food no longer held much appeal; she could go for days on occasional snacks. The dog had a healthy appetite but watching him eat made her queasy. He was whining again and pawing the door, gazing at her with reproachful eyes. The message he gave her she could not ignore; it was time for another walk.

Muttering and cursing she rose to her feet, steadying herself on the back of the chair, feeling the acid burn in her throat because her stomach was empty. The day was mellow; a great orange sun hung in the sky like a party balloon. The cows in the meadow were starting to moo because it was nearing their feed time.

'Damn,' said Auriol, lacing her shoes and wondering where she had left the lead. It was up and down all day with this blasted dog.

5

In the village they knew her as Crazy Betty, the woman who lived on her own in the woods and had done for longer than most of them could remember. She was bent now and gnarled like an ancient tree, with wild grey hair in a frizz round her head and washed-out eyes that had once been a vivid blue. She seemed entirely content with her lot as she sat by her Romany caravan, playing tunes from a bygone age on a battered old penny whistle. Her campsite there was very remote, her neighbours being the woodland wildlife with whom she shared her meagre existence.

She had two close allies in this retreat whose welfare now was her main concern – Satan and Lucifer – and who, like her, rarely emerged before nightfall. During daylight hours both went to ground in the densest part of the darkest wood but they always responded to Betty's distinctive call. Mostly she lived from hand to mouth, scraping a living however she could. Her needs were fulfilled by the bountiful moor: her larder as well as her refuge.

She knew how to set a trap for a hare, to tickle river trout under the stones, to comb the hedges for whortleberries and beechnuts. She could also milk a cow in a field without alerting the farmer's wife. The villagers had become used to her, less an oddity now than a treasured fixture. A group of them kept an eye on her health and found her light work when the temperatures dived and living outdoors on the moor became an ordeal. Effie Willcox had known her for years, the strange doolally creature who came from nowhere.

She was, though, sharper than credited for and knew those woods like the back of her hand having lived this way since her earliest years, an outcast whom nobody wanted. Few people knew who she actually was. Her closest friends were the animals, the only creatures she felt she could properly trust. She spent many hours in the heart of the wood, coaxing them gently with her songs until they drew near enough to allow her to pet them. Often Lucifer posted guard, strategically poised on the branch of a tree, huge eyes swivelling, constantly on the alert.

Once she'd had a French governess who had taught

her music and needlework and fancy manners to grace the best drawing rooms. But those times were long gone, a distant dream submerged beneath sediment in her raddled mind. She had spent her youth in the African sun which was where she acquired her affinity with nature. Unloved and unwanted, they let her run wild. Her crazy mutterings even now were spiked with a sprinkling of Swahili. These days the vicar and Effie Willcox conspired to help her grow old with grace but Betty's spirit was stubborn and wild. She would not accept she was failing.

As daylight faded and night drew in, so she would start her nocturnal walk, gliding silently through the trees with little more substance than a shadow. She might be confused but she knew beyond doubt that this was where she belonged by right. Nothing could drive her away, not even the builders.

After seventy years of wasteful neglect, the land on which the manor once stood had been vandalised by charlatans to make way for a brand-new terrace of jerry-built houses. They had come in force with their digging machines and cleared the site with unnatural haste, eradicating all trace of its historic past. This land had been farmed and, before that, mined as far back in time as the Bronze Age. The soil was soaked with her ancestors' blood as well as the sweat of their toil. Crazy Betty might not know much but she knew who she was and that they had stolen her birthright. All she lacked was proof that it was legally hers, which was one of the reasons she clung to Effie who was educated and very wise. She also knew without doubt that Effie could be trusted.

Once the builders were done, the new settlers moved in with their town-bred habits and vulgar ways. They used their patios as outdoor kitchens; she heard the clatter of grills and pans and smelled the pervasive barbecue smoke that began each evening's ritual throughout the summer. What did they know of the glorious past, these interlopers who had bought a cut-price dream? The insult to her ancestors angered her. Their voices betrayed that they weren't from these parts. They were louder, brasher: some nouveau riche. They lived crowded together like pigs in a sty, lowering the tone of the place.

She could hear their laughter and the sounds of them eating as she set off each night to patrol the estate. They rarely saw her, she was careful of that, but if they did they gave her no thought, just an old gypsy woman passing by. When the moon was full she came into her own and made a regular pilgrimage to the churchyard. She carried a basket of gardening tools and spent the night in a labour of love, taking care of the spiritual needs of the only soul with which she still had a connection.

*   *   *

Tonight the moon was huge and bright. It sailed through the trees like a stately ship, flooding the moor with light as clear as daylight. She slipped through the gate that was rarely used and followed the track till she reached the signpost where the two paths diverged. There she paused to assess the scene and make doubly sure that the coast was clear before taking the footpath along the river where she climbed the stile into the farmyard. The dogs approached but did not bark, just wagged their tails and licked her hand then followed her silently through to the road before slinking back to their kennels. Now Lucifer suddenly swooped from the trees, leading the way like a great white moth in the moonlight. He stayed with her almost as far as the bridge before arcing back to the woods again. He'd be watching for her return to escort her home. Satan was somewhere off on the moor, his life a constant enigma to her though she knew he was never too far away and rarely out of earshot.

She stood for a while on the narrow stone bridge where legend had it a battle was fought, the neighing of wounded horses heard to this day. It was peaceful now with no one about, in the country they go to bed early. The hill grew steadily harder to climb, especially so when her joints seized up. Dressed in rags and a battered felt hat, she looked like a walking refuse bin, a piece of old carpet swathed around her as a cape. At the top she paused to regain her breath and looked fondly back at the sleeping village that had, when she needed it most, provided shelter. She had travelled the world and come to rest here, where the bones of her ancestors lay. She had no intention of ever moving on.

Crab-like she made her way to the church, past the pepper-pot market house in the square around which the village was clustered. She passed the Three Crowns, its doors now shut, where Violet Endecott's portrait hung, challenging all with that bold confrontational stare. Somewhere nearby a cockerel crowed; the nights were shortening as the solstice approached. The lych-gate creaked but nobody heard. The sleepers here were all under the ground. The church stood silent with tendrils of mist like cotton wool round its steeple.

There was no time to waste. She had work to do before that dratted bird could crow again.

6

The first thing Erin did every day, having put on the coffee and fed the cat, was go upstairs and check her computer for emails. Nobody ever phoned her here; very few people knew where she was. Her story had been that her mother in Cork was ill. The fact that her mother did not exist had raised no comment from anyone. People were used to her not being there, it went with the territory. She had a mobile she rarely used, it was only in case of emergency, and the landline was forbidden in case it was tapped. Which left her with only email as her link to the outside world.

Rod, of course, knew where she was. Also Amy, her valiant PA, now holding the fort as she had for two years while Erin travelled the world as a roving reporter. They were aware how cut off she felt and how much she hated having to hide. She'd done nothing more than voice an opinion, the job she was paid to do. Rod, who once emailed her five times a day, had reduced it to a sporadic trickle. She knew he had only her safety at heart but that didn't make it any easier to take. And these days even the wonderful Amy also seemed very remote.

As exiles went, it might have been worse – especially as it was now the height of summer – but she hungered for the clamour and bustle of Wapping. Gossip was part of a journalist's life, the essence of what it was all about. She spent the main part of her time on the move, filing copy wherever she could, endeavouring always to keep a very low profile. But the cosy base to which she returned, and where her mind and her heart were now, was the small cramped cubicle overlooking the Thames near Tower Bridge. Devon was fine, the air was pure and the wildlife transported her back to her youth: butterflies she had forgotten about and buzzards with the wingspan of small gliders. What she mainly lacked was binoculars; she would search for some in the village store. Even the somnolent humming of bees transported her back to her childhood.

Erin's grandfather, Seamus O'Leary, had been a very distinguished man, a founding member of the IRA as well as a literary giant. These days his name was synonymous with some of the very greatest Irish writers. From her earliest years she sat on his knee and listened to how things had been in the days when he'd waged a personal war to win independence for his comrades. Later he'd modified his views but had never entirely disengaged from the dangerous machinations of Irish politics. He believed in, and had drummed into her, the power of truth and the defence of the weak. From him she had learnt her sense of fair play and any writing talent she had was doubtless due to him too. Though she'd never aspire to fill his shoes, she was carrying on in a similar vein and hoped that, were he alive today, he'd applaud the stand she was taking.

Having trained in Dublin as a journalist, she travelled widely in subsequent years, covering stories for RTE News that had thrust her into the limelight. Most recently she had specialised in what formerly had been the Soviet bloc which had led, through a series of fortunate breaks, to this job with the *Globe*. She loved the work; it was stimulating and stretched her resources to breaking point. She also enjoyed the element of danger that kept her on her toes.

In many ways she was due this break, having not had time off in a couple of years. Whenever she started making plans they sent her back to the front line. In that final meeting she'd had with Rod, a rushed half-hour in a backstreet pub, he'd expressly asked her not to write and publish under her name.

'We can't have your byline cropping up. Your distinctive style would be recognised. If you feel you can't not write, try fiction or confine it to a diary.'

'I'll write,' she insisted, 'and just not file my copy.' Journalists write, it is in their blood. It's like asking a songbird not to sing. At the very least, she might save things for her memoirs.

Rod was looking tired and strained. His skin was flaky and under one eye a nerve was visibly twitching. It was nine years now since they first hooked up and became, almost overnight, illicit lovers. She always had been attracted to older men. Rod was frustrated by being fast-tracked and thrust into the job at the top due to the paper's recent acquisition. He missed the risks that Erin took, the thrill of the battlefront. Circumstances divided them but kept their relationship fresh and very erotic.

Before she left they had sat her down and emphasised the basic rules. Whatever she did she must not risk her own or anyone else's life. The enemy they were fighting now was famed for its cold-blooded ruthlessness. No matter how cordial the entente, she must not take any chances.

She had no idea why they'd chosen this house except that it was supposedly safe and that she would be under twenty-four-hour surveillance.

'How will I recognise them?' she asked. This unnamed army defending her. In a gated community such as this they would surely be hard to hide.

'You won't,' she was told. 'For security reasons. But be assured they are there for you.'

'And if I should ever need them?'

'Ring this number.'

It all seemed absurdly cloak-and-dagger but the order had come from the very top. Not even Rod seemed to find it at all amusing.

'Where will they be?' Erin wanted to know.

'Closer than you might imagine.'

Jenny had not worked with Phil before. He was seconded from Special Branch whereas she was from the Tavistock force which made her more or less local. They had met a few times on the firing range where he had impressed her with his skills. You could feel secure with a man like that at your side. Though perhaps not so close; their living arrangements were taking some getting accustomed to. He was cleaning his gun on the kitchen table while she was attempting to iron. They were doing their utmost to adapt. The best thing was he could be very amusing.

'What's this about?' She cocked her head, hearing faint movements through the wall. The cat had been out on the terrace for some time.

'Something political, I believe. Not for the likes of us to know. Can't complain, though, about this cushy billet.'

'Provided it doesn't go on too long.' She missed her horse and the Tavistock crowd plus the regular Thursday night quiz in the local.

'You mean provided they knock her off fast,' said Phil, the counterfeit doctor, with a grin.

'Something like that.' She jerked out the plug and passed him an armful of ironed shirts. She disapproved of the helpless male but didn't mind doing her bit while the iron was hot. It was odd this, living together so close, though their sleeping arrangements were decorous. She had the whole of the top floor ensuite while he made do lower down with the guest room and bathroom.

At base they had asked if she fancied him which she'd batted off with a slightly feigned shudder. Not her type: she preferred them a little less rugged. But Phil was okay as such things went. So far they were rubbing along surprisingly well.

Erin tried reaching Amy by mobile but wasn't able to get a signal. Round here was very hilly, as she had been warned. Later she'd walk to the lower meadow, maybe she'd be more successful there. She felt rather fragile, badly in need of a hug. The thing with Rod had electrified her; a single encounter and she had been hooked. With his hooded eyes and world-weary air, she had found him entirely hypnotic. She'd been working in Dublin at the time, where he presented a popular politics programme. She was thrilled when invited to take part and had been such a hit he had asked her back to join the regular panel. Erin liked radio a lot, was volatile and articulate, kept up to date with current affairs and was always ready with an original opinion. Thus it became a weekly thing. They were very much on the same wavelength.

Rod's principal banner was saving the world and he put all his energy into the cause, doing his utmost to rattle his listeners' cages. Erin deflected his wilder extremes, reining him in when he went too far. Together they made a consummate team which led, inevitably, to an illicit affair. He was married; the best ones were, at least in her experience so far. But it wasn't an issue, not at the time. She was still only twenty-seven. She was free to travel and do as she liked. They met when they could and had brilliant sex and as he rose up the ladder, he took her with him. So when he was poached by the *Irish Times* and invited her to join him there, she hardly needed to give it a second thought.

Now she both missed and needed him. As well as her mentor, Rod was her closest friend. She could deal with the fact he might never be free but, not being able to talk to him was more than she could bear, the way she felt now.

Finally she got through to Amy, who answered sounding her usual bright self.

'Hi!' she screamed when she heard Erin's voice. Then, in a whisper, 'Are you quite sure this is safe?'

'Idiot,' said Erin. 'I'm on Dartmoor, you goose. Not in the Gaza Strip or war-torn Baghdad.' She was grinning already. She loved this girl who had worked at her side for the past two years, checking her mail and taking her calls. Without her she couldn't have coped. 'Just touching base. What's up?' Erin said. 'I'm sick of being a social pariah. I wish you'd come down and cheer me up. You're exactly the tonic I need.'

Amy laughed in her gurgling way. 'We miss you dreadfully too,' she said. 'I'd be down like a shot if there weren't so much going on.'

'What kind of thing?'

'Top secret,' said Amy. 'I don't think I ought to tell you over the phone.'

'Spoilsport.' At least she was doing her job. Amy had promise, was likely to go very far. Erin could picture her now at her desk, surrounded by cuttings and reference books, with those huge dark eyes and unruly curls that made her look more like a pop star.

Instead of what? She paused to consider. Instead of an Erin O'Leary in the making.

'Is Rod around? He never picks up.' She kept it casual but Amy knew, more than anyone on their floor, exactly how things were between them.

'Hang on a sec and I'll check,' she said, instantly putting Erin on hold. After a pause she came back to say he was out. She asked if Erin had heard the news; another Russian dissident had been murdered.

'Crikey, no. How awful,' said Erin, a prickle of fear running down her spine. She longed to be back there in Wapping instead of stuck here. 'What happened?' she asked but the details were vague. The press had been asked not to mention it yet though Rod was preparing a leader for the *Globe*.

'I am not quite certain.' Amy was cautious, as well she should be; top marks to her. 'I think it was a bullet this time. At close range.'

Less macabre than plutonium or whatever it was they had used last time but nasty all the same.

'Tell him I called,' was all she said. She would try to catch up with him later.

They were getting more dangerous by the second, these so-called friends of our government who were taking over London with their vast wealth. She longed to be able to cover the story but the veto had been very carefully spelled out. She must curb her terrible writing itch and think about something else.

She settled on the sofa to read and Perseus graciously moved beside her. Without his consoling presence, she might have gone mad. The night was bright; she could see the trees, bent almost in half by a slicing wind. Even in summer the moor made its presence felt. Somebody passed: she heard faint steps crunching along the gravel path. She tried to see who it was but they had gone.

In order to read, she switched on the lamp which obscured her view through the filmy drapes. Anyone looking in would see her but she could no longer see out. Perseus mewed; it was suppertime. He knew to the second when food was due. She laughed and went to fill his bowl and consider the state of the fridge.

Just vegetables and chicken breasts. She was growing bored with the local fare. Tonight it would be another stir-fry, at least it was something to do. She picked fresh herbs and chopped them up, then added garlic and heated the pan. At which point the lights went out and she was in darkness. She had no idea where the fuse box was, they hadn't bothered with details like that. Next door's van was parked outside. She made a rapid decision.

'Sorry to bother you,' Erin began, but number four was in darkness too.

'It happens all the time,' said the neighbour. 'Come in.'

She had candles burning and also a torch so could demonstrate how the fuse box worked. These houses were identical which was handy. The lights came on. Erin glanced around. Their house was even less furnished than hers. It looked as if they had only just moved in. All they had on the kitchen shelf were a couple of mugs and a jar of instant coffee.

The neighbour looked pleasant and roughly her age. Erin had only encountered her once before. She seemed faintly awkward although it wasn't clear why. A man came pounding down the stairs, dressed in a formal suit and wearing a tie.

'Oh,' he said, stopping dead in his tracks, for a moment stuck for something to say. It flashed through Erin's mind that they might not be legal.

'Your neighbour,' she said, extending her hand, used now to leaving things just at that. If they wanted to know more details, they would ask. He was a doctor in Exeter where Jenny, the wife, also worked, he explained. Instinctively Erin checked and she wore no ring. His handshake was unusually firm, perhaps he was a surgeon. Congenial enough; she thanked them both and accepted the offer of candles and matches. Tomorrow, she laughed as she bade them goodnight, she'd stock up on the essentials.

7

There she goes, thought Sylvia sourly, flaunting herself in those skinny jeans, displaying all she's got to whoever is out there. She had taken against the new neighbour on sight though couldn't have honestly justified why. She was younger, which might be it, and in greater shape, with reddish gold hair that owed nothing whatever to art. Added to which she was on her own which always rang instant alarm bells. Sylvia couldn't stand competition. She had glimpsed the look on her husband's face as he helped the fit new neighbour with her shopping. She stood at the window and watched her now, casually strolling across the lawn, without a care in the world. She wondered why she was here in the back of beyond.

She couldn't decide what to wear today. Lately she'd started putting on weight due to the hefty portions they served, usually garnished with chips.

She was taking too little exercise also, having had to forgo her pilates class. Country living would be her death; she relied too much on her car. Miserably she flicked through the closet rails, hating everything hanging there. Most of the time she saw only Gerald but still liked to look her best. In the end she slid into a shapeless smock, later she would change to something more fetching. She still had most of the day to make a decision. The truth was she found it lonely here with nothing but views of that bleak black moor.

Back home there had always been something going on. Apart from coffee, tennis and bridge, there was usually some sort of social event: a matinee or a leisurely lunch with friends. Sylvia didn't have intimates; they were rarely more than acquaintances selected on the basis of social cachet. They came and went as the seasons changed, largely depending on what their husbands did. Gerald worked for a merchant bank – private, she stressed, not just run of the mill – so standards of who they mixed with must be maintained. Her diary worked round her Christmas card list; she revised and shed and added names according to how the stock market rose and fell. This sudden uprooting had thrown her off-course. She realised glumly she'd have to start over again.

Her dream of a cosy shared retirement, at last

spending quality time together, still seemed very remote. Gerald grew more and more withdrawn. She guessed he was missing his business life even though it had been his decision to opt for early retirement. Now he was feverishly building new contacts. She wished he would tell about his plans, she could do for him what she did so well and organise social soirées. Entertaining was something she loved though here there was no readymade set. She still hadn't really got to know her neighbours.

Gerald was down in the Ring o'Bells, socialising for all he was worth, networking like a pro. This was the village's principal pub, friendlier than the other three, where he was hell-bent on joining the coterie. He splashed around what money he had on the basis of something he'd always known: no lunch, not even here, is ever free. He was the new kid on the block, trying to enter the status quo. He wanted to join their poker game and they were taking their time. But a round of whiskies could only ease his way.

What he sought was recognition and an entrée into their tight little clique. To join, however, he needed the right connections. The fact of having no work to do filled him with paralysing fear. He couldn't imagine a future without a job. Sylvia didn't know all the facts and he dreaded the day when she might find out. Early retirement had not been his choice but something they'd forced on him.

When *Neighbours* ended and he still wasn't back, Sylvia poured herself a drink and settled on the sofa to call her daughters. Francesca first, since she was the elder with two sturdy boys aged six and four, and afterwards Lucy, whose daughter was only nine months. The usual chaos prevailed in both homes so Sylvia kept things short and sweet. How were they all? Just checking in. Neither ever made her feel terribly welcome. She was always careful what she said since both were still very much their daddy's girls.

Daddy was fine, had been out all day. Was liking retirement very much though still had plenty of irons in the fire and was building up quite a local social life. Francesca didn't have time for this. The boys were scrapping, her mood was strained. She was disappointed her father was out, there was something she needed to ask him.

'Try me,' said Sylvia indulgently, sherry in hand and a smile on her face.

'We want to take them to Disneyland and wonder if Daddy can help.'

It was always something. Sylvia frowned. They treated Gerald like a money pit while both had husbands with supposedly good jobs.

'What sort of sum are we talking about?' She was hoping for a new car herself.

'By train from Ashford a thousand would possibly do it.'

'He *is* retired.' She did not approve. Kevin should raise the money himself. They had already spent a fortune on two weddings.

'But we're thinking about a house extension. The boys need more space to express themselves.' From the noise they were currently making, she did have a point.

'I'll ask him when he gets back,' Sylvia said. 'But don't rely on him saying yes. He's got quite a lot on his plate right now. I don't want him over-extending.'

'Mum, you live in the country now.' Francesca's voice had developed a whine. 'There can't be much down there worth spending it on.'

Lucy's problem was dental work. She needed crowns on her two front teeth. 'I'm not going near the NHS,' she said.

They didn't care about Sylvia at all. She was quite dejected when she hung up. All they cared about was the cash Gerald kept doling out. It was as well they had something put by as she liked to be able to spoil the kids. But neither daughter ever thought to ask her how she was.

* * *

A man sat silently in the corner, deep in a book in a small pool of light, a dog at his feet and a stout ash cane at his side. Country gentry: he looked the part. His tweeds, though old, were extremely well cut though also understated. The book he was reading was leather-bound and he wore pince-nez on his well-bred nose. He didn't look old though his hair was dusted with silver. The pub's proprietor, behind the bar, strolled over and had a few words with him. Gerald studied their pleasant exchange, soaking in every detail. Someone of note from his general bearing and the easy smile as he chatted away. After a while, he pocketed the book, clicked to the dog and bade the landlord goodnight.

'Who was that man?' Gerald asked when he paid, guilty when he realised the time and remembered Sylvia had been alone all day.

'Oh, that's the Commander,' the landlord said. 'He lives down here but is often away. A lovely bloke though he keeps very much to himself.'

'A naval commander?'

'I guess so,' he said. 'Though he can't have seen active service in quite a while.'

Gerald pondered as he drove home. His initial assumption was proving right. Down here there were very rich pickings to be had, provided he played his cards right.

*   *   *

The next time Gerald encountered him, the Commander came wandering up from the woods with a gun slung over his shoulder. Gerald was outside washing his car (observed by Sylvia from upstairs) and the two men had an exchange on the state of the weather.

'Do you live round here?' Gerald asked.

The Commander nodded towards the gatehouse then wandered on with a smile, leaving Gerald exultant. What an extraordinary piece of luck. For once the fates must be smiling on him.

'Who was that?' Sylvia wanted to know.

'A man I met in a pub.'

Already he was devising a plan, one that was bound to appeal to his wife. It was long overdue that they hosted a cocktail party.

'But who do we know down here?' she asked, delighted but at the same time scared. She hadn't yet got her contacts list up to scratch.

'The neighbours,' he said. A perfect excuse. That good-looking redhead two doors down would certainly be on the list. He'd been waiting for a chance to know her better.

Sylvia was torn. She had nothing to wear but this was what she had wanted for so long, a chance to make her mark on the local nobs. They would have it catered and do it in style. A Sunday lunchtime was probably best and the guests could mingle outside on the croquet lawn. Canapés, she scribbled a note, and maybe also a chocolate fountain. A barman hired from one of the pubs who knew how to mix a real cocktail. Correction: get one from Gidleigh Park, the swankiest hostelry in the locale, situated conveniently just down the road. Worth it, whatever the extra cost, if only for the prestige.

And if it should rain? Perhaps a marquee in which case she'd throw in a string quartet. She had been to a wedding where a quartet played and very nice it was too. Not as intrusive as a band, tasteful and more refined. Though where to find one in this neck of the woods was something she'd have to investigate. She had met a woman at a bring-and-buy sale who played the harp at private functions. If only she'd thought to take her telephone number.

Sylvia's musings were interrupted by Gerald enquiring when supper would be. He had some business to tidy up and would be sure to get back in time.

Unaware of his wife's cogitations, Gerald was making plans of his own. This was the perfect moment to pounce while the Commander was still on the scene, a chance to know him better without looking pushy. What he had in mind was a small affair, guests carefully picked from the Ring o'Bells, with a handful of affluent landowners subtly mixed in. He might also lure down a few London friends who owed him a favour or two, to add distinction. Thirty at most, the crème de la crème. Some of the neighbours, though carefully vetted; he didn't much fancy the thought of that couple in shorts. The tall blonde widow from number one, provided she left the hound at home, should also prove quite a talking point though he hadn't yet made her acquaintance. He had glimpsed her occasionally out for a walk. She always looked somewhat off-puttingly grim but it couldn't be denied that she was a real looker.

The bar was disappointingly empty, none of the regulars having yet shown. Gerald ordered an Irish whisky and flicked through the parish magazine. August was pretty much dead in Kent though possibly that was not the case here, what with the summer crowds and the perfect weather. On the Thursday before the bank holiday the village show was tradition-ally held. It might make sense to fix it for then when everyone of note was bound to be present. Pimm's on the patio would be his choice, which he would mix himself in a jug. None of the fancy palaver Sylvia favoured. No barman, no finger food, no fuss. Just peanuts and potato crisps. It was time she took on board that he was retired.

He finished his drink and checked the time. Ten

to seven; he would have to go. The bar was still almost deserted.

'Is there anything on in the village tonight?'

The barman considered then shook his head. 'It's just the time of year,' he said. 'Many folk are away.'

Where, Gerald wondered, did you go to get away from a place like this? Perhaps up to London to look at the queen or take in the cricket at Lord's. He felt a wistful longing to be there too.

'Another drink?' the barman enquired but Gerald morosely shook his head.

'Best get back to the lady wife.' Or there'd likely be a rumpus.

The table was strewn with cookery books though the meal was already in the oven. Sylvia, sherry in hand, was compiling lists.

'What are you up to?' Gerald asked, pouring himself another drink. He was disappointed his foray had turned out fruitless.

'Making plans,' said Sylvia, frowning over her lengthening list. It was ages since they had entertained; she was having to concentrate.

'Do you think we should have the curtains cleaned?'

She was crazy; they hadn't been up a year. And down here there was no pollution. The house was pristine.

'No need to go overboard,' he warned, seeing the dangerous glint in her eye. There was no stopping Sylvia once she started spending.

'Shall we include the girls?' she said. It might take their minds off Disneyland. One lot could stay in a B & B unless they'd prefer a tent.

'No,' said Gerald who certainly didn't want children.

Finally they both agreed; if they had any neighbours it must be them all. You couldn't pick and choose in an enclave like this. Since they hoped to hold the party outside, everyone would know what was going on.

Sylvia was bleating about what to wear but Gerald considered it naff to dress up. Casual was the code for drinks in the country. He also vetoed the string quartet and if it rained they could move indoors. He needed to keep a check on her or else she would land him in debt. As it was, he was taking a fairly wild gamble and banking all on one roll of the dice. Instinct told him his mark should be the Commander.

8

Sharing a room was a new experience. Lisa and Ned were trying their best to adjust to the situation. Luckily both were tidy which helped a lot. He always suggested she go up first and sort herself out in privacy then, after a reasonable interval, he would join her. Lisa, having put on her pyjamas, brushed her teeth and cleansed her face, tried to be under the covers when he appeared. She was usually reading when he came in and smiled benignly over her book or else she had switched off her bedside lamp and made a good show of seeming to be asleep. On those occasions he got the message and moved as silently as he could, doing his utmost not to disturb her when he got into the bed. Normally he liked to read too but, being considerate, left off his lamp and made it an early night.

But when she was reading he talked to her about the minutia of his day and then she would close her book and listen politely. Mostly he didn't have much to add to what he'd already told her at supper so he filled her in on what he was doing at work. She would watch as he neatly folded his clothes and stowed his shirt in the laundry bag, then placed his watch and change on the bedside table. Like her, he kept his pyjamas in the bathroom. Next would come the trickiest part; did they or didn't they want to make love? Both were too shy to be proactive so, more often than not, they did not.

Lisa would pick up her book again and Ned would switch to his reading glasses and both would settle for a nice cosy read before switching off the light.

'Goodnight,' he would say and peck her cheek, carefully marking his place in the book.

'Goodnight,' she would whisper, snuggling down. 'See you in the morning.'

It wasn't the way she'd imagined it, marriage between two consenting adults in the privacy of their own home with no one listening in. Occasionally, though, he would roll across and envelop her in a clumsy hug after which nature usually took its course. In the dark with no words spoken, as if it were something not quite nice. It wasn't a subject they ever discussed. Once it was done they turned their backs and Lisa would lie awake for hours, worrying where she'd gone wrong.

Ned was a draughtsman when they met, working in the town-planning department at St Pancras Town Hall. Lisa was purely administrative. She shuffled papers and dished out forms, did tedious chores and made endless cups of tea. There was quite a spirited life below stairs, on the whole the other clerks were a genial bunch. They quickly fastened on Ned's good looks and made him the subject of prurient speculation. He seemed remote, a romantic figure who kept himself very much to himself. Edward Thornton, architect, or so in their dreams he would one day be. They liked his pale abstracted stare and lack of self-importance. There were speculations about his sex life; which way, for instance, did he swing? One by one they chatted him up, waylaying him in the work's canteen or fixing it so they left with him or followed him to the bus.

He lived in Purley, liked nature programmes; his conversation gave little away. At breaks they pooled their information. He read a lot, or so he said. At lunchtime he usually stayed at his desk and worked or did the crossword. Buzz buzz buzz, the rumours went. Their interest in Ned Thornton steadily grew.

Lisa was as intrigued as the rest but hadn't the bottle to chat him up. She perceived, though, in his off-handedness an element of reserve. She was shy; he might be too. There must be some way of finding out. It didn't quite happen. She left the job and went to work in a stationery shop. Better prospects, classier too, though ultimately quite boring.

In the upheaval of changing jobs, Lisa entirely forgot about Ned. Never bothered to say goodbye, was gone without even a backward glance. Later, when the job fell through, he did occasionally cross her mind. By then, though, he had also moved on. She hadn't known how to reach him.

She often thought back to the Council days and the bawdy discussions they used to have about whether or not he was gay. She regretted not having stayed in touch with the other girls; she had no one to whisper with now. Nobody else in the world, in fact, except Ned. It was probably simply a matter of time, she consoled herself as she lay in the dark listening to the comforting sound of his breathing. He must love her since he had married her. It had happened so fast she'd been overwhelmed. The truth, to which she closed her mind, was that she had done most of the running. She'd convinced him that he should settle down. He'd be lonely living away from town. He had no one else in the world now his mother was dead. To her surprise he had taken the bait and graciously allowed himself to be caught. They were both alone, in the prime of their lives, had similar tastes and got on well. There seemed to be nothing to stop them being together.

Lisa sighed and tried to drop off. From what she'd deduced from the books she had read, quite often it did take time.

'Better hurry or you'll be late.' Lisa tapped on the bathroom door. Ned was having his morning soak and hated to be disturbed. She could hear him listening to Radio 3 so, when he didn't respond, she tapped again. 'The coffee's ready, I'm cooking your eggs so you'd better hurry or else they'll be cold. How many pieces of toast shall I make? One or two?'

She heard him mutter so tapped again. 'Can't quite catch what you're saying, you'll have to speak up.'

'One,' he shouted but she made it two. He was looking slightly peaky these days. Part of her job as his wife was to fatten him up.

Down in the kitchen she'd set the table with china she'd bought in the village shop. Matching mugs and plates with sheep on them. Cute. She poured the coffee, he'd soon be down, and ladled the eggs on to one of the plates. She would make do herself with unbuttered toast. She needed to watch her waistline. Being married was quite a chore, more than she'd ever expected. As a single girl she'd skipped breakfast altogether. In the old days she'd have a cigarette but that was something Ned wouldn't allow. Along with her marriage vows came new restrictions.

He was down at last in his workday suit, a light-weight linen picked out by her. The silver-grey went well with his eyes. She thought he looked very handsome.

'Take an umbrella in case it rains.' The forecast was dry but what did they know? These days it rained throughout the year. The seasons were all screwed up.

Abstractedly he ate his eggs, one ear still tuned to Radio 3. He carried the transistor around, a throwback, she supposed, to his single days. Except that then he had had his mother, someone he never spoke about. If she ever tried asking about his past, Ned fell instantly silent. He pushed back his chair; it was time he was off.

'Wait,' she said. 'You've got egg on your tie.' She carefully sponged away the spot then pecked him on the cheek.

'You look very nice,' she said with approval. 'Have a good day and drive carefully.'

She stood in the doorway to wave him off then went back inside to clear the plates. Another day with nothing planned but she was not complaining.

After she'd tidied and put things away, hoovered the staircase and shaken the mats, Lisa turned her mind to the rooms upstairs. There were two guest bedrooms on the second floor, beneath the one they used themselves, as well as a separate bathroom and Ned's study. The door to the study was usually closed which meant the landing was very dark. If she opened it up, the light would shine through from both the front and back of the house. This she tried, with a wooden wedge to prevent it automatically closing. These houses were built to new EEC rules designed to prevent fire spreading. She liked the effect when the sun poured through and opened the door to the opposite bedroom. She would gather some flowers for the small oak table to complete the country house look.

Well pleased, she wandered into the study, looking for further improvements to make. All this room contained was a desk topped by a draughtsman's easel. When Ned worked here he kept the door closed and the view he had was across the carport. She leaned on the sill. He could watch people coming and going. She looked around; it was very bare with plain white walls and white-painted shelves. There were metal cabinets stuffed (she found) with his drawings. Idly Lisa riffled through. She had never looked at his work before. It was mainly architectural stuff, joists and architraves and mouldings. Suddenly curious, she started to burrow, going through each of the drawers in turn. There was a lot about Ned she still didn't know.

The cabinets revealed nothing new so she moved, instead, to the artist's folders stacked behind the door. These contained sketches in charcoal and pencil: Ned's more creative side. Lisa's attention was properly caught. She popped downstairs to make fresh coffee then settled down to trawl through her husband's past.

The first thing he noticed when he came home was the charcoal sketch taped to the kitchen wall.

'What the . . . ?' He stopped in his tracks, appalled, letting the briefcase slide to the floor. His face was suddenly ashen and drawn; he looked a good ten years older.

'It's lovely,' she said. 'I found it upstairs.' She came up behind him and slid her arms round his chest.

He flicked her off like an annoying fly. 'How dare you touch my things?' he said. 'I thought you under- stood my study was private.'

Lisa, rebuffed, went icily quiet. She wasn't accustomed to being ticked off. This was her marriage too, they should have no secrets. Instantly she went on the defence.

'What have you got to hide?' she asked. 'I assume that's your mother. I see a strong resemblance.'

The sketch was slick, from a practised hand, the subject glancing up from a book, caught in an instant, sudden surprise on her face. Her hair was glossy and dark like Ned's; the luminous eyes, without a doubt, were his too.

'She was quite a beauty.' Which came as no surprise.

'Leave that alone.' He snatched the sketch and ripped it to pieces, dropping them into the garbage. Lisa was shocked; he was out of control with emotion. She reached out a tentative hand to him but he shrugged her off and turned away.

'Never go into my study,' he said through clenched teeth.

My study too, she was tempted to say, though bit it back when she saw his face. He was pulling on his walking boots. He headed towards the door.

'Your supper,' she cried but he didn't turn. Helplessly she watched him stride off to the woods.

Lisa was sorting through the mail while Ned got ready to go to work.

'There's an invitation here from the Brennans,' she said.

He didn't react, seemed preoccupied. Things between them had been a bit tense since the night she had dared interfere with the sketch of his mother. The door to his study remained firmly shut, making the landing very dark which meant the demise of any living plant. She had compromised by replacing real flowers with silk ones. They hadn't mentioned his mother again. He had made it clear it was a very sore subject. When he'd returned from his angry walk he had seemed slightly calmer as well as less stressed.

She had cooked a vegetable casserole which was simmering in the oven.

'Something smells good.' He smiled at her and then meticulously washed his hands in the little cloakroom across the hall where they kept their outdoor things. She liked the fact that he was so clean and always smelled faintly of soap.

She had lit candles and opened the wine and changed into a prettier frock. She'd also brushed her hair and put on make-up. Marriage, to her, remained a challenge into which she was throwing the best of herself. She would do what it took to make it work, having no alternative. Ned's sudden flare-up made her see how much about him she still didn't know. If she asked too many questions he got rattled.

'An invitation to what?' he asked, his main attention on Radio 3. It seemed he sometimes used music as a defence.

'Drinks and canapés.' She checked the date. 'Sunday morning. In . . . six weeks' time.' She wondered if it was some sort of celebration.

'Must we go?' He wasn't keen, not being very gregarious. In company she'd noticed he always clammed up.

'I think we should. It is nice of them.' She wanted to be a part of this group. 'And since it's next door we really can't not go.'

The weather was golden and serene. Lisa spent her mornings outside working on the patio, rearranging the rock plants. She had never had a garden before; all she knew was from a book and a gardening column cut from the daily paper. The postman brought the paper each day, a tall lithe youth with a surfer's tan, golden curls like a young archangel and a necklet of tiny blue shells. Peter, his name was; he liked to chat. Everything moved at a leisurely pace. He caught her up on the local news as well as the weather forecast. She started keeping an eye out for him, was at the door when she saw his van and he always greeted her with a wave as though they really were friends.

He worried about her being alone without the car, which her husband took. 'You ought to have wheels of your own,' he said. 'Stuck in this lonely place.' He offered to run small errands for her but Lisa told him she was all right.

'My husband gets home at a reasonable hour,' she explained. Emphasising her marital status made her feel very grown up.

The truth was Ned wasn't often there, not at a time that was useful to her. This wasn't London with its flexible opening hours. Occasionally she would ask him to shop on the journey home from Newton Abbot, would give him a list of anything urgent she needed. He did it, though always without a word and never, she felt, with very much grace. He seemed to consider it women's work, not part of his role as her partner. Since he'd been raised as an only child, as far as she knew without a father, it seemed quite likely he had been very spoilt. But she wasn't sure since he never let on, never mentioned his mother at all. He only said she had been a beauty and her death, several years ago, had come as a shock.

A cat appeared and Lisa froze. She had always been slightly nervous of them in case they jumped or tried to scratch her face. This one strolled in from the garden next door, picking his way on delicate paws from stone to stone on the sun-baked crazy paving. Lisa sat back and stared at him and he, in turned, stared back at her. He had the most beautiful topaz eyes as well as exotic markings.

'Well, you're a beauty.' She closed the doors to prevent him wandering into her house then, after a while, continued with her weeding. He must belong to the woman next door who lived alone and looked around her own age. They hadn't spoken but Peter had filled her in. She'd arrived, he said, at the dead of night and no one had seen her moving in. No furniture van or the usual paraphernalia. She certainly kept herself to herself. Despite the thinness of the walls, Lisa was hardly aware there was anyone there. Now, though, she took a cautious peek and saw that the terrace doors were ajar. Someone inside was working on a computer.

After a while, the neighbour emerged, stretching before she called the cat. Awkwardly Lisa rose and revealed herself.

'Is this who you're looking for?' she asked.

'It most certainly is. Come here,' she said to Perseus, then turned to Lisa. 'Erin O'Leary.' She held out her hand. 'I've been lent the house for the summer.'

She had rust-coloured hair that she wore tied back, perfect teeth and a glorious smile. Lisa introduced herself then went on with her weeding.

'I met the woman next door,' she said when Ned arrived home late, looking cross. 'Not the Brennans. The one on the other side.'

She could see he wasn't remotely concerned. His journey had been disrupted, he said, because of some vast piece of farm equipment that shouldn't be out at that hour. She still found his sudden petulant moods unnerving.

'It held me up for miles,' he said. 'The traffic's backed

up to Moretonhampstead.' His hair was ruffled and his clear pale eyes glowed with an inner rage. He hadn't remembered to pick up the things she'd specifically asked for from the shops, which meant the hotpot would lack its most vital ingredient. She poured him a drink, the dutiful wife, which Ned ignored. He went upstairs. She heard the bang of the study door, followed by absolute silence. She turned down the oven and switched on the news. Supposedly marriage was all about sharing but they still had a considerable distance to go.

9

Auriol stood at her kitchen window watching the happenings in the drive. The door of the gate-house stood wide open and a golden retriever was bouncing about outside. It was obvious someone was living there now, she was keen to get a glimpse of who it was. She didn't have to wait very long. A man emerged, talking into a phone and paused in the porch while he finished the call in full view of her house. She popped upstairs for a better look, the view from the boxroom was less obscured. He was even-featured with silvering hair, in tweeds and a combat jacket. Under his arm he carried a shotgun. The dog was now settling into the back of a Range Rover parked outside.

The man stuck the gun in the back of the car then climbed into the driving seat and reversed. Auriol guessed he was sixtyish though he might be younger:

that hair colour could be deceptive. Whatever age, he looked pretty good. Her spirits perceptibly lifted. She had always been one for a good-looking man and he was the best she had seen since arriving here. She hoped there wasn't a wife in tow. At least they both had dogs, which might break the ice. In the short time Jasper had been with her she sometimes found him a social asset. No matter how badly behaved he might be, strangers found him enchanting. She would keep an eye out for this gun-toting neighbour. At the very least, she might get a peek inside his house.

As he drove towards them, the gates swung open then automatically closed again. There was no more action that she could see. With luck, he was there on his own. Not that it made much difference to her, she was through with men in a major way though was finding it hard to adjust to being alone. The catastrophe that had wrecked her life had hit her out of a clear blue sky. The last thing she needed now was another liaison.

They had met when she was twenty-seven and he two years younger, though self-assured. He was also four inches shorter. He wandered into the Sloane Street shop, where she was embroiled with a well-heeled client, and made no secret of eavesdropping on her spiel.

'I like your style.' He sounded sincere. 'You're the type of high-class totty I might find useful.'

She glanced at him, in his chain-store suit, cut-price trainers and garish tie, then glacially dismissed him.

'Can I help you?' Her eyes were cold and she stared quite pointedly over his head. She was holding the fort alone and exceedingly busy.

'I don't know, darling. Can you?' he asked, leaning forward, his hands on her desk, giving her a very thorough once over.

Her withering look should have done the trick – she was known in the circles that mattered for her *froideur* – but he was brassier than the rest, had bluffed his way through life with his barrow-boy charm.

'Why not join me for a drink and I'll fill you in on my long-term plans.' Ignoring her scandalised look, he shovelled up brochures. 'I'll pick you up around six,' he said, 'and we'll pop across to the Carlton Tower. Tell the boyfriend you'll be home late.' And he left.

He was waiting, reading a newspaper in the doorway of the Armani shop, when she left that night at ten past six, having already forgotten. He dropped the paper into a bin and fell into step beside her.

'All right, then? I don't have long unless you're free for dinner, of course.'

She didn't know why she had swallowed it, she had

had no shortage of male admirers, but something about his brazen cheek amused and also intrigued her. She wouldn't join him for dinner, she said, but could spare time for a very quick drink. They were still installed at a Rib Room table when the restaurant closed at eleven.

She moved her easel out to the terrace from which point the gatehouse was out of sight. He was likely to be on the moor all day and, in any case, Jasper would sound the alarm when he heard the Range Rover return. Not that she cared one way or the other. All that really concerned her now was getting to grips with her art.

At ten she heard the postman's van so went back into the house to greet him. Peter, with his seraphic smile, had become an important feature of her day. Along with her mail, which was usually just junk, he brought the paper and up-to-date village gossip.

'Lovely weather.' He dug in his bag and handed her a cream envelope. 'It's from number seven.' He nodded towards that house.

Auriol laughed. It bore no stamp which meant her neighbour was cutting costs. 'What is it?' she asked.

'A party invitation.'

'And have they included the whole corral?'

Peter grinned. 'Pretty much so.' There wasn't very much that got past him.

She ripped it open. It was weeks ahead. She wondered what it might signify; some kind of anniversary maybe, though, if so, it was pushy to include total strangers. It might, however, be worth dropping in just to suss out the neighbours. He was the one with the breezy manner and she was uptight and had clearly had work. That 'startled chipmunk' look was a dead giveaway.

At noon she stopped for a G and T and also to fill Jasper's water bowl. All this painting was thirsty work with the heat and the concentration. She brought her lunch (just a chunk of cheese) out to the easel and ate as she worked. She'd been right about the focal point, those larches positioned the view. Somewhere nearby a woodpecker tapped relentlessly like a pneumatic drill. She looked for it but couldn't locate where it was. The clouds were high and the sun was bright. An inspirationally lucid day. Painting defused her rage and helped her relax. She mixed her colours as she sipped her drink then daubed straight on to the canvas.

She thought about the gatehouse again and who its glamorous owner could be and why, with a house like that, he was so little there. Most of the neighbours lived here full-time. Peter had filled her in on them. In the main they were newly retired, fulfilling a lifetime's dream. But he at the gatehouse did not fit that role. Peter was bound to know; she would check it out.

At five she took another break and strolled round the patio, stretching her legs. Jasper perked up. She fetched his lead, she might as well take him out now. She didn't bother to lock the doors, just pulled them to in case of deer. There were several neighbours chatting outside and they waved.

She crossed the lawn and forded the stream which was, at this stage, little more than a trickle. Further on it merged with the River Teign. On the opposite bank the woods began. Jasper raced ahead of her into the trees. This was paradise for a dog with so many novelties to explore. It cheered her to see him nosing his way through the thicket. What she mainly missed was the city buzz that even Cheltenham had provided. People and shops and a social life, with a stylish house and a man she was crazy about. Her decision to remain childless had not been an issue. Not until now when she faced a void with nobody in her life but a tiresome dog.

Their chemistry had been lightning swift. They had more in common than she could have guessed. What he mainly lacked was a guiding hand and a gentle push in the right direction to unlock the real potential that lurked beneath the cheesy veneer. His insight into the property world had mesmerised her in one so young, a bricklayer's son who'd grown up in the backstreets of Plymouth. Having cut his teeth in his father's trade, apprenticed from the age of sixteen, he had learnt to assess a potential site within a very tight margin. He had married early, at twenty-one, and thus had commitments beyond his means. He also possessed a restless spirit and an overwhelming desire for financial success. The combination of his drive allied to Auriol's social skills was exactly the kind of cocktail he had been seeking.

She showed him round their exclusive rentals and he made notes for future use. She also taught him how to dress and get a decent haircut.

'You're class, you are.' He was proud of her but also attached to his infant sons. Jilly, his wife, he was willing to ditch but he wasn't so sure about the boys. Auriol, full of self-confidence, was not prepared to be messed about. She would think about being his business partner but strictly without any strings. She liked the idea of combining their skills, her business nous with his native cunning, but drew the line at becoming his bit on the side.

Jasper was acting oddly again, digging frenetically in the grass, stopping only to bark and jerk something around. Life for a dog was an endless game. Auriol loved to see him enjoying himself.

'What is it?' she asked, striding over to take a look.

He wagged his tail but refused to drop whatever it was he had clenched in his jaws. It looked very dead: another predator's leavings. Grabbing his collar, she hauled him off, gingerly stirring the lustreless fur with her toe. A sad dead squirrel in a dreadful state with half its entrails ripped out. Nature could be very cruel at times. She looked for somewhere to bury the corpse. She didn't want him bringing it home as a trophy. She kicked it into a natural trench, gathering ferns to cover the spot, all the time restraining the dog now barking in frustration. Poor little wretch, it was only young. She looked more closely and then recoiled. Whatever had got to it first had gouged out its eyes.

The sun was setting as she trudged home. They had walked much further than she had planned though Jasper didn't seem tired at all and still bounced with boisterous spirits. Now she felt calmer and less fraught; she knew that, in time, her heart would heal, that people survived worse things. She picked her way through the darkening wood, in search of the place where the paths diverged. One fork led to the Whiddon Down road, the other to the local pub at which point a stile led into the neighbouring field.

She opened the gate that led into their woods then fought her way through a sea of tall ferns, careful where she put her feet as she couldn't see what lay beneath. Beyond, the path was still staked out from when it had been the manor's grounds. Now she could just see the roof of her house which meant she was almost home.

'Jasper?' She looked around for the dog whose peregrinations had suddenly ceased. She hoped whatever he'd found this time wouldn't be quite so gruesome. He was totally rigid, ears alert, growling aggressively in his throat. She placed a restraining hand on his head and strained to discover the reason. She sensed slight movement on the path though couldn't see anything through the trees. Just a fleeting impression of somebody passing.

Jasper continued refusing to budge, so in the end she abandoned him there. There was no one about; the terrace was clear and there weren't any cars in the drive. She felt sudden unease though wasn't sure why. She couldn't shake off the sight of that vandalised squirrel.

10

Betty proceeded along the path that led from the gate-house and up to the woods, passing behind the terrace of newly built houses. She knew their construction both inside and out, having staked out the site since the first sod was cut and watched the wrecking ball demolish the walls of the ancient manor. Houses back then had been built to last. Had it not been for the ravaging fire that had swept through it seventy years before, it would have been still in its prime. Even so its ruined shell had survived, refuge to cattle and prisoners of war, a grand old landmark three miles out of the village. For years she had parked her caravan here, sheltering from the winter storms that gusted down from the moor. She had lit her primus stove in the outhouse and wandered the rooms that were redolent with age, the ballroom with its great curved doors where long-dead Violet had danced with her handsome prince.

When the army of Polish navvies moved in she had stolen away in the dead of night, though continued to keep a regular check on proceedings. She watched the destruction of her home, the slapdash manner of its execution, the corners cut to meet an impossible deadline. They ripped out fireplaces that had survived and what was left of the old stained glass, reducing to rubble the mansion's elegant lines. They opened it up by flattening walls, removing the roof and exposing the beams. The beautiful woodwork that had survived was stripped out panel by panel. They lifted the floorboards and gouged out the plumbing, revealing its workings to outside view. The doors and windows were sent to the salvage yard. By the time they were through it was just a wasteland where ghosts still danced by the moon's bright light and the dying screams of a generation were borne away on the breeze.

They desecrated a work of art, a sixteenth-century monument, for a rapid sale in an auction house to a greedy uncaring contractor. They speeded things up to such a degree that the only part of it left untouched were the cellars which somehow they managed to overlook. Which was where Betty chose now to roam at night, in the complex as spacious as Victorian sewers, covering almost two acres beneath the floorboards.

* * *

Elfrieda sat in her swivel chair under the light of her anglepoise lamp, carefully cataloguing new stock which was piled around her in stacks. An itinerant hiker and two local bookworms were quietly browsing in separate corners. Effie loved the tranquillity of the place. Betty came in with her mop and pail and waited until the librarian looked up.

'Gracious,' Effie exclaimed. 'Is it that time already?'

Betty said nothing, just stared at the floor, whistling quietly under her breath. She lived in a permanent time warp these days, almost entirely detached from affairs of the world.

'I'll let you get on with it,' Effie said, struggling into her old tweed jacket. 'Back in an hour. If I'm needed I'll be in the pub.'

She picked up her bag and grabbed a book. She felt, in any case, like a break. With a half of shandy and a bite to eat she'd be able to keep her eye on the comings and goings.

The landlord hailed her as she came in. 'All right?' he asked as he pulled a pint.

'Can't complain.' She ordered her regular Ploughman's.

The street door opened and a man walked in, silver-haired with a dog at his heels. 'Effie!' he cried in unfeigned delight. 'What a stroke of luck. I was hoping I might catch you.' She shifted up and he took his place beside her.

They went back decades, the pair of them, having played together at nursery school, though his family moved away when his mother remarried. Piers Compayne – former diplomat, now semi-retired, working on his memoirs – lived in the gatehouse of Endecott Park on the rare occasions that he could find the time. He had a healthy respect for Effie whose eccentricities cloaked a very fine mind.

So, having ordered, 'Tell me the news,' he said. He enjoyed her company more than most, relying on her as his main informant on these fleeting visits.

Effie peered over her specs at him. 'What,' she asked, 'did you have in mind? Livestock prices? Stocks and shares? Rumours of foot-and-mouth?'

He laughed. She was great at this guessing game but today he hadn't much time to spare. He had sought her out with one subject in mind: recent comings and goings at Endecott Park.

She filled him in on the little she knew; most of the houses were occupied now though few of the residents seemed like the reading sort. 'But you tell me. You live there,' she said. 'If you came more often you would know them too.'

'I don't have the time.'

'You travel too much.'

'It goes with the territory, my dear. I would be here a lot more frequently if I could.'

'I thought you were thinking about retiring.'

He shrugged.

They had worked together, on and off, for years. She, more than anyone, knew what he did. And that he rarely wasted time, his own or anyone else's. Since he was here, there was something afoot though she knew enough not to ask too much. She would find out soon enough when he needed her help.

So instead they talked about other things: the shooting, the weather, the village show, the highlight of the year that both tried not to miss.

'Will you be here?'

'I shall certainly try though my time, as you know, isn't always my own.'

'I shall be doing my regular stint,' said Effie. 'On the gate.'

'That's the spirit.' He sipped his beer. She liked to appear a bit of a joke though her mind was as razor sharp as it ever had been. He was fond of her; she kept him on his toes.

'Any more manifestations?' he asked, a gleam of amusement in his eye. He indicated the portrait over the bar.

'Occasionally. You know how it is. Most often on nights when the moon is full. Or else when she feels in the mood, she is very strong willed.' She stared at him with those innocent eyes, refusing to say any more.

'And do you still hold your seances?' Only he would dare go this far. It contradicted her erudition, this fascination with other worlds, but he knew her temperament well enough not to make jokes.

'Indeed I do and you'd be surprised at the level of contact we have achieved. The vicar doesn't approve but he's old-fashioned.'

The Commander chuckled and knocked back his beer. He found it hard to relax, even here, for long. He said goodbye and clicked to the dog. They went their separate ways; Effie strolled back to the library. The place was clean and Betty had gone. She settled down to her work again, thinking about dear Piers. Whatever his reasons for being here, which sooner or later he would reveal, he knew he could always count on her for support.

Betty smelled fresh blood as she walked through the glade so stopped in her tracks and sniffed the air. All her senses remained acute despite her advancing years. It was dark in the shadows around her home and the roosting starlings had ceased their noise. Rustling in the bracken announced that she wasn't entirely alone.

'Is that you?' She whispered the words then waited in silence for some sort of sign. He was somewhere close; she sensed his powerful presence.

When nothing happened Betty walked on and

hauled herself up the steps of the caravan. It was hard on her poor old knees these days but she wouldn't choose to live anywhere else. They had tried to move her into a home, the vicar and Effie who both meant so well but she knew she would die if she lost the freedom to roam. It wasn't locked; no one came this way and her two loyal guardians would send invaders packing. Besides, she owned nothing that anyone else would want. She fumbled around and lit the lamp which threw a dull yellow light on the floor. Enough for her to find her way through piles of rubbish to where she slept on a thin, worn mattress in one corner. She had no bedroom nor bathroom as such and cooked her food in the open air, not like those trespassers up at the house but over a fire made of grass and twigs as she'd been taught by the gypsies. Afterwards she would stamp it out, making sure she had left no trace that anyone human had ever passed this way.

The thought of a fire raised her appetite. She returned to sit on the caravan's steps, enjoying the musk of the warm night air, alert to any sounds of stealthy movement. When nothing emerged, she found her whistle and started playing a plaintive tune. That, she found, often did the trick. It let them know she was back.

11

The sun was slanting through the blinds. Erin looked at the clock; it was not yet six. Too good, though, for lingering on in bed. She leapt straight out and under the shower. Perseus was draped across the pillow, his narrowed kohl-rimmed eyes like topaz slits.

'Chop chop,' she told him, dressing fast. 'This weather's too good to miss.'

Being here had its advantages, especially on a day like this. Clerkenwell would be a living hell, the tube like a can of sardines. She raced downstairs and opened the doors then stepped outside and took massive breaths. The air was as clean and fresh as a toothpaste commercial. She ought to be exercising more; perhaps she'd invest in a skipping rope. She touched her toes rapidly twenty times while Perseus washed his face. On the other hand she walked a lot, more than she ever had in her life. She was into the rhythm now of those six-mile round trips. Everyone else in the complex had cars but so far no one had offered a lift. They waved to her as she staggered past, hefting her knapsack full of supplies, but seemed to imagine she did it from choice, if they thought about it at all. Not that she cared; she was far too proud ever to be an encumbrance.

And since she had nothing important to do except scribble notes for some mythical book, exploring the neighbourhood kept her out of trouble and still on her toes. There had been no signs of the enemy yet, no horse's heads or crows nailed to her door, not even a spooky late-night call with nothing but heavy breathing. Sometimes she wanted the action to start in order to get it over with but even Rod had little to add on that front where she was concerned.

Things were hotting up, though, where the action was. You could scarcely open a paper these days without reading something unsettling about the regime. Erin had pioneered untapped sources, several of which had been rounded up and given a Kremlin grilling or worse. It was getting extremely alarming. Even an unbiased paper like hers, with offices dotted all over the world and a strong international financial base, was treading with extra caution. Her viewpoint had been strictly personal, yet still they had killed off the story.

Initially she had run to Rod, accusing his board of rank cowardice. Tyrants should not be allowed to win; without free speech they might all wind up in the salt mines. He took her point and calmed her down. Editorially he backed her one hundred per cent. The problem lay with them upstairs, their own Toronto-based oligarchs, the *Globe* being financed now by Canadian money. At an earlier time she might have stormed out and sold her story to someone with balls but Rod was a man whose opinion she respected, and also loved. He explained to her in his erudite way that politics sometimes do have to encroach upon the freedom of speech the British hold sacred.

'There are forces beyond our control. Which does not make us pusillanimous cowards. It's more that we don't always get to see the full picture, not at first.'

Erin demurred but he was the boss. In her heart she had to agree he was probably right.

Here, though, was a different thing. No way would those Russkies penetrate rural Devon.

She decided to walk to Fingle Bridge, had been planning that since the very first day but somehow hadn't yet managed to fit it in. It was true what they said, that time, like water, finds its own level and fills its own space. Now, though, looked like the ideal day. As soon as she'd had her breakfast she would be off.

Erin stood at the window, nursing a coffee, and watched her neighbours set off to work; the athletic doctor from number four and Lisa's pallid husband from number six. Him she had not set eyes on before, he was some sort of architect Lisa had said though looked, with his rimless glasses, more like a teacher. Nice, she thought as he unlocked his car, thoughtful and rather good looking. That was a couple she wondered about, newly married according to Peter, both around forty give or take a year. Things were slowly developing here at the spectator level.

A card had arrived only yesterday from the older couple at number seven, inviting her in for lunchtime drinks on a Sunday in several weeks' time. The husband had always been very effusive, though she sensed the wife did not share his view. She had met that kind of woman before, scared stiff of losing her husband. It seemed she had no life of her own, stuck down here in this dreary place with nothing to occupy her except idle gossip. Which meant, poor soul, she must be starved since nothing of any consequence ever happened.

She stuck her mug in the sink to soak, pulled on her trainers and grabbed her keys. Perseus was drowsing in the sun and didn't notice she'd closed the terrace doors.

The walk by the river to Fingle Bridge was flat and

comfortable to manoeuvre with a natural path upkept by the National Trust. The sun was bright but the trees kept things cool and halfway along Erin came to a weir where salmon were actively leaping. She slowed her pace and watched, enthralled, something she'd never seen before: bountiful nature at its most enticing. There weren't too many people around, only a straggle of booted hikers, mostly foreign, weighed down with cameras and rucksacks.

After two hours precisely she reached the bridge – picturesque, built of weathered stone, a crossing point over the river for four hundred years. The waters here were shallow and fast and studded with fish that were easily seen. Bare-legged children with shrimping nets were racing round like naiads trying to catch them. There were wooden tables outside on the lawn which ran right down to the water's edge. Erin bagged one then went inside to order herself some lunch.

She was nicely settled with sandwich and beer when she spotted a dog she recognised, a dark brown Labrador leaping around and causing chaos among the fishing children. His owner, seated a few yards away, seemed to be absorbed in sketching the bridge. One of her neighbours, Erin thought, though she'd seen her only a couple of times. Blonde and striking with very fine eyes and perfectly chiselled cheekbones. Not someone she normally would be drawn to; she hated the haughty London catwalk type. The dog, however, had no such restraint and when he had finished annoying the kids, he bounded over and shook himself all over her.

Which was when his owner finally turned and saw Erin. Loudly protesting, she leapt to her feet and tried, without success, to call him to heel.

'I am dreadfully sorry. This blasted dog. Here.' She brought over a handful of tissues and tried to wipe Erin down.

Erin laughed. There was no harm done. All she had on were her oldest jeans and a T-shirt. 'Won't you please join me for a drink?' In fact, she preferred to drink alone but, since they were neighbours, it seemed the polite thing to say.

Her neighbour paused; she was hesitant too but couldn't really get out of it now. 'Wait a second and I'll fetch my stuff,' she said. 'Then I'd really love to.'

She became more human once she'd loosened up with a gin and tonic that went down fast. And insisted on buying a second round when she went inside for another. She was really beautiful when she smiled though with serious worry lines round her mouth. Late forties, Erin guessed, though in excellent shape. Formal introductions were made and the pair shook hands, exchanging their relevant details.

'Are you the one with the beautiful cat?'

'I am,' said Erin. 'Perseus. I hadn't realised he travelled so far afield.'

'Jasper would love to play with him but Perseus always stands his ground. Jasper is somewhat over the top but soft as butter inside.'

Erin looked at Auriol's sketch. 'You are seriously good,' she said, sincerely impressed.

Auriol laughed. 'I am out of practice. I used to paint in my early youth but gave it up in favour of my career.' She had dealt in property, she explained, working as half of a partnership. She made no reference to a husband; Erin knew not to ask.

Erin admitted to being a journalist, currently on a sabbatical. She was finding it hard not to have to cope with deadlines. Auriol said she sympathised; time had hung heavily on her hands too but now she was getting her act together by taking up painting again. She was finding it very therapeutic, it was bringing new purpose to her life. She drained her glass and went in for another drink.

She drank too much, that was clear to see though not Erin's business to mention it. Except that she'd come by car so should not be driving.

In the event they compromised, both of them taking a bit of a risk since legally neither should be in charge of a car. Erin drove and Auriol kept watch, Jasper standing guard at the rear. The road was narrow and overgrown and rose very steeply up from the riverbed. Fortunately there was little traffic on a weekday afternoon at this time of day. And, by car, the journey was twenty minutes, as opposed to Erin's exhausting two-hour hike. They reached the park without any mishap and Erin quietly released her breath as Auriol opened the gates by remote control. Safely home; she was glad of it but equally pleased to have made such a nice new connection. Good conversation here was sparse. Erin looked forward to knowing her better.

She watched while Auriol parked the car, she was sober enough to deal with that, then invited her in for another drink or a coffee.

They sat on the terrace to watch the sunset, a glorious performance that never failed to impress. At moments like this country living came into its own. The moor lapsed into an indigo blue, concealing whatever secrets it held, and nocturnal creatures started to stir as the birds retired to their nests. Fiery arrows of scarlet and gold split the horizon across the sky. The grove of larches that held centre stage morphed into solid blackness.

'It's amazing how fast the night sets in,' said Erin, accustomed to city lighting. 'I wouldn't like to be caught out there when it does.'

They were fortunate in being enclosed by iron gates and surrounding walls. Though hardly foolproof (few places were) it must, on the whole, put off the average marauder. Certainly no one unauthorised could gain easy entry.

'Why did you choose to move down here?' Erin had already stated her case, that friends had lent her the house for a break. Now it was Auriol's turn.

Auriol paused and stared into her glass. 'It wasn't really my choice,' she said. She was the one who had found the place but circumstances had forced her hand. The bitter divorce had rent them apart and she had been left with the remnants. She hated the place. It made her quite ill to see the damage the builders had wrought, sloppy workmanship overlooked in the cause of selling the low-grade houses at a considerable profit. This wasn't the way she'd envisaged things when she'd first seen photographs of the ruin and made an exploratory expedition in order to fulfil a dream. Endecott Manor was legendary with quite a distinguished historical past. Auriol had planned to restore it to its full glory.

She gritted her teeth and emptied her glass then glanced up hopefully for a refill. Erin considered then went inside for the bottle. They were safely home and it wasn't her business to preach to a virtual stranger. Sometime, when she knew Auriol better, she would tell her how she had come to lose her own licence. Though in her case things had not been what they seemed; someone, she was convinced, had spiked her drink.

They chatted on in a casual way, enjoying the mildness of the night, women with quite a lot in common, as it slowly began to emerge. Both had been recently starved of like-minded conversation. Having let on that she was a writer, Erin expanded on her career without giving too much detail away since she still didn't know who to trust. She talked a little about what she'd done, avoiding identifying her field or even naming the paper for which she worked. She acknowledged there was a man in her life, not a husband – at least not her own – but the inspiration and strength behind all she did. Auriol, being newly divorced, was instantly critical of her state. Semi-detached was not good enough. Her advice: get rid of him fast.

Not so easy, Erin explained, aside from which he was her boss. It was he who had engineered her move to Devon. And why would that be? Since she had no answer, Erin just changed the subject.

Instantly curious, Auriol asked more but Erin was still not ready to trust a stranger. She batted the ball straight back to her, subjecting her to her own searching questions. Starting with why, if she hated the place, she'd decided to move here at all. Auriol sighed. This called for another drink.

It was, however, now getting late. Jasper, alone at home, would be pining. She had dropped him off there out of deference to Erin's cat. Actually, Perseus wouldn't have cared having swiftly adapted to outdoor life. He spent much of his day out of sight in the woods, slaughtering baby rabbits and shrews and either eating them on the spot or bringing their carcasses home. Auriol shuddered when Erin explained. Her thoughts went back to the savaged squirrel. She doubted that could have been Perseus, though. Not even a talented Burmese cat could mutilate at that level.

12

It was very nearly the end of the month; the Brennans' cocktail party was scheduled for Sunday. The weather was holding up, a huge relief. Sylvia hated the thought of strangers tracking their dirt throughout her immaculate house. The neighbours, at least, could come round the back without setting foot in the house at all, assuming the rain held off which at present seemed likely. They expected forty; twelve from the Park plus a handful of villagers carefully handpicked and Gerald's circle of drinking pals which would, he very much hoped, include the Commander. His financial situation was dire; without an immediate infusion of cash, he could not maintain this lifestyle.

He hadn't let Sylvia know, of course, just insisted she try to economise. Her grandiose plans had been drastically trimmed, though on the pretext of taste. He was keen she shouldn't know how things were, had even lied about taking early retirement. The truth was grim; he was on remand with a possible jail sentence over his head depending on whether or not they decided to sue. They had caught him with his hand in the till, or so the senior partner said. He might still wriggle out of the charge if he found some way to replace the money he'd stolen. Because the firm was privately owned they had kept it out of the papers.

He had spun the family a far-fetched tale about overwork and seeing the light, not wanting to grind himself into the dust while his grandchildren were still so young. The daughters had grumbled but Sylvia was pleased though she'd been amazed by the speed of the move. He knew how much she regretted The Firs and wished she would learn to adapt. If only she'd get a worthwhile hobby, though a paying job would be preferable. But she had no skills, had been barely nineteen when he'd snatched her out of the typing pool. It had always been his Achilles heel; if he'd learnt to resist a pretty face, he wouldn't be in this situation now.

Sylvia fretted over everything: the weather, the numbers, the water feature and if the village-made canapés would be all right. Since Gerald had killed off her Gidleigh Park plan and imposed a laughable budget instead, she seriously wondered if she would dare show her face in public again. Perhaps in this village but not back in Kent where a hostess was socially crucified if her vol-au-vents failed to rise. She had found a woman in the village deli – a Pole, she thought, as her English was bad – who had undertaken the order without a flicker. Gerald would do his nut when he heard: forty covers at six pounds a head. Cheap at the price though he'd hardly see it that way. He thought that, since she had little to do, she could spend whole days making falafels and baby Yorkshire puddings with horseradish sauce. Sylvia grimaced; that wasn't her thing. After fancy lunches she drew the line.

She had ordered the cava, cut-price from Tesco who'd agreed to deliver from Newton Abbot, but was leaving it to her lord and master to organise the serious stuff for his friends. Sylvia hardly drank at all, just the occasional lunchtime sherry and again in the evening while waiting for Gerald to come back, half-cut, from the pub. There was not much else you could do in these parts if you sat around half the evening, waiting to eat.

She counted the glasses; they had enough so she rinsed them and left them on teacloths to dry. She'd have flower heads floating in fingerbowls because of the canapés. The guests wouldn't wear coats which was one relief nor, if they stayed on the patio, trek dirt inside. One by one she ticked off the points: no need for ashtrays, an excellent thing. And strawberries, dipped in the local cream, could be eaten as finger food. Over and over she checked the list; eight responses from Endecott Park, all of them coming except the Commander who had not, thus far, replied. She stood at the window and watched for the postman who hadn't been by for a couple of days. She suspected that, with the weather this good, he was skiving off, surfing over at Croyde Bay.

Some of the neighbours she still didn't know: the pair who only came down at weekends and the older couple she thought were retired who seemed to have numerous children. Nice enough from the look of them. She only had four more days and then she'd find out.

In the event, the Commander declined. On Friday evening he dropped a note through their door. Unforeseen business in London, it said, he was truly sorry but it couldn't be helped. He hoped he could compensate at some future time. Sylvia was secretly slightly relieved; she wouldn't have known what to say to him. She had glimpsed him a couple of times with his dog and he did look unnervingly daunting. Gerald, though, seemed unusually vexed and smashed the note into a crumpled ball. What did he mean by business? he snarled. He'd assumed the man was retired. It didn't matter, one less to feed; she still had her mind on those canapés but Gerald was in a grump for the rest of the evening. It was not before time he'd retired, she reflected, even down here he still appeared pretty tense.

On Saturday evening the Polish girl came with cardboard boxes containing the food. Sylvia had already cleared space in the fridge. Kasia her name was. She was graceful and slim and wore her hair in a single thick blonde plait. She looked at the house with interest and enquired about the neighbours. Were all the houses now sold, she wanted to know. Sylvia told her as far as she knew, wondering what business it could be of hers. There was no way a Polish immigrant, surely, could ever afford these prices. But the food looked great; Sylvia took a peek and was very favourably impressed. If they tasted as good as they looked, she would use her again.

Gerald was out which was just as well. She hated the way he looked at these girls and chatted them up like the strumpets they probably were. She pursed her lips. They were all over England now like a rash, infiltrating the countryside too. She wondered why a girl with those looks would have chosen a quiet place like this. Not her business though she'd done a good job. When she offered to come back next morning and help, Sylvia struggled and then gave in. Gerald might scold but what did he know? She could use a hand clearing dishes and refilling glasses.

* * *

Sunday, to her relief, dawned fine though the moor was veiled in a vapour of mist. With luck it signalled a brilliant day and the mist would lift before the guests arrived. Sylvia, up at the crack of six, walked round the patio in her robe, sipping camomile tea to steady her nerves. It was no big deal, she had done it before more times than she could even count yet this time, she didn't know why, she was not at her ease. It was only a handful of village folk, people she hoped she would get to know better. She'd been longing for some sort of social life. With luck, this party would open the requisite doors. The bathrooms were sparkling, her outfit was pressed and Gerald had even polished his shoes. He seemed to be in a better mood; she could swear she had heard him humming. She couldn't account for her nervousness, though. Perhaps it was just that she wanted so much to fit in.

Polish Kasia came at eleven, immaculate in white blouse and black skirt, and set to work efficiently, polishing glasses. Gerald, who'd already had his say predictably about the expense, nevertheless was clearly impressed. His mood took an upward swing. He busied himself removing corks and insisted Kasia sample the bubbly. She thanked him but never drank on duty, she said.

First to arrive were the two from next door, the ponytailed wife with her hair flowing free and her uptight husband, immaculate in a grey suit. She was carrying chocolate truffles and he a bottle of cheap champagne. Both seemed awkward and not at their ease. Sylvia ushered them through and into the garden. Gerald and Kasia poured the drinks and Sylvia carried out nibbles and nuts. She would wait until the others arrived before serving canapés.

Cars began to pull up outside and Erin and Auriol strolled in together, engaged in lively conversation having met outside on the path. Sylvia slowly began to relax. As she'd hoped, the weather was perfect.

The villagers, in particular, were keen to see what the builders had done. They all knew about the manor, of course, and the fire that had destroyed it. Most had lived in these parts for generations.

'I remember my mother telling me you could hear the screams of those trapped inside. Thirty-seven were lost that night, all youngsters.'

Names were mentioned and everyone sighed. Not a lot happened in deepest Devon and families were so intertwined, many had lost close kin.

'You can hear them still,' the postmistress said, 'on a stormy night when the wind's in a certain direction.' She was stout and red-cheeked with a thatch of grey hair and not a flicker of irony in her expression.

Erin and Auriol swapped a glance which Kasia

intercepted. All three grinned and discreetly averted their faces. Here we go, thought Erin, amused. You couldn't go long in a village like this without beginning to hear the spooky stories. With her own Irish roots, she was not one to mock; back home in Dublin the Little People were very much run of the mill. But doom-ridden spectres were what the moor was most famed for. Skeleton horses and great black hounds, the hairy hands that had caused many motorists to swerve. Hooded figures with hollowed-out eyes or, even worse, no faces at all. It was all great fun on a bright August day but wait until winter crept in.

Now someone was talking about this place and the odd occurrences since renovations began. One night, when the foreman was leaving the site and had stopped at the gates to let himself out, he turned to see all the houses lit up despite the fact that none was yet occupied.

Some kind of short circuit, one householder said. Such things could happen on building sites.

Maybe, said another, but that didn't explain how once he had returned from abroad to find his television set on and blaring.

'Ooer,' said Erin, sotto voce.

'Bollocks,' said Gerald, banging his fist. Though lately he had been feeling a lot less secure about many things.

Auriol turned to Erin and said, 'It's all down to shoddy workmanship.'

'Cutting costs?' She was not surprised.

Auriol rolled her eyes. 'If you only knew.'

'Go on, tell me.' She sensed a story which the journalist in her could never resist and she, alone of the residents here, did not own her house.

'Not here,' said Auriol, shaking her head. It would certainly not go down well with her hosts if they overheard her slagging off the houses. Sylvia Brennan was a scream with her too-low neckline and too-short skirt. Talk about mutton dressed up as lamb, she must be heading for sixty. And she certainly didn't like younger, more glamorous women. Aware of her glare, Auriol grabbed Erin's elbow and diplomatically steered her away until they were well out of earshot and could relax.

The spooky stories were Sylvia's cue. She was longing to mention the Endecott Ghost who, she had heard, patrolled these grounds and was also seen in the graveyard. Gerald might scoff but what did he know? She preferred to believe the country folk who remembered the actual fire of the 1930s.

'Tell me about Violet Endecott,' she asked the villagers standing there. 'Is it true that she danced with the Prince of Wales? In this house?'

She loved the idea of a royal connection, would

have been much happier buying the house had she known. And even the prospect of meeting a ghost was made less daunting now that she knew that the dead person could have been a queen.

The villagers nodded in unison and said that the stories were certainly true. Though the ghost only walked at the time of a full moon.

'Like tonight?'

'Tonight, indeed.'

'But,' said the postmistress, serious now, 'if you want to know more about these things ask the village librarian, Effie Willcox.'

'And she would know?'

'She most certainly would.' They looked at each other and nodded again. ''Tis Effie who summons her up from the dead. So they say.'

'Balderdash,' muttered Gerald crossly, annoyed that his party was taking this turn. The Commander's absence was vexing enough without all this spinster's hokum. His wife was already quite silly enough without getting notions like this in her head. He wished now he'd listened to her and invited the vicar.

It was time they all left. He had done his bit but the biggest fish had not taken the bait. He looked around for the sexy Pole but she appeared to have gone.

13

'You talk too much,' said Ned severely.

She had only been doing her bit, Lisa tried to explain. Due to the fact, which was not her fault, that they had been the first to arrive. He was always like that: too punctual, also too quick to leave. Left to herself, she would have preferred to have been an elegant twelve minutes late. She had sensed her hostess was caught on the hop; her smile had been bright but not entirely sincere. She had worn an aquamarine floral print with a neckline a shade too low. And ten years too young.

'Do come in,' she had fluted politely, watching to see where they put their feet. The fitted carpets were cream, decidedly naff.

Lisa noted the finger bowls with floating decapitated flower heads and the three-piece suite in eau-de-Nil watered silk. 'She thinks she's back in Bromley,' Lisa hissed but Ned remained stiffly poker-faced. He said very little and only drank half a glass. It was new to them both going out like this, Mr and Mrs, a married pair, something Lisa had dreamed of most of her life. She was proud of Ned in his well-cut suit, though a little too formal for such an occasion. Their host was wearing a blazer and flannels and some kind of regimental tie though none of the other men wore jackets and one, the guy from two doors down, had even come in shorts. Nice legs, though; he wore them well and had a healthy all-over tan. He looked to her like a surfer, as did his wife.

They chatted a bit. They were much of an age and had only moved in at the end of May. She sensed they might be newlyweds, too; there was something slightly formal about the way they interacted. He was a doctor in Exeter and she did something medical too. She had seemed quite vague about what it was so Lisa hadn't pressed her. And when the redhead from number five had wandered over to join their group, both the medics had moved away and shortly after had left.

'We must go too,' said Ned abruptly, placing his glass on the Polish girl's tray. Lisa, enjoying herself, was surprised. They had still only been there less than an hour and had nothing else planned for the day. She followed him, though, obediently like the dutiful wife she was trying to be but resented the way he spoke to her once they were home.

'Don't tell me how to behave,' she snapped. 'At least I made an effort to mix. It was nice of them to invite us at all considering we hardly know them.'

She could still hear voices on the Brennans' patio which meant she had better not go outside. She would have to wait until the coast was clear.

'I don't like people knowing our business,' said Ned.

'What business?' asked Lisa, opening the fridge in the hope of finding something to eat. She hadn't even thought about lunch since it wasn't often they got to go out at weekends.

'Too much gossip,' he muttered sourly. For reasons she couldn't deduce, he seemed fairly put out. 'I am going to get the papers,' he said and went.

Lisa flounced upstairs to change and tie her hair back in its ponytail. There were times she just didn't understand Ned at all. She liked being part of this small enclave with neighbours with whom she had some rapport. It was different for him; he was out all day while she was imprisoned here, with nothing to do. She had done as much as she could to the house, was waiting now for an influx of funds to pay for those extra little touches, like cushions for the bedrooms. Although she liked being somebody's wife, she resented not having money of her own.

* * *

One of the things that had drawn him to her was that she was always immaculate. He had noticed that when they worked together, all those years ago. She never had money in those days yet managed to keep herself neat and trim. She wore her hair, always squeaky clean, tied back from her elfin face. It was, in fact, that little-girl look that had caught his attention in the first place. Now they were married and lived down here she often wore jeans, which were practical, but she always changed into a skirt before he came home. As marriages went, it was not that bad. Neither was used to much intimacy but both were learning to rub along without too much overt discord. It helped, of course, that he had a job that took him away from the house for so long. The thought of cohabiting constantly made him feel claustrophobic.

He had seen the way the woman next door was always hovering just offstage, never taking her eyes off her fatuous husband. How they had managed to last this long – thirty-five years he had heard her boast – was more than Ned could even contemplate. Of course, having children made a difference, other people sharing the house. Lisa, luckily, was too old for that to have been an option for them but if she had made an issue of it he wouldn't have married her. Even so, he still wasn't sure why he'd allowed her to hook him. Lassitude, largely, and solitude. His mother had left a huge hole in his life and Lisa had happened along at the relevant moment. He wasn't complaining. It worked well enough. He liked the things she had done to the house, as well as coming home to a meal on the table.

He had been away when they'd met up again, years that were still just a blank in his mind, and Lisa had caught him at his most vulnerable. When she'd pounced on him in that crowded train, to start with he hadn't a clue who she was though she'd struck a distant chord with her nervous chatter. St Pancras Town Hall and that dreary job. She was one of the faceless council workers who, at the time, had all looked much the same. He did remember her neatness, though, and the fine-boned hands with the well-kept nails. Such details made an impression on Ned, especially at that time. She had fluttered round him and talked a lot, implying a closeness he didn't recall but so much had happened in a few months. He had just been through a fairly traumatic time.

It was Lisa who had suggested the drink – a chance to catch up on old times, she said – and, largely through inertia, he had agreed. His life was sterile, his mind a blank. He was touched by the way she had flirted with him in a clumsy childlike way he found appealing. This was no woman of the world but a shy young thing who belied her years. When she smiled at him from under her fringe his heart had gone out to her.

He had reached a watershed in his life, unsure of which direction to take having walked out of the St Pancras job due to a personal crisis. He was hovering on the edge of despair and, without her there, might have not come through but she had taken charge of his life for which he still remained grateful. It had turned into a whirlwind romance with Lisa making most of the moves. For one so initially shy, she had overwhelmed him. He had to admit she was quite a girl. That drive down to Newton Abbot had sealed his fate.

By the time he returned after almost an hour (she suspected he'd stopped for a drink in the pub) Lisa had put the scratchings of lunch on the table. Liver sausage and shop-bought hummus, tomatoes and lettuce and mayonnaise. Not a feast but he'd just have to lump it having dragged her home from a perfectly reasonable party. He seemed in a far more amiable mood, patted her shoulder as he passed, scrubbed his hands vigorously in the cloakroom then removed his jacket and rolled up his sleeves. It was, after all, still Sunday. He suggested they go for a walk on the moor and Lisa, relieved that his mood had passed, gladly agreed. Neither was hungry, the meal would keep. It would do them both good to have some exercise.

The moor, in late summer, was green and benign with rock formations and coarse grass dotted with sheep and adorable ponies, grazing. Ned and Lisa followed the path that led to the highest local tor from which they had an amazing view over foothills of scrubby moorland. A trickle of hikers came stomping past, taking it seriously, studying maps. Forty miles away was the famous prison. The only time they had driven that far the mist was so thick they could barely make out the granite walls of the institution, fabled for being escape-proof. A grim place to be incarcerated, especially out of season. Lisa shivered; despite the heat, up here there was always a stiff breeze blowing which could, without warning, turn into a serious gale. There were also peat bogs that sucked you down. Hikers, caught in a sudden mist, had been known to disappear without trace though their bodies occasionally surfaced. They had not yet experienced a winter here, still had that pleasure to come.

Again she shivered and reached for Ned's hand. She would never have chosen to live down here were it not for him and the fact of his work location. He looked at her with faint surprise. It was clear that his sulky mood had passed. He wasn't a very tactile man but he didn't recoil, as he sometimes did, from her touch.

'Surely you can't be cold,' he said.

'No,' said Lisa. 'It's just this place. I think someone just walked over my grave.' And even though she smiled she wasn't joking.

Ned said nothing, just walked on though kept his fingers entwined with hers. She would have to learn to live with him as he was. She longed for him to understand that marriage included companionship. They needed to know each other better, to share more. He listened to music and read a lot, both of them solitary pursuits, and he went for walks on his own at night in order to help him unwind. Sometimes she offered to go with him but he never seemed very keen on that. There were things he needed to think about, he said. There was nothing communal they could do, not even a cinema anywhere near and neither went to church or had a hobby. Perhaps they should take up tennis or golf. Even the thought of it made her smile. He asked her what was funny. She said, Nothing.

She squeezed his hand and walked closer to him, leaning her head against his arm. She longed for him to give her a hug but the thought clearly never occurred. He just kept striding along in a world of his own.

The temperature dropped as the moon rose high, bathing the world in its bright, cold light. Lisa shivered and said it was time to go back. They sat outside for their makeshift meal and she lit candles as a festive touch. There wasn't a sound from the house next door; they were doubtless sleeping it off.

They ate in silence, absorbing the view as all around them the night closed in and the larches beyond the lawn merged into the background. The scent of jasmine hung in the air, more pervasive than during the day, and Lisa, with a sharp prickling of nerves, sensed eyes in the darkness watching.

'What?' asked Ned sharply, sensing her tension, stretching across to squeeze her hand. He had the right instincts after all, in time she would get him trained.

'Nothing,' she said. 'Just a premonition. I feel so vulnerable sitting out here with nothing between us and the moor and heaven only knows what.' Even though it was so bright, the moon created pockets of shadow so that nothing looked quite the same as it did in the daytime. The stories they'd heard started filtering back, of the terrible fire and the people who'd died generations ago on the spot where they sat. A night-bird sounded its eerie call and down at the farmyard a dog started barking. None of the houses along the terrace showed light.

'Now you are just being stupid,' said Ned. 'People spend fortunes on places like this. You surely can't miss city life with all that filthy pollution.'

He was treating her like a child again. Lisa was

about to reply when she heard the sound of light foot-steps coming towards them. Both leaned forwards, straining their ears and Ned discreetly wiped crumbs from his mouth, but the feet went rapidly past their gate without stopping. All either could see, by the light of the moon, was a shadowy figure of indeter-minate sex.

'How very odd.' Ned rose to his feet and walked a few paces towards the gate. But the path, quite white in the moonlight, was now empty. Whoever it was had disappeared or vaulted the hedge to the croquet lawn without so much as acknowledging that they were there. Which, in a gated community, was unusual not to say rude.

Lisa, feeling suddenly spooked, gathered her cardigan round her shoulders, stacked the tray and carried their dishes indoors.

14

The party, to Auriol's surprise and delight, was lots more fun than she'd ever have guessed, largely due to the presence of Erin with whom she was starting to feel a definite bond. She hadn't expected a kindred spirit in such a godforsaken place, had only gone in the first place because she was lonely. She had also liked meeting the Polish girl, who was far too intelligent for that job, and been vastly amused by her hostess's affectations. The water feature, the finger-bowls, the fact they had not been invited indoors except to use the 'little girls' room' at Sylvia's arch invitation, had combined to put her into a rare good mood. The husband, of course, was a total buffoon, parading in his RAC tie as though it were one of the smarter regiments. He had fancied her, she was used to that, had stood too close and sweated too much and had wanted to know why a woman like her was living there on her own. None of your business, she'd nearly said, but instead had looked him straight in the eye and told him that she had recently lost her husband. Which was not, in fact, a total whopper, all she omitted to tell him were the details.

Predictably Gerald had lowered his voice, embarrassed by his own clumsiness, and, having muttered condolences, had declared himself at her service. If there was anything he could do, something she needed, by night or day, she only had to ask. Soon he would slip her his business card, she knew the procedure all too well, and, when his wife wasn't looking this way, discreetly press her hand. Just the idea of it made her laugh; men like that were pathetic.

The villagers, too, had cheered her up with their stories of spooky shenanigans. There were worse things in heaven and earth, goodness knows, than a ghost. A genuine ghost, if there was such a thing, was not flesh and blood and could therefore not harm you. Unless, of course, it *scared* you to death which had to be relatively rare. What Auriol faced in real life was a lot more upsetting than anything supernatural. One of these days she might tell Erin; there were things she needed to get off her chest and she sensed her new friend was a warrior like herself.

The neighbours had seemed a congenial bunch though she'd missed the silver-haired cutie from the gatehouse. It was just her luck that he hadn't been there, she'd been stuck instead with her bumptious host whereas he was the only one she had seen who was even halfway attractive. The doctor was far too outdoorsy for her and the one with the rimless specs looked too intellectual. Besides, they had both had wives in tow. Auriol wasn't remotely that desperate yet.

Erin was great; Auriol liked her a lot. She was fun and feisty and awesomely bright though covered it up in an effortless way, another point in her favour. She liked the Irish, they had great charm and she sensed they shared the same humour, too. She had seen the glint in Erin's eye when Gerald was strutting his stuff. There was something she was concealing, though. She had picked that up at Fingle Bridge and later when they had drinks together outside. She knew enough to recognise when someone was holding her at arm's length though she couldn't complain; she was doing it too, though in a less obvious way. It wasn't that they didn't get on, her instinct told her they would be friends. They simply needed to trust each other more first. Which they would do when the time was right. It certainly brightened her sojourn down here knowing she had a potential soulmate so near.

People intrigued her; it took all sorts and a motley crew had been gathered today, thrown together haphazardly by the machinations of fate. She knew her stuff from her marketing days, could sum up a stranger at a glance and assess his worth to within ten thousand or so. The Brennans, for instance, were not what they seemed. She liked to play Lady Bountiful and flash around her dubious taste whereas he was a man with a weight of concern on his mind. Not a bad man, good at heart despite his tendency to grope, somebody she might yet turn to if in trouble. Both were socially insecure. Behind its pretentious veneer, the house was a joke. Auriol, who came from privileged stock, recognised parvenu posers when she met them. Which was not to say there was anything wrong in a person trying to better himself. She, who had worked with it at first hand, had become a firm believer.

Jasper was waiting. She grabbed his lead. What she needed now was a breath of fresh air to clear the alcohol from her brain and liver. One benefit of living down here was the multitude of picturesque walks. It was only a question of mood and available time. Smiling, she let herself out of the back and walked down the lawn to the gap in the hedge which accessed the farm and the footpath that led to the pub. No doubt in the twenty minutes it took, her alcohol level would need topping up and, hell, it was Sunday. Who was there to criticise but the dog?

* * *

Drink had become quite a part of her life lately in order to help her forget. Living alone was something she was not used to. She had always worked hard and lived hard as well and could hold her own with the best of them, master-minding stupendous deals after a night on the town. She had partied hard with the rest of her set and topped up her energies with cocaine, which had never meant anything more to her than a recreational drug. She had never allowed it to take control, was far too savvy to follow that route and had always been able to stop when she'd had enough. Since the divorce she had cut out the drugs altogether, to be on the safe side.

But she liked to drink and refused to cut down, knowing that she was the best judge of that and if she should have one too many, who cared? She'd be sober again in the morning. Sometimes she even forgot to eat, getting her calories from the gin, and if she felt rough when she awoke, she simply went back to sleep. She had no deadlines any more, no meetings to go to nor calls to return. She had let her share of the business go into the general melting pot, had wallowed a bit and then emerged with only a fraction of what she had once been worth. The battle was bitter and she had lost. She hated herself for admitting it but the person she saw in the mirror each day was a loser.

And so she drank. She had lost it all in a final gamble that hadn't worked out. She had wanted to teach him a lesson but he had won. There was no point in crying crocodile tears; she had known the risks when she took him on. She had lowered her guard and forgotten how ruthless he was. There was no one else she could blame for landing herself in the back of beyond. The booze helped numb the pain till she'd had too much.

But meeting Erin had made her think; by driving her home when she shouldn't have done, having lost her licence, Erin had jeopardised herself to take care of a virtual stranger. She'd made Auriol see where she was going wrong, no longer having respect for herself, and to what depths she'd allowed her morale to sink. Encouraged by that unselfish act, Auriol determined to help herself by cutting down on her drinking before it spiralled out of control. Which was already making her feel much better.

Back from her walk with a clearer head having, after all, resisted the pub, Auriol gathered together a laundry load. She lugged it down to the brand-new machine, all fixtures and fittings having come with the house, filled it up and switched it on at which point the lights all failed and the freezer fused. Auriol cursed; this was nothing new, it happened quite regularly on this site. The neighbours had told her at the party they had the same problems too. When one house went, the others did too, like a string of cheap Christmas-tree lights. Fortunately, Auriol knew how to cope and kept the requisite toolkit handy. Which was just as well since the engineer had to drive all the way from Newton Abbot and could not, therefore, be relied upon to turn up.

This all went back to what she had said; it was the fault of the cowboy builders who had cut every corner they possibly could in order to add to their profit. The gutter pipe leaked, the fire was fake. The first time she turned it on it had fallen apart. The floors were flimsy, the walls too thin and none of the kitchen equipment was very effective. The contractors, Swann Homes, were charlatans run by an out and out crook.

Normally she would go for the gin. This time she made herself coffee instead. 'Start as she meant to go on' was to be her new mantra. What hurt her most was the loss of her pride for this building venture had been her own dream, a brainchild which somehow she'd managed to abort. Having seen the old manor in its derelict state, inspiration had instantly struck. The site was prime and set in marvellous grounds. The views all round were magnificent. Dartmoor was rising fast on the property ladder.

'Let's buy it,' she'd said. 'We can't go wrong.' It had

been a once in a lifetime chance. By the end of that same afternoon the deal was completed. Which was part of the magic of working with him; they thought as one and knew when to strike. When there was something they wanted, neither held back. The irony being that, for all her smarts, the thought had never once crossed her mind that what he had done to poor Jilly he might do to her. She had blithely married a conscienceless man without properly thinking things through.

What she'd had in mind when they'd bought the land was three elegant houses, possibly four, each one different from the rest, one of which they would keep for themselves for when they eventually retired. She would make this her permanent base, was sick of Cheltenham, would like a change, while he continued moving around expanding their business empire. She had always been a forward planner, had put up with a lot, it was her turn now. Now that they'd finally made it legal, she wanted the world to know.

To begin with he'd gone along with her plan so she'd found a reputable architect and together they had created the dream on paper. Three sections made better sense than four. The original manor had been vast but gracious living came at a price and Auriol had been loath to skimp now that they actually owned it. They were doing well, it was worth the risk. Property prices were rising fast. They would occupy one wing and divide the other in half. She threw herself into this mammoth project, gripped with a passion she'd not known before. And, by so doing, she took her eye off the ball.

She couldn't believe she had been such a fool, had not even noticed the danger signs until disaster struck. Kimberley something, the girl's name was: a flibberti-gibbet he had picked up somewhere, blonde like her and twenty-seven, the age she had been herself when they had met. She was vacuous but her daddy was rich, an Essex-born impresario of sorts. Auriol made a still bigger mistake by losing her rag and insisting on a divorce. If she'd kept her cool she'd have talked him round. Money had always come first with him. Then, though, she'd fallen to pieces with rage and they'd ended up splitting their empire.

Big mistake. She could see that now. She had put aside having children for him and when they had finished fighting she lost out again. He kept the bimbo and bought her out; the business had always been in his name. Even the manor had to be split though not in the way she had planned. It was chopped up into nine equal parts, one of which was part of her settle-ment. He made a killing while she lost her dream and was left with a house that she didn't much like. And the dog he no longer wanted.

15

By tradition, the village show was held the week preceding Bank Holiday Monday. This year the weather was doing them proud: a cloudless sky, the trees in full leaf. Nature putting on a gala performance. The site was owned by the National Trust, overshadowed by Castle Drogo and flanked by the River Teign. The show had been an annual event for close on a hundred years. The whole of the local community was likely to turn out in style.

Effie was manning the entry gate, spectacles perched at the end of her nose, selling admission tickets. Despite the heat she wore her tweeds; you never knew when the weather might change. Beside her sat Dora, the farmer's wife, whose land abutted the manor's estate. Her roots, like Effie's, went back for generations. Effie was more than ever alert; her dear friend, Piers, had been called away and would not, alas, be at the show after all. He had couriered her a cryptic note containing very precise instructions. He needed her to act as his eyes and ears. Something was up; he didn't say what but Piers had fingers in numerous pies. The facade of genial country squire was more than a little deceptive.

Watch and listen; she was expert at that. They had been in more scrapes together than she could recall.

Erin and Auriol strolled down the drive and across the fields with Jasper in tow, romping around their feet. Farm machinery came rumbling by, all gussied up for its annual display, the drivers for once wearing polished boots and pressed jackets. Not much work would be done in these parts today.

Erin, for once, was in excellent spirits, despite the fact she had still not spoken to Rod. He had emailed twice, just to be in touch, though with no endearments or any real news, sounding from his cursory scribble bothered and very stressed. Erin's heart softened: she loved the man, could imagine how tough it must be for him knowing she was in danger he couldn't control. It frustrated her to be stuck down here but, in her more lucid moments, she understood. It was part of his job, as editor, to protect her. All had gone quiet on the Russian front which was not to say she could lower her guard. Assassins might strike at any time no matter how cautious she was. Here, however, she felt quite safe though missed Rod unbearably.

Auriol was in a frivolous mood, determined to have a good day out. Her personal problems would keep until after the show. One of these days she'd confide in Erin, till then she intended to put it on hold. Jasper joyfully raced around, glad to have their combined attention. Erin stooped and tossed him a stick which he caught in mid-air and rushed back to place at her feet.

'Careful,' warned Auriol, 'or he'll have you at it all day.'

'I don't mind.' Erin found him cute; though she was mainly a cat person, Jasper was growing on her. If she spent any length of time down here she might even get a dog herself – subject, of course, to Perseus's approval.

They were nearly there. There were volunteers directing cars into parking slots and a couple of women sat at the gate, selling tickets. One of them, the farmer's wife, recognised Auriol and her dog so Auriol introduced her to Erin, her neighbour.

Effie, who never forgot a face, knew precisely who Erin was. 'You haven't been in to see me yet,' she scolded.

'Sorry,' said Erin. 'There hasn't been time.' Though

what she'd been up to she couldn't have said. It was hard to believe she had been here almost three months.

Effie looked at the pair of them, attractive independent women doing whatever they wanted to with their lives. She could tell from the cut of Auriol's clothes that this was another sophisticate, down from London for whatever reason, slumming it in the country. She noticed she wore no wedding ring and acted as though she owned the world with her chilly good looks and confrontational stare. Fascinating, both of them; she would like to know them better.

'Are you here for long?' she asked Auriol, knowing exactly how Erin was fixed. Here for the summer, she'd said, in a borrowed house.

'Here indefinitely,' Auriol said, showing her perfect teeth in a rueful smile. 'Unless, of course, I can get some mug to take the house off my hands.' She glanced at Erin who also laughed though both were too classy to labour the point. It was rude to make fun of the village in front of the locals.

Effie looked at them pointedly and said perhaps she would see them in church. There was plenty of community work if they hadn't enough to do.

'Well, that's us sorted,' whispered Erin as they took their tickets and moved through the gate. 'Basket weaving or making jam. Your choice.'

Together they drifted round the show, Jasper now

safely back on his lead to stop him interfering with the livestock. There were pens of sheep and cows and pigs and some glorious llamas with soulful eyes. Erin suggested they take one home and let it loose in the grounds. It would make an exotic talking-point as well as save them money in mowing bills.

'Someone would have to clear up its mess. The deer are bad enough, as it is.'

'Sylvia could be in charge of it. She seems quite an expert at shovelling shit.' Both cracked up, in agreement about their neighbour.

They watched the judges run practised hands over hocks and withers and studying teeth, then moved away to look at the morris dancers. A troupe of men in distinctive clothes leapt up and down with their hankies and bells, bashing tambourines and tooting whistles. Auriol and Erin collapsed as one, then stifled their giggles and quickly moved on.

'Do you think you could fancy one?' asked Erin.

'No,' said Auriol. 'Though I can't put my finger on why.'

Close at hand was a tarot tent where Madame Hortense would read your cards. 'I'll treat you,' Auriol said but Erin declined. Even though it was all just a load of claptrap, she didn't feel comfortable playing with fate. Not while she knew that she might be a sitting target.

* * *

Kasia was in the refreshments tent, serving homemade cakes from the deli. She acknowledged them with a professional smile, handed them menus then went away. She looked very *soignée* and well turned out, as chic as anyone in a five-star hotel.

They ordered coffee. 'I like that girl. She is smart and savvy, too good to be here. She ought to be working at Gidleigh Park or, better still, the Caprice.' Auriol had an eye for such things, had only ever moved in the smartest circles.

Erin agreed. 'I wonder why she is doing such menial work,' she said. It could only be due to her being an immigrant.

'But why is she here at all?' Auriol wondered aloud.

'Perhaps there's a boyfriend,' Erin said. Though where she had met him was anyone's guess. The Polish invasion of qualified workers was spreading all over the country.

'Ask her,' prompted Auriol, curious too.

So Erin did when Kasia brought them cakes and coffee that was unusually good. 'You should be running a place of your own,' she said. 'So why are you here?'

Kasia pondered. 'I like it,' she said. 'Polish countryside not so good.' She waved her hand round the tent. 'Better standard of living.'

So why not London? But they didn't pursue it, none

of their business in any case. But she spoke and dressed like somebody more than a waitress.

Crazy Betty was working backstage, clearing plates and washing them up, scuttling out like a frightened rat to fill up her big tin tray. She looked a mess in her old worn clothes, filched from somebody's duster drawer, but Kasia had kitted her out in a starched linen apron.

'It's good to see her working indoors.' Auriol had met her more than once while walking the dog in the woods. A strange gnarled creature of uncertain age, muttering and chattering to the birds, occasionally whistling like a songbird herself. In London they would have rounded her up or else she'd be sleeping rough on the streets. Here they treated her kindly as one of their own.

It was late afternoon and they were on their way home, full of good cheer having stopped at the pub, as easy and relaxed together as sisters. Barriers were lowered and secrets shared: Erin that Rod was a married man, Auriol that she was not the widow she allowed the world to believe. Erin knew where she should draw the line so said not a word about being in hiding. Auriol had an agenda, too, of which she would not divulge. They might be sisters under the skin yet neither knew how much she dared trust the other.

They followed the path that bordered the farm and then the shortcut that led through the woods. There they were faced once again with the ferns, taller still having not been scythed, Erin leading with Jasper close on her heels. Soon their own properties came into view, slate-grey tiles glinting in the sun, partially obscured by the clump of larches.

Erin halted and drew deep breaths, waiting for Auriol to catch up. 'Would you do it again?' she asked. 'Sell up in town and move to the country proper?'

'No,' said Auriol. 'Not a chance. If it weren't for you, I would hate living here. For one thing, I haven't met anyone else on my wavelength.'

Erin agreed. She had guessed as much and felt exactly the same. The neighbours were pleasant but lacked the essential humour.

'What about you?' asked Auriol. 'Is it feasible you might ever make such a move?'

Erin's reply surprised even herself, having not before now really thought it through. 'I quite enjoy having to rough it here without any shops or even a car. Living where I do, in the centre of things, you learn to take so much for granted.' Her job, a very good salary, the Clerkenwell loft, an expense account. A man she adored who adored her too but also the freedom to do as she liked without too many restrictions. Plus a licence to travel widely and have her byline on everything she wrote. The last bit she didn't tell Auriol, though. It was still too soon to reveal who she really was.

They soldiered on, Erin still in the lead, now able to see where she'd walked before. Ahead of them were the stakes that marked the manor's original driveway. Just round the bend they would find the clump of bamboo.

'Result!' she cried, her thumb in the air, then she lost her footing and fell headlong, something concealed in the ferns having snared her ankle.

'Drunk again,' said Auriol, laughing until she caught sight of Erin's face. And saw the way the dog was over-reacting.

Who it had been was not easy to say due to the damage done to the face. The nose had been pulped and knocked askew, both eyeballs rearranged. But the sun-baked curls, now matted with blood, and the blue shell necklet rang instant bells. They stared in silence at what had been done to lovely Peter the postman.

Autumn

16

It was the second week of September though the sky remained purest cerulean blue with hazy sunshine and the scent of apples wafting up from the orchard. There was a definite nip in the air. At night Erin closed all the windows and shivered and, even during the day, wore cashmere socks. This was the West Country at its best, glorious as the days grew shorter with the leaves on the turn and a faint whiff of bonfire smoke. She wondered where the woodpecker was, had not been aware of him now for several days. Perhaps he had emigrated; she couldn't blame him.

The village was still abuzz with the murder which had drawn together the neighbours in Endecott Park. Peter had been universally liked and his terrible death had occurred on their land. From what they heard, the police had no leads and were playing their cards very close to their chests. Gerald took it upon himself to check them out every day or so and pass on what he found out to the residents. Each in turn had been interviewed but no one, so far, had shed any light. The last time Peter had been seen alive was on the Saturday, five days before the show. His van was found parked in its usual place, in the narrow lane leading to the Sandy Park Inn which was where he often met his friends at weekends.

What he'd been doing late at night, which it was assumed was when he had died, was something not even his mother could account for. The killer would not have been after the mail; the post office closed for the whole weekend and Peter only had the use of the van as a favour. After all, as she pointed out, he worked all hours for them.

He was not a raver, did not take drugs and, although he admired a pretty face, did not have a regular girl-friend, as far as she knew. His main recreation throughout the summer was the surfing on the North Devon coast, hence his permanent tan and superlative fitness. In the winter he worked part-time in a carpentry shop.

'It's really shocking,' Gerald agreed as he passed on the gossip from house to house. At crisis times he came into his own, being a natural meddler. The crime rate round here was virtually nil. It was only by chance that Erin had stumbled upon him.

*   *   *

Literally stumbled. It wasn't a joke. Erin was suddenly horribly scared. The ruthless violence of his death – his throat had been slashed almost through to his spine – kept her awake and sweating, unable to sleep. All she was able to tell the police were the basic facts about finding the corpse, to all of which, luckily, Auriol had been witness. The mutilation of the face had happened, she fervently prayed, post-mortem. Only somebody totally sick could have done something like that. It threw her into a quandary as to whether or not she should fill them in about her own, so far unstated, situation. The police should be safe yet she couldn't be sure. Instructions from base had been explicit. Without formal authorisation, she should trust no one.

She tried several times to get through to Rod who still hadn't emailed or picked up her calls though news of the murder must surely have hit the nationals. So far her own name had not appeared though it could only be a matter of time, after which her contrived anonymity would be blown. Worse, though, was the disturbing fact that a maniac killer was loose round here, much more alarming than local fables of big black dogs or dismembered hands. Country folk were much simpler in their fears.

Though knowing she mustn't give too much away, she turned to Auriol for support. Being equally involved, Auriol was naturally similarly shaken. Her solution was always the same; despite her recent private resolve, she poured them both a massive gin even though it was not yet eleven. Comforted, Erin knocked hers back and didn't say no to a refill.

'Well,' she said, looking out at the moor and raising her glass in an ironic toast, 'here's to the rural idyll and glorious Devon.'

'Come now,' said Auriol, 'it's just a fluke.' She couldn't have Erin losing her nerve, she needed her far too much as her new best friend. Yet deep inside she was shaken too with a nasty suspicion she dared not yet share. In a way she had almost expected this. It had seemed too easy to escape down here and believe all her troubles were over.

Why Peter, though? He didn't fit in. She knew him only from their cheery morning encounters. And everyone else knew him just as well so where was the motivation? She must not let her fears get out of hand. She needed to put a brave face on things. 'It can be only coincidence', she said, 'that he died on our land.'

Erin, however, was not convinced. Trust no one, they had specifically said, which included everyone here.

And then, miraculously, out of the blue Erin's mobile rang and it was Rod. Finally, after these anxious weeks of waiting.

'I'm sorry, my darling,' were his opening words. 'But I had to go to Canada for a briefing.' Which didn't explain why he couldn't have called from there or sent an email.

Erin, however, was so relieved just to hear his voice after so much time that she bit back her fears and simply explained what had happened. He had heard already, hence his call, though dismissed it as pure coincidence. On the whole, assassins did not carry knives. They were deadlier and more devious, which he misguidedly seemed to consider a joke.

'I know it's tough.' His voice was smooth; he was trying his hardest to keep her calm. 'But it's still essential, my love, that you stay undercover.'

She did not agree, was sick of it all, she loathed it here and was longing to leave. 'If I promise to be careful,' she begged, but knew from his tone that he wasn't going to budge.

'I daren't put your life at further risk. It's not just you but the principle. I am in charge and responsible for my staff. It is that simple.'

Not simple at all. 'But I miss you,' she said, fighting hard to hold back her tears, determined that he should not hear her weaken. 'Can't you at least come down? I need to see you.'

'Afraid not,' he said. 'There's a crisis on. Something I can't discuss over the phone. It shouldn't be long.

I have reason to think this situation may soon resolve itself.'

Which was all, he explained, he could tell her over the phone. She must simply hang in there till she got the all clear and know he had only her best interests at heart. The important thing was he loved her; she must not forget that.

Did he, however? She was now not so sure, had a nasty suspicion of being sidelined, but Rod was under much pressure and had to hang up.

'You will hear from me soon, I promise,' he said. Then told her again how he felt.

This time Erin was so pissed off she gambled and let off steam to Auriol. As far as she felt she dared go, that is; she still held back on the relevant dangerous details. She was in a spot of bother, she said, which was why she was here in this borrowed house. The married man she had hinted at was her boss.

Auriol tutted, had suspected as much, had seen the way Erin's eyes lit up whenever she talked about work. This was a woman with much to give: Irish, free-thinking, red-headed as well, still in her thirties and passionate; wasted down here on her own. It was never wise to mix business and love. Only trouble could come of that and she, more than most, knew what she was talking about. She still wasn't clear what Erin did except she was some sort of journalist; Erin had been deliberately vague. Auriol imagined a woman's mag.

But the man in question, how close was he? Erin admitted as close as it gets. Too close for comfort, to tell the truth. The focal point of her universe if she were really honest. Auriol hugged her; she understood, more perhaps than she would say. The pain that was eating away at her too was only partly to do with her boiling rage. What they needed now was a real heart to heart, though preferably not in this horrible house. They could go for a walk if the woods weren't full of the uniformed mob and most of the grounds taped off for investigation. So instead she suggested Fingle Bridge, no more than fifteen minutes by car, where they could have a leisurely lunch and Jasper could romp with the fishes.

Jenny, watching them drive away from her unseen position within the van, urgently checked with control for updated instructions. This was an unforeseen happening; fraternising with the neighbours. Do nothing, she was told, until they return. They must not involve themselves with this death that had no connection with why they were here. She risked blowing her cover if she talked to the local police.

But, she explained, the party had left and was now outside their protection zone.

No problem, came the reply. Just remain alert.

Phil, who was itching to get involved – he could use some action, was stifled here – nevertheless went along with what they were told. He changed into his gardening gear; at least he could watch what was going on from the comfort of his own patio though there wasn't that much to see. Overalled experts with sniffer dogs surfaced occasionally from the woods and the area where the body had lain was now concealed by a tent. Orders were orders but, just in case, he kept his revolver stuck in his belt. It seemed an unlikely coincidence that danger should strike more than once.

17

Sylvia was snooping, as was her wont, keen to know what was going on. The police had made official visits to everyone in the complex. All they'd been told were the barest facts; someone had died in their private grounds and his body had been discovered under the ferns. Peter Stevens, a local man known to them all as he brought the post, twenty-four, the son of a widowed mother.

Was it true that his throat had been slit? The sombre policeman refused to say. He was there to establish their whereabouts on that night. Sylvia shuddered, vicariously thrilled. Finally they had some action here. Were there any significant leads? The officer flatly refused to speculate.

Where had she been that particular night? Home as always, no need to check. They rarely went out at all since they'd moved down here. Gerald, too, though if she were honest she could not put a finger on when he'd come home. He was spending more and more time in the pub though she saw no reason to let the police know that. She confirmed they had been together that night though, if it should come to a court of law, it would be his word against hers. There were, after all, limits.

Riveting stuff. She ran to the phone to update both daughters on what had occurred. News that she hoped would not be met with their customary lack of approval. She was disappointed. Lucy was out and Francesca, as always, bursting with angst. Money, or rather the lack of it, and the regular unsubtle hint that her father might help. No real interest in Sylvia's news, not even the fact that a murder had been committed right on her doorstep.

Gerald returned in a more buoyant mood having soaked up news in the public bar. The postboy's gruesome death came top in the areas of public debate. Numerous theories were being put forth, a few of them weirder than the rest, ranging from simple robbery to interference from a higher source. Flying saucers and all that guff; here they were steeped in the twilight zone. Gerald, for once, was ready for lunch. He opened a beer and settled down to relate to Sylvia the more outlandish stories.

'Nothing straightforward happens here. It was either the Hound of the Baskervilles or some vengeful spirit, back from the dead, settling an ancient score.'

'By killing the postman?' It did seem extreme though Sylvia could suspend disbelief having always been faintly gullible with not very much to occupy her mind.

He held back the nastier details, though, that someone had ripped out the poor fellow's eyes. And that the head, when they'd moved the corpse, had practically fallen off. He could cope with unvarnished violence, with which the streets of the city were rife, but graphic sadism of this kind turned even Gerald's stomach. Talk about red in tooth and claw. Not even nature at her worst was quite as perverse as that.

One positive thing he had found out, though; the Commander was back unexpectedly. He had flown into Exeter late last night and lights had been seen in the gatehouse. He would not let him slip away again. Gerald was busily making plans. This time, whatever it took, he would pin him down.

It was time for a visit to Annie's Place though her roots were fine and a cut not yet due. Sylvia wanted to hear the gossip, the details that Gerald had overlooked. You could not expect all the nuances from a man. Besides, she was getting cabin fever having not talked to anyone in a week. No one of any consequence; she didn't include her husband. Apart from the murder, Sylvia was keen to test the social atmosphere since her party. They had dropped her notes and a couple had called but it wasn't the same as meeting them face to face.

The salon, as always, was fully booked but they squeezed her in at a quarter to one. It would mean making Gerald wait for his lunch but Sylvia wasn't concerned. It wouldn't hurt him to fend for himself or even eat at the Ring o'Bells which she was sure, in any case, he would prefer. He spent so much of his time there now he was part of the fixtures and fittings.

Annie, as usual, was in full flow though she lowered her voice when Sylvia came in. 'I'll be with you in a minute,' she called, directing her to a chair. The listeners round her all leaned closer to catch the tail end of her story.

Sylvia picked up a magazine, straining her ears to overhear. She was disappointed, after all these months, not to be treated as one of them. She had, after all, invited them all to her house. A few of them smiled and acknowledged her but nobody even bothered to ask how she was. All ears were glued to Annie and her story.

Annie was regaling them with a creepy thing that had happened to her uncle one night when driving home very late from Moretonhampstead. Such things were always one person removed, thought Sylvia sniffily, listening in. You never met anyone in real life who had actually seen a ghost. Not that she didn't believe in them; local lore was packed with stories. But she found Peter's horrible murder far more upsetting.

The uncle's story was simply this: he'd been driving along the old turnpike road when a man stepped out, straight into the path of his car. The uncle had swerved but felt a dull thud and was sickened to think he had mowed the poor devil down. But when he got out to investigate, the road was empty; there wasn't a sign of anyone having been there. Nothing at all. No blood, no dent, no undergrowth that might conceal a body. Only the open road on a clear moonlit night.

'And,' continued Annie with relish, 'when he stopped for a brandy to calm his nerves, there were folk in the pub who told a similar story. Turns out it's a famous accident spot where, over the years, many people have died. The thing about my uncle is he saw the man close up in detail and heard a very definite bang as he stumbled against the car.' Her spellbound audience hung on her words, enthralled.

Gerald would have dismissed it as bunkum but Sylvia was more easily swayed. She found these Dartmoor stories extremely disturbing. Almost everyone had one to tell be it piskies, werewolves or great black

171

cats; it could be something to do with the lack of street lighting. But she minded more that they shut her out. By now they should treat her with proper respect, part of the local community, entitled to recognition. When it was her turn in the chair, she cut out the gossip and gave curt instructions as to how exactly she wanted her hair to look. No letting Annie do her own thing, relaxing while she experimented and laughing along with her jokes like one of the gang. She sensed she wasn't popular, the other clients were starting to leave and Annie herself was reduced to an awkward silence. Regretting that she had messed things up, Sylvia tried too late to get a conversation rolling. But Annie seemed now to have nothing to say, had one eye on the clock for her next appointment.

Which was always the problem with this sort of place. It could take generations to be accepted.

Gerald was having problems too becoming part of the coterie. Despite the number of rounds he bought and the hours he spent in the Ring o'Bells, he still felt a rank outsider. Even those he had entertained seemed to clam up when he appeared though he noticed they rarely declined an offer of drinks. Gerald, though, was a man of the world. If that was what it took, he would pay the price. He was well aware at this stage in his life that he needed them more than they needed him. His future hung on his hopes of becoming accepted.

He had heard the Commander was back, he said, glancing around for some confirmation but nobody even let on that they knew who he meant. Even the barman's back was turned as he busied himself with changing a barrel. Gerald's words seemed to fall into empty air. He shrugged and wondered what more he could do. Perhaps he had better go home after all. He stood more chance of encountering him there since they were, after all, near neighbours. It occurred to him to call at the house. Country manners were more relaxed and he had already made the initial connection.

So he blustered about and paid his bill, cheerily taking his leave of them. They sat in silence and watched him go then, catching each other's eye, exchanged a grin. One thing was clear to the lot of them without anyone having to spell it out: no matter how long he stayed around and bought them drinks as an obvious bribe, a man as flashy as Gerald Brennan would never be accepted into their set.

18

The police were back he saw as he parked the car. Ned recognised the one in charge and strolled across to greet him. Sergeant Hollis, if that was right, a burly chap of roughly his age who had called the previous night making routine inquiries. They had found a body in nearby woodland, identified as a local chap, and were now conducting a closer investigation. Ned had been out, not yet back from work, but Lisa had given them chapter and verse of her own movements around the time they assumed the murder had occurred. She'd been cooking supper, as she always did, while listening to *The Archers*. Ned found it touching how hard she was trying to fit in. Not that they socialised very much; he found the neighbours a spurious crowd, some endeavouring to appear what they clearly were not. Lisa accused him of snobbery but Ned was merely fastidious, preferring to keep himself to himself until he knew people better.

'Good evening, Inspector. Any news?' he asked with his silvery smile. The rimless lenses were very slightly tinted.

'Sergeant, sir. And the answer is no though we have established the cause of death.' The facial wounds had been superficial though he didn't go into details.

'Poor young chap. We never met though he and my wife were on quite good terms. He was very obliging, I understand, and occasionally ran her errands.'

The policeman nodded and scribbled a note. He had met the wife who had told him that too. He appreciated their cooperation. 'Nasty business, especially here where residents leave their doors unlocked. I wouldn't advise that, sir, as I'm sure you'd agree.'

'Indeed I do.' There was not much sense in paying to live in a gated park and then forgetting to close the stable door. Ned shook his hand. He was usually home around seven, he said, should there be further questions.

She was wearing pink and looked very young with her freshly washed hair hanging loose on her shoulders. Ned pecked her cheek – she wore almost no make-up – and went upstairs to divest himself of his suit.

'Something smells good.' His mood was benign and

Lisa was pleased when he uncorked the wine. She liked it when he came home in an affable mood.

'Good day, dear?'

He gave a shrug. His days were all very similar. He liked the job, which was not too taxing, as well as the pleasant drive home. Unless, of course, he encountered traffic disruptions.

Lisa had cooked his favourite meal, baked lamb with tomatoes and rosemary, so he chose a light red that would go very comfortably with it. He set the bottle on the table to breathe, then went to wash his hands again. The cloakroom, he observed with approval, was spotless. She was not a bad wife, he had chosen well. After living four months together, he still had no serious quibbles.

Except when she tried to mother him which almost instantly stuck in his craw. Sometimes she treated him like a very small boy. She was giving him now that proprietary smile that occasionally threatened to unhinge him.

'Now eat it all up, you are far too thin. I noticed the way your trousers hang. You're supposed to put on weight when you're newly married.' She leaned across and stroked his cheek, her look unusually provocative. Ned felt himself instantly tensing and choked on his wine. He wanted to scream at her to back off, that now was not the time to be making advances.

Instead he leaned over and sliced the bread. 'I saw the police outside,' he said. 'They don't appear to have got very far with their inquiry.'

Lisa sighed as she tidied up. She was getting nowhere in the intimacy stakes. Whenever she tried to up things a notch, she was all too aware of her husband backing off. It had been four months, a third of a year. She had hoped to have made some progress by now. She had read the books and the magazines which told her that patience was the key. Though she didn't want to scare him off, she was starting to grow disheartened at having to wait. In the films she had seen and the books she had read there was almost always a resolution by the end. She had soaked in the bath and washed her hair then drenched herself in expensive scent. The underpinnings she wore were from her trousseau. No one had loved her as a child. She only dimly remembered her mother, and her father, long before he died, had taken his interest elsewhere.

She gritted her teeth; she would soldier on. She had made her bed and must lie in it. If it were the last thing she did, Lisa was determined to make Ned love her.

His mother, Helge, had treated him like that, humouring him when she wanted something, trying to bribe him with her pretence at love. Eat your greens or wash your hands, do your homework or practise your scales. Instructions, though stern, had always come sugar-coated. A chocolate bar or a Dinky toy, whatever it took to bring him to heel in the fastest and least trou-blesome way that would not interrupt her work. It made him feel he was in the way, that she had more important things on her mind: patients to see or the house to clean or else a paper to write by the following day. She trotted him out when it suited her, her darling boy who looked so like her with his classic features and straight dark hair and the silvery eyes she said he had got from his father.

His mother didn't get on with men, had trivial-ised them in a radical way, displaying her contempt with little restraint. As a Jungian therapist of note, she had forged a career of great distinction since leaving her native Oslo and moving to London. His father, Charles Thornton, was a classicist she only married in order to have a child. He had played no role at all in Ned's life, had died before Ned was old enough to question the set-up or even want to meet him.

Ned had lived with his mother the whole of his life until her death five years ago when he was in his late thirties and she not quite at the apex of her career. Though he never discussed it with anyone, he was still adjusting to the loss. He'd been seeing someone privately about his emotional state.

Lisa had been an experiment he still devoutly hoped would work out. He needed a woman in his life though would never find one who could fill the gap created by Helge's death.

Now he looked round the door and beamed. 'That was lovely, dear. An excellent meal. It's a perfect night. How would you like a walk?'

He had the newspaper in his hand and Mozart playing on Radio 3. He never so much as cleared the table; presumably she had his mother to blame for that.

Lisa, pulling off rubber gloves, turned to him brightly and forced a smile. 'Wait while I put on my walking boots,' she said.

'No need for that. It is growing dark.' The nights were already drawing in. 'I thought', he said with his luminous smile, 'that we might stroll down to the lower meadow and check out the situation with the police.'

Lisa recoiled. What a gruesome thought. The last thing she wanted to see was the murder site. She had looked upon Peter as a friend and hadn't yet come to terms with his horrible death. She bit back her reservations, though, would do whatever it took to make Ned happy.

'If you'll wait,' she said, 'I'll pop up and fetch my wrap.'

19

The shock of seeing the poor dead postman jerked Auriol into a new awareness. Life continued around her while she smouldered. Or, rather, death; she could not erase the memory of that horribly brutalised face. He had been so young and enthusiastic, the age a son of her own might have been. Now she acknowledged how much she had missed out in life. And all because of a misplaced love, a passion that had grown out of control, though this was no time to be beating up on herself. Something seriously bad was happening and she had a suspicion she might have unwittingly triggered it off herself. The flip side of passion can be very ugly. She paced the floor in the early hours, for once entirely sober.

Someone out there must have reason to kill. She refused to believe Peter's murder was purely random. The village might talk about ancient myths but Auriol came from a seamier world and recognised a warning shot when she saw one. It was someone with access to these grounds, though doubtless the postman had his own key. The police would know the details without her prompting. Her mind tracked back to three years ago when they'd bought the land as a safe investment, largely to satisfy her romantic whim. Then she had been at her fighting best, determined nothing should get in the way of a dream that had taken so long to come to fruition. Forces of evil she thought had withdrawn she sensed were now regrouping on the horizon. Even if she did it alone, it was imperative that they should be stopped.

Auriol dressed to face the day. Her hand was steady, her eye was bright. She unlocked the door and whistled the dog. They were taking an early walk. Conflict was something that she enjoyed, always had and always would. All her fighting instincts came flooding back. She'd allowed herself to be victimised but that was now firmly in the past; enough was more than enough. Don't tangle with me, she snarled to herself as she crossed the lawn and skirted the woods. The makeshift tent was still there, repelling invaders.

'Morning, miss,' said a weary cop, intimating with delicacy that she must not cross the official blue-and-white tape.

'Morning,' she said with her brightest smile. 'I bet you've had quite a night of it here. You are more than welcome at my place for coffee as soon as you come off duty.'

She wasn't quite certain what she was after but suddenly longed to be back in the fray. If they trusted her and would share information she might even give them a lead or two. She already had an idea of where they should look.

They didn't come though she'd thought they might; instead they sent their regrets. Too busy sifting the clues, she assumed, though she might have saved them a lot of wasted time. No matter. She'd do it on her own, was accustomed to getting her way in the end. There was lots she could teach a bunch of halfwit cops in a sleepy village.

'You sound cheerful,' Erin said, roused from her sleep at an early hour. She couldn't believe it was Auriol on the phone.

'Do me a favour and come with me. I'll be outside waiting in half an hour. There is something I need to investigate. I could use some moral support.'

Erin's attention was instantly caught. She loved a challenge of any kind and helping her friend with whatever it was might take her mind off her own danger. For danger it was; she was positive now that the postman's death was no coincidence. Someone was attempting to flush her out. These were well-known tactics the Soviets used to show their enemies who was boss. They must suspect where she was and were breaking her cover.

A wild excitement coursed through her as she stood beneath a scalding shower. Her senses had started to atrophy here, she had been too long off the job. She wondered whether she should tell Rod, then recalled his insouciance. If he loved her too little to come when she called she would sort things out by herself.

Auriol was waiting, bright-eyed and alert, standing beside her car, the keys in her hand. Jasper was already stowed in the back and he greeted Erin with a hopeful yelp. This was his pal from the other day who had given him so much attention.

'Thanks for coming.' Auriol's smile was broad. 'Sorry to drag you out of your bed.'

'I have the rest of my life to sleep,' said Erin, getting in.

It was not yet seven. She glanced around the empty complex, still fast asleep. The Range Rover was parked outside the gatehouse.

'Someone's up early.' She indicated but Auriol was slowing down for the gates which automatically opened to let them out.

'He must have arrived last night,' Auriol said. 'I haven't seen hide nor hair of him since the week before the show.' She glowed with health and determination, groomed and prepared for what lay ahead. Erin had never seen her so vitalised.

'Where are we going?'

'Wait and see. I hope you are free for the rest of the day.' She edged into the early traffic heading for Whiddon Down. And after that to the motorway. 'I can't let you know too much,' said Auriol. 'Yet.'

When they reached the outskirts of Exeter the rush hour proper was underway. Auriol tightened her grip on the wheel and tried to curb her impatience. Erin, intrigued, was content to wait, surprised at how Auriol's mood had improved. From being a lush on the brink of despair, she had overnight metamorphosed to a steely-eyed killer. Whatever it was that was driving her now was not something Erin would care to have to deal with.

Auriol bypassed the city, knowing it well, and came at St David's obliquely. In the deep ravine where the station lay were acres of faceless industrial estate divided into separate lots by neon signs and chain fencing. Auriol slowed and consulted the map; things had changed since she'd been here last but she soon found whatever it was that she sought and put down her foot again. Then took a sudden sharp turn to the left, up a steep back alley that was a dead end and terminated in a grassy space fronted by a stone wall. She leapt from the car, slamming the door, and went to peer over the wall. After a pause, Erin followed her, mystified and curious to know what her friend could possibly be after here in this uninspiring terrain. She suddenly seemed to be in a world of her own.

Below them lay the railway tracks, bordered by the industrial estate; miles of identical Nissen huts set in a concrete jungle. She was searching for something though didn't say what and all of a sudden located it. Triumphantly she clutched Erin's sleeve and indicated a parking lot beneath them.

'See that,' she exclaimed. 'The yellow car.' All Erin could see was a distant blur. 'The famous primrose Lagonda, his pride and joy.'

'Where are we looking? At what, I mean?'

'Believe it or not, the HQ of Swann Homes. He never was one for ostentation except, of course, for the car. He always was a sleazy git. It's those little details that give him away.' Her face, when she turned, was a mask of vindictiveness.

'Why are we here?' Erin still didn't know, had never seen Auriol so hyped up.

'Just checking out the lie of the land. I had an instinct that the bastard was back.'

20

Betty watched the policemen at work and skirted the crime scene, unseen by them. Having felt invisible all her life, at this she was now an expert. She saw the forensic experts arrive and later leave with a body bag. In the afternoon a local team came up to the site for the fingertip search. They were being very thorough; she was impressed.

She had known him well, since a tiny child, the polite young man with the pleasing smile who had many times stopped just to pass the time of day. She never received any mail, of course, so he hadn't precisely known who she was except Crazy Betty who lived in the woods and was one sandwich short of a picnic. More credit, then, to him for his courtesy.

She felt sad for the mother, already a widow, for losing a child at that tender age, knew only too well the trauma it must have caused her. For Betty had been the replacement child whose conception had seemed like a miracle, born to a mother of forty-two within a year of her first daughter's tragic death. Glorious Violet, their future hope, had perished at a similar age in the terrible fire that had also destroyed the manor.

They had given Betty the exact same name, Violet Elizabeth, sharing her birth sign, and endowed her with the same qualities: the gaiety, the precociousness and the charm. She had been conceived as a replica but all she'd achieved was a pale pastiche with washed-out colours and none of the spirit the first child had possessed. Small wonder her parents had turned their backs, her mother later succumbing to grief after her father gambled away what should have been rightly hers. They had raised her in a foreign land to which they had fled in their terrible grief and later died there, leaving her alone with no one to turn to.

Like a homing pigeon, she had found her way here and taken up residence in the place she knew by instinct should be hers by right. Very few people knew who she was and she had deliberately kept her identity secret. But these were her roots and this was her land. She had settled here for the rest of her life. And now another disaster had struck on the same spot as the first. Another tragically early death even more gruesome than the first. At least the destruction of the house could have been accidental.

She was only ever an afterthought, born to parents too old to cope. In modern times she'd be categorised as neglected, if not abused. Mama spent her days in a darkened room, hiding away from the African sun, lamenting the cool green countryside of the Devon where she had grown up. The baby she wasn't able to love was raised by servants who were cautious though kind. Knowing how overly precious she was, they could not allow her too close.

Her father, fifty when she was born, was already prey to the heart disease that was to carry him off in just a few years. Unable to deal with an active child, he had passed his afternoons at the club, playing poker and harking back to the good old days before the onset of war. Mama found God and a handsome priest; Father Domleo was constantly there, attempting to stem her unassuageable grief. If one of her children had had to die . . . The thought, though obscene, had hung in the air and Betty was sharp enough to have picked it up. She had always known, from an early age, had heard the whispers when nobody knew she was there. Had grown up aware how much she had failed to fulfil her reason for living.

Her only confidante was Odile, exiled from France

as the Germans advanced, now employed in Happy Valley to raise the unwanted child. Odile was sallow, tight-lipped and tense but her musical skills were superlative. She had taught the lonely child to play to very high standards indeed. They passed their days in the dreary schoolroom, practising scales and later far more. Due to the heat the house was dark as the blinds were drawn for most of the day, though the morning mists Mama so much loved fostered the feeling of England.

Having abandoned all they owned, the Endecotts found they could not return to Dartmoor because of the intervening war. The house was a ruin, their daughter dead, her grave neglected on the windswept moor. Four thousand miles away, in the heat, the mother could not stop grieving.

'She was such a spirited child,' she sobbed while the fawning padre caressed her hand. They would sit in the half-light, sipping tea, and she would dab her eyes with cologne-soaked lace while the baby, conceived to fulfil a need, cried in the nursery unheard.

'Did I mention she danced with the Prince of Wales?' The litany was unstoppable. It wasn't only the daughter's death that had left the mother so deprived.

Betty was still only seventeen when her mother thoughtlessly passed away, leaving her the plantation house and what little remained of her father's estate once his gambling debts had been settled. There was no one in Kenya to whom she could turn nor was there family that she knew of. Communications with home had ceased when her parents did their overnight flit and the intervention of war had sealed the split. Even Odile had relocated to Uganda.

Betty, entirely alone in the world, was faced with making an adult decision. She paid off the servants and sold the house, dispersing its contents for less than their worth, then left with a few possessions for what she called home. Having never been out of the Valley before, she was dazzled by London's awesome size so spent just one night in a cheap hotel before catching a train down to Devon. From Exeter a pony and trap conveyed her the last twenty miles to the village in which her family had lived since records began.

At first she drifted aimlessly until, wandering into the nearest pub, she was stopped in her tracks when she came face to face with the painting of her sister. A dramatic portrayal that leapt off the wall of a vibrant young woman whose challenging eyes arrested the attention of all who entered. She virtually breathed.

'Violet Endecott,' said the barman, intrigued by the young girl's apparent shock. 'Quite a character in her time, so they say.'

190

Betty said nothing, just stood there and stared while the landlord brought her lemonade. This land had been owned by her ancestors, not only the manor but much of the village as well. This was her sister hanging here in a public bar for the world to see. She had seen old lithographs of the manor before its untimely destruction. She was still underage yet knew her rights. One of her forebears, after all, had been a Pilgrim Father.

The burnt-out ruin existed still. The second she saw it, it felt like home though Betty had no way of proving who she was. Someone must have the deeds to the land but no one here even knew she'd been born, though all remembered her sister's death on the night of the terrible fire. So she found cheap lodgings and went to ground, supporting herself by doing odd jobs. And over the intervening years had transmogrified into the wild-eyed creature she was now. No one had ever cared about her. She had passed her long and lonely life living hand to mouth.

That was fifty years ago. New generations had grown up and gone. Betty was part of the local landscape and everyone knew who she was. Or thought they did: just an ageing crone who sang to herself and whistled tunes that, had they listened, possessed quite a musical flair. She had found a decrepit caravan, once gaudily painted, now falling apart, with a short flight of steps to a cosy main room, a chimney and wood-burning stove. Here she had taken up residence, in an empty glade in the Endecott woods, close to the spot where her sister, Violet, had perished. Her friends were the animals and birds. She slept through the day and rose with the moon to ramble around her estate, keeping watch over things.

Something was definitely going on; the powers of evil had now encroached and the atmosphere in this peaceful haven had changed. Since the cowboy builders had come on the scene, there was noise and dirt and general disruption. No one was what they seemed any more. She was starting to be afraid. The vicar and Effie looked out for her and would prefer she go into a home. But Betty's free spirit refused to be tamed. As long as she still had breath in her body, she would live on the land that she owned.

Or die defending it, should it come to that.

21

It was Erin's day for her weekly shop; she was into a practised regime. What she couldn't carry she now ordered from Tesco, though they had to come over from Newton Abbot and she still preferred to eat local stuff when she could. The weather was bright with a nip in the air so she tugged on boots and got out the trusty knapsack. She could have asked Auriol for a lift but was now well-used to the six-mile slog, also rather enjoyed the exercise. She had plenty to think about today: the murder and also Auriol's revelations. She had swung overnight from a sozzled depressive into being a spirited warrior queen though had not, as yet, divulged the salient details. All Erin deduced from their Exeter jaunt was that the proprietor of Swann Homes was not a person with whom to get involved.

She would fill her in later, Auriol had said, reversing

the car and speeding off. She insisted on treating Erin to lunch at the fancy Royal Clarence Hotel where prices hit London levels. Which was fine with Erin who felt like a bit of spoiling. They laughed and joked and had a good time though Auriol hardly drank because she was driving. She was witty and sharp and now very controlled and through the laughter her beauty showed, giving Erin a glimpse of what she must have once been. She was nearing fifty, admitted to that, but now could have been a good fifteen years less. Erin's age, in fact, give or take a year. In fighting form and ready to settle some long outstanding scores.

'Once everything's sorted I'll sell the house, get out of here and move back to town. The truth is, this isn't the dream I thought I'd bought into.' Which, for the moment, was all she would say. In time she would dish the dirt on the man she had loved but now despised.

All of this ran through Erin's mind as she set off cheerfully into the woods, skirting the field that scared Auriol's dog for reasons they couldn't work out. It was strange how at home she felt these days, having lived here almost a third of a year. Her longing for London had virtually ceased; she was growing acclimatised. Even the hike seemed less arduous; she managed it now in two-thirds of the time and climbed the steep hill to the village square without having to pause for breath. Back in town she might get a bike; she was fitter now than she'd been in years and felt that much better for it.

Rod was still never far from her thoughts though lately she'd stopped feeling quite so bereft. Though she studied the newspapers every day and kept tabs on the Internet, she had failed to find any references to the danger she was avoiding. She wondered where her protectors were, had seen not a sign of them since she arrived. Amy, too, was a lot less often in contact. Erin sighed. It was par for the course, her fault entirely for taking up this profession.

She was through the woods and approaching the weir. The path seemed easier every time and she hailed a couple of walkers she'd met before. They stopped for a chat to discuss the terrain. She felt she was part of the village now and was losing the desperate need to get back to her work. Though her mind was toying with various ideas that might sometime develop into books.

She stopped at the deli to pick up some pies she could easily heat in the microwave. Kasia was there on her own and seemed pleased to see her. She insisted on serving her coffee outside and joined her since it was early yet and very few shoppers were out. The deli was beautifully situated, at the foot of stone steps leading up to the church and right next door to the post office and the bus stop. A perfect point for observing village life.

Kasia, as always, was immaculate in a starched white pinny and plain black dress with her thick blonde hair woven into her trademark plait. She brought out cheesecake, freshly made, and insisted that it was on the house. Like everything else she cooked, it was excellent.

'I can't imagine why you stay down here, mouldering away in this tiny place. You could make a killing in Exeter,' said Erin. 'Or even London.'

As far as she knew, Kasia lived alone. There had been no mention of any attachments. And yet she was not just efficient but gorgeous too.

Kasia shrugged. 'Is good down here. Country people very nice.'

Erin was curious why she had come in the first place.

Kasia's English was still very patchy. Quite often she seemed not to understand. 'I leave my country to look for work here,' she said.

Erin gave up. After all, it wasn't her business.

She wandered home by the longer route, across the bridge at the foot of the hill and along the path on the other side of the river. Here there were fields of golden corn waiting for harvest, not far off, and a handful of cows that had wandered down from the meadow. She hummed with contentment as she walked, enjoying the brilliance of the day and planning the lunch she would eat outside on the terrace. She couldn't complain; she was still on full pay and was learning to think of her exile as a vacation.

The water flowed swiftly beneath the willows. She reached the first of the kissing-gates and bundled her knapsack through. A man approached on the narrow path, fit and well-groomed in a shooting jacket, leather boots that came up to the knee and a rifle slung over one shoulder. Beside him walked a panting golden retriever.

'Good morning.' Politely he raised his cap and the sun gleamed off his silvering hair. The eyes were blue, Erin noticed that, and the smile relaxed and good-humoured.

'A great day for shooting.' She hadn't a clue but it seemed appropriate in the circumstances.

'Indeed,' he said, allowing her past. 'I believe we are neighbours up at Endecott Park.'

The man from the gatehouse, she should have known. Now she could see why he'd caught Auriol's eye, good-looking though of indeterminate age. She offered her hand. 'Erin O'Leary. Down for a few months' sabbatical.'

He looked at her long and hard before letting her

go. 'We must meet some time. Come in for a drink. I am only there very occasionally. Piers Compayne, by the way, and this is Rufus.'

Dishy indeed. She was very impressed and flattered by that appraising stare. She liked his style and the cut of his clothes, made by a first-rate tailor. She wondered why he came down here at all since he looked very much a man of the world. Older than her though clearly still in his prime. Piers Compayne. The name rang bells though, just for the moment, she couldn't think why. She could hardly wait to tell Auriol, who would be jealous.

Someone else was approaching now, moving swiftly with silent tread, face entirely obscured by a hooded cloak. The path was narrow so Erin paused and stood to one side with a friendly smile but the walker passed by without so much as a glance in her direction. Odd behaviour somewhere like this where almost everyone knew each other or, if they didn't, greeted you all the same. When she reached the second kissing-gate and turned to manoeuvre the narrow space, she saw with slight surprise that the walker had gone.

22

Gerald eventually got his chance, quite by accident; Sylvia was out and he saw the Commander on his way home with his dog. Quick as lightning Gerald was in there, stopping only to change his clothes and put on his RAC tie. He strolled in a very nonchalant fashion along to the gatehouse and rang the bell. The sun was suitably close to the yardarm though still a tad early for lunch.

'Gotcha!' he murmured under his breath as the bell resounded and set the dog barking inside.

After what seemed a very long wait, the Commander answered, phone in hand, and hesitated, uncertain of Gerald's name. 'Hello,' he said, looking faintly surprised, obviously waiting for Gerald to speak. No instant invitation inside, not even a friendly greeting. Gerald, flustered, stumbled his cue by asking him lamely how he was.

'I'm fine,' said his neighbour. 'Won't you come in?' And only then fully opened the door to admit him.

Gerald, embarrassed, had nothing to say, just stood there, in the immaculate hall, looking round. The Commander, still on the telephone, wandered away and left him there frantically thinking of some excuse for this impromptu visit.

'Well now.' Having completed the call, the Commander reappeared and stood there smiling.

'Um,' said Gerald, feeling a fool. 'I was wondering if you might still be here in November, for Guy Fawkes Night.' He improvised as fast as he could. 'We were thinking of having a few folks round. Fireworks, you know. That sort of thing. We thought a communal bonfire might be nice.'

The Commander watched his confusion but did not help.

'Drink?' he asked, after too long a pause, and led the way, reluctantly, into an attractive morning room. The house was Georgian and very well-kept, with furniture in impeccable taste set off by delicate floral prints and newly restored oak floors. On a sideboard stood a tray with bottles arrayed. Gerald chose gin and his host withdrew and came back carrying a lemon and ice. He indicated that Gerald should sit and he sank into an armchair. Mission accomplished but how the hell would he ever be able to talk his way out of this one?

He was saved by the bell. The telephone rang. The Commander answered and took it outside. 'Sorry,' he said on his return. 'It was something I had to deal with.' He was obviously busy and not in a mood for much chat.

'So this party,' he said, watching Gerald flounder, too suave and well-bred to score points off him though only a fool would believe that he couldn't see through his flimsy excuse. 'I am sorry I missed the last one. It couldn't be helped.'

'No problem.' Gerald was anxious to please. Having forced his way in, he was hoping to stay. A bonfire night party made actually rather good sense and need not be expensive. If he asked the neighbours to bring their own fireworks, with luck they'd bring bottles as well.

Gerald beamed and had a look round while his host remained standing and not at his ease. He poured himself a small Scotch which he quickly knocked back. 'I can't be sure I'll be here,' he said. 'Though I'll certainly come if I am.' He looked as though he considered the subject closed.

'Nice place you've got here.' Gerald got up and paced, frantically still fighting for time. He couldn't afford to lose this chance to get to know the man better. He was hoping he'd offer to show him round but no such invitation was forthcoming. And time was creeping on; he would soon have to leave. And then the telephone rang again and the Commander shrugged and left him to it. Seizing his chance, Gerald quickly started exploring.

Through the door was a dining room which led, in its turn, to a library which was where the Commander was taking the call which sounded like being a long one. Gerald, no connoisseur of such things, nevertheless could recognise class when he saw it. There were logs in the fireplace, ready to light, and bowls of chrysanthemums in each room but no other sign he could see of a feminine touch. Wait till Sylvia got on his case; she would be in her element making the place more cosy.

The phone call ended. The Commander returned. 'Sorry,' he said. 'There's a crisis on.'

'I thought you were retired,' Gerald said. 'A diplomat writing his memoirs.'

'Something like that,' the Commander agreed. 'Now, if you wouldn't mind, I am rather busy.'

'Mind if I just wash my hands?' Gerald asked as the telephone rang again.

He found the cloakroom all by himself: scarlet and panelled, with linen towels.

Beside it a half-closed door led into a room in semi-darkness. He couldn't resist it, just had to peek, his host wouldn't even know where he was. He opened the door and looked inside then stopped in his tracks in amazement. The room was an office with blinds fully drawn to protect the massive technology: a mainframe computer that half-filled the space, covered with lights flashing on and off, clearly in full operation. A telex machine was working away, spewing out pages at breakneck speed. One whole wall was taken up by a full-sized cinema screen.

'Blimey!' said Gerald, backing away, stupefied by what he had seen.

'Satisfied?' asked the Commander crisply, glancing now quite pointedly at his watch.

'I've looked him up in *Who's Who*,' Gerald said. 'It doesn't say much about what he does except that he is a former diplomat.' Which was what he had thought.

'We'll ask him to dinner,' Sylvia said. 'He's bound to be more expansive then.' Though who she would ask along with him she couldn't immediately think. Not the redhead, that was for sure. Nor the widow from number one. The vicar, perhaps, though she didn't really know him. This was her chance, though, for social advancement. Whatever she did, she must get it right. Social occasions like this were rare especially here in the sticks.

Which meant a worried few days for her, cookbooks perused and a date set with Annie well in advance to get her colour done. She mustn't be caught on the hop and found to be wanting. Gerald paced and muttered and swore, deep in some turbulence of his own, details of which he still didn't share with her. He was losing weight and he didn't sleep. He disappeared for much of the day, leaving her alone in her own private hell. What she felt she needed was a hostess course, to spruce up her entertaining skills. She had been too long out of the social whirl; it was now fourteen months since they'd moved down here and, apart from the party, she hadn't had anyone in. Nor had the children been down many times though the place had been planned as a weekend retreat for them all. Too far, said both daughters, and too much hassle. Whitstable would have been a more popular choice.

Now it was already autumn again. Soon the nights would be drawing in and the daylight hours would shrink to a miserable few. No one would want to drive all this way; she was trapped again like a rat in a drain. Even Exeter seemed too far since she'd nobody there to visit. Gerald still urged her to join a class but she turned up her nose at what was on offer. Flower arranging was something she took in her stride. She saw herself as a seasoned hostess if only Gerald would deliver the goods and find her some guests who were worthy of all that effort.

The Commander, however, was proving elusive and November still several weeks off. The thought of a fireworks party filled her with gloom. Mud all over her fitted carpets and smoke seeping in from the bonfire outside. It was bound to drizzle, it always did, which would wreck her hairdo and spoil the food which she'd have to serve inside. She didn't know anyone well enough to ask for a hand with the entertaining. The Polish waitress would cost too much and it wasn't that sort of occasion.

Gerald fretted and Sylvia sulked. The country idyll was turning into a nightmare.

23

Lisa was competitive too, though nowhere near in
Sylvia's league. She would be content with a perfect
home and a husband she could be proud of. Who
was proud of her too; that was her secret concern.
She thought he loved her, he said he did but only
when she asked him outright and even then he trivial-
ised the subject. 'Wait till the ring is on the finger'
was one of the edicts of Lisa's youth. Her stepmother
used it a lot and she ought to know. She had hooked
Lisa's father in just a few months after Lisa's mother
died prematurely and both the half-sisters had also
found husbands quickly. By playing by their mother's
rules, she supposed.

Lisa was not much of a flirt; she was too uptight
to put it about though, in her slightly stand-offish way,
some men found her appealing. She had learnt the
hard way not to come on too strong. She had longed

for a husband and children, too, having been deprived of a mother's love and emotionally neglected most of her life. But her earnest manner put suitors off; often by only the second date she already appeared too keen.

'When shall I see you again?' she would ask. 'Why not come over for supper next week?' And if they agreed she'd, as likely as not, have another social suggestion up her sleeve: theatre tickets or a private view. Suitors sometimes found disentangling themselves very sticky. When several dates in a row dropped her flat, she retreated into her shell.

Her wish for a child had never been strong; she wasn't by nature at all maternal, found even the basics messy and distasteful. The same applied to pets; she had never had one. Nor wanted one though the cat next door was kind of cute and kept wandering in or sunning himself on her patio while she was gardening. Perseus: he had a lovely face and a steady purr like a sewing machine and he wasn't forever leaping on her or making demands for food.

Ned liked animals, so he said, and often watched nature programmes on television. He fed the deer when they came to the house and went for solitary walks on the moor, occasionally bringing back a baby rabbit or injured bird. These he would tend to then let go. It wasn't fair, he explained, to keep them imprisoned. Lisa very much liked this aspect of him: gentler and more in touch with his feminine side. But he put down his foot about having a pet of their own. Too much trouble and too much mess. Like her, he preferred an immaculate house. Both took their shoes off at the front door and only wore slippers inside. A child or an animal wouldn't have fitted at all.

But Ned was gone for most of the day for five days out of seven, leaving her lonely. She read magazines and cleaned a lot, tended the patio which didn't take long but after that fretted for something more to occupy her time. She didn't approve of daytime TV (unlike her neighbour who watched it all day. Lisa could hear the monotonous mumbling through the thin wall). She hadn't even the use of a car since Ned drove to work in it during the week, which meant she was marooned until his return. One between them had seemed enough before they had made the move down here but the buses were few and far between and came at irregular times. She had no money of her own; her meagre savings had all been used in putting together a trousseau for the wedding. But Ned had money, or so she thought, though he wasn't forthcoming about such things. Even though she was now his wife, he rarely discussed finances. Nevertheless, this could not go on. She was going to need some transport of her own.

*   *   *

Lisa was still appalled by Peter's death as, indeed, was everyone else. She had grown to look forward to his regular visits. He had always been such a cheery soul, ready to help with whatever it was, picked up her outgoing mail and delivered the papers. The stand-in postman was sullen and terse, too overworked even to pass the time of day. He was having to do an extra round which was hardly Lisa's fault. Nor did he ever offer to run her errands.

The police occasionally came to the door, checking out facts they had checked before, asking the same tedious questions over again. Lisa's alibi never changed though she had no other corroboration. She had been at home alone that night, as she invariably was.

'Ask the neighbours,' she told the cop. 'The lights were on and I have no car.' She would hardly be out there in the woods, killing postmen.

'Purely routine,' the policeman said, weary too of the repetition. He apologised for taking her time and always refused to come in for a cup of tea. Which was also a bit of a disappointment; she could do with the company. And then she remembered that Sunday night after the party, two weeks ago, and the unidentified visitor who had passed them on the path.

'We were sitting outside at dusk,' she explained, 'my husband and I, having Sunday tea. And someone walked past though we couldn't see who it was. They didn't speak.'

'Heading which way?'

'To the left,' she said. Along the path that skirted the terrace and, yes, now she thought about it, down to the woods. Or up to the drive. From where they sat, because it was dark, they hadn't been able to see.

'One of the neighbours?' He took out his pad.

'We couldn't tell but I really don't think so. Any of those would stop and have a word.' It was only polite.

He made a note, though it didn't mean much. It could have been anyone, friend or foe, but without identification had little meaning. It was also before the murder had taken place.

Lisa shivered after he'd left and warmed the pot for a cup of tea. One of the reasons they'd wanted the house was the fact of extra security through being within a gated community.

Through Perseus, Lisa grew to know Erin, who would sometimes chat as she sat outside reading and soaking up what remained of the sun. She also appeared to have time on her hands though walked long distances down to the village and often took all-day hikes across the moor. Lisa was curious as to why she was there, marooned alone without a car in a house she had explained was not even her own. Which was why she wasn't bothering to do it up.

'It's not my house so what's the point?' she said when Lisa came round for a drink. She worked on her laptop at the livingroom table. She was some kind of writer, she didn't say what, not currently working but doing research. Erin had loads of books, piled on the floor, and also masses of papers. She had lovely red hair and a sunny smile and was fit from all the walking she did. Her Irish brogue was also very beguiling.

Lisa liked her a lot. She seemed awfully brainy but did not throw her learning around and went out of her way to encourage Lisa to talk. Erin lived in London and travelled a lot, had hated the country at the start but was very slowly becoming acclimatised.

'You'll be sorry to leave.'

'Well, I won't say that. Though I do confess there are things I am going to miss.'

'When will you go?'

'I have no idea. The decision, alas, is not in my hands.' She didn't offer an explanation and Lisa didn't ask.

An odd way to live your life, she thought, smug because at least she did have Ned.

24

Auriol was suddenly down from her high. Brave was one thing but not on her own. Whatever courage she might have shown had been with Erin's backup. Now the murder was two weeks old and, with police activity tailing off, she was taking a more balanced view of the recent occurrence. At first she had thought it might be a sign that a man she knew to be ruthless was back, a calling card to warn her that he still had her in his sights. He was totally bent, as she knew for a fact, and owned this land on a flimsy premise that would hardly survive much legal investigation. She knew because she'd been part of the plan though was not too proud any more of that role. But then they had been a team and extremely effective.

She had been young and defiantly proud, coolly careless about the law, focused only on getting what she wanted. All that had mattered then had been the endgame. They were ruthless and bold and made fortunes from dubious dealings. Auriol had learnt her lesson by falling hard and seeing the loss of a life-time's work. But she'd also been a fool all along by loving a man she had known wasn't straight and there-fore not to be trusted. A little of this she had hinted at to Erin without going into much detail. Until she was certain of her facts she'd be wise to watch what she said.

She was sure it was him until Erin let slip that she was in some sort of trouble herself and also holding back on significant details. Until they both dared lay their cards on the table and trust each other with what they knew, they might be at cross-purposes, even risking each other's life. An odd dilemma. Who would have thought that total strangers who got on so well would end up, by chance, living side by side here in the middle of nowhere. It was almost funny. She had thought she'd escaped but was, it appeared, still in it up to her neck.

The question now was what to reveal and how much she dared trust Erin. Right from the start she had warmed to her from that first time on the river-bank, watching the crazy dog chase after the fishes. She had liked Erin's looks, with her reddish-gold hair and the honesty in her candid eyes, also her voice with the lyrical Irish brogue. Erin, she instantly recognised, was everything she might aspire to be were she ten years younger and starting all over again. Fearless, honourable and plain-speaking, not afraid to stand up for her principles. She hadn't gone into what she did or even her reasons for being down here but Auriol was an expert at character assessment. Perhaps not in her private life but certainly in the marketplace, it was one of the reasons for her impressive success. She could sum up a stranger in seconds and get it spot on.

They had become instantaneous friends, each recognising a kindred spirit in the small mismatched community into which they had both been thrown. They were two smart independent women, both successful at what they did. Why then, Auriol wanted to know, did Erin have this apparent blind spot about her personal life? It was something she'd seen many times before: a woman who seemed to have everything else, stuck in a dead-end relationship unlikely to have any future. Erin loved him, he wasn't free. End of story; she should walk away. Nothing was ever going to change, the oldest story in the book. Auriol frequently marvelled at how weak even really intelligent women could be.

The telephone rang: Erin, on cue, with something hugely important to say. Too good to waste over the telephone; she was hoping Auriol might be free for at least a pre-lunch drink. Auriol was. She leapt at the chance to find out more about Erin.

Erin's news was encouraging; she had met the Commander face to face and very charming he was, indisputably dishy. *Too old for me but perfect for you*, that was her unspoken implication. Without a doubt the best she had seen down here.

'I wonder why he's here,' Auriol said, once they were settled outside with their drinks.

'I can answer that,' said Erin. 'He owns the house.' She was struggling with the sun umbrella. 'He said to drop by for a drink sometime. Perhaps we should fix it that you come along as well.'

'Too obvious.' Auriol was worldly wise. The way to interest any man was never to chase him, which Erin already knew. She had simply been doing her usual thing and excluding herself on the grounds of not being free. One of these days they were going to have to discuss it.

'So how come he's hardly ever here? What does he do with the rest of his time? It seems a terrible waste of a beautiful house.'

'I would guess he shoots. He had a gun. Though *what* he shoots is anyone's guess.' Postmen in their prime, perhaps, as long as they were in season. Something still nagged at the back of her brain. Piers Compayne. She definitely knew the name.

'And you're certain there wasn't a wife in tow?'

'No, only a dog. A nice one.'

Erin didn't mention the other walker who she wasn't able to get out of her mind, who had swept straight past without even so much as a nod. Something about that fleeting encounter had deeply disturbed her, she wasn't sure why, but it chilled her to the bone just recalling it now.

Auriol was laughing. 'After you, mate.' She was still not ready for even a passing flirtation.

'But you saw him first.'

'Which does not give me rights.' Thanks but no thanks; she was not getting into a contest.

They giggled a bit and both agreed that if Erin was right and he wasn't attached, then it wasn't just them but everyone else who'd be beating a path to his door. Wait till Sylvia Brennan clocked him. She'd be throwing another party.

'Just one more thing.' Auriol picked up her keys then halted indecisively in the doorway. She sensed she was treading on delicate ground yet longed to find out what was on Erin's mind. She covered it well but seemed very keyed up. Not only now but all the time, the more so, she fancied, since the recent murder, which made good sense. She never, for instance, sat with her back to the moor, not only because of the view. She gave the impression of constantly watching for something.

'I know it's none of my business,' she said. 'And forgive me if I speak out of turn, but I sense there are things you're not telling me. I hate to pry but if you will trust me you might find it therapeutic.'

There, it was said. And she saw she had scored a bullseye. Erin's eyes flickered and, just for a second, she looked as though she might spill the beans.

But the moment passed quickly. 'I haven't a clue what you're talking about,' Erin said.

25

At night Betty tried to jam her door; it was fairly futile but the hinges creaked so would give her at least some warning if anyone came. Not that she would have much defence against a killer out for her blood. She was terrified in case she'd been recognised. She quaked in her shoes; she was old and infirm and wouldn't be able to put up a fight. It was also autumn with lengthening nights and a lethal searing wind blowing down from the moor. Draughts invaded her eggshell home with icy, insidious fingers. Even if she weren't hacked to death, she couldn't be sure of surviving another winter.

The postman, poor soul, had hardly screamed, had been caught unawares in the depths of the wood though why he had been there at that time of night she really couldn't imagine. All she had heard was a distant disturbance then the terrible sounds of his dying breaths. Whatever it was that had done that to him must have been hardly human. The memory made her tremble still; her ancient fingers shook as she wired up the latch.

The small thatched cottage was dimly lit and showed no signs of anyone home. The windows were closed but she found the front door on the latch. She ventured inside. The dogs weren't there though the car was parked round the back. The kettle perched on the ancient hob was stone cold. She, however, was in no hurry but perfectly happy to sit and wait. For Betty time moved on a totally different plane.

Footsteps pounded along the path with joyful barks as the door flew wide and a tall stooped woman entered then stopped in her tracks. Effie Willcox opened her arms and greeted Betty with real delight. 'You are here already. I was walking the dogs,' she said. She switched on lamps in the gathering dusk and struck a match to light the stove in order to heat the kettle. The dogs gulped noisily from their bowls then went to lie side by side in the warmth. Winter would soon be here, it was growing colder.

'It won't take a second to make the tea.' She had bought cream cakes as a special treat, knowing how easy it was to please the increasingly frail old woman. Effie had known her all her life, was a child when

Betty appeared on the scene and had grown up accustomed to having her always around. She understood her. Effie knew all there was to know about Betty's continuing tragic belief that the Endecott land should really be hers since there weren't any other claimants. The last of the line, the long-dead Violet, lay buried up there in the churchyard. The last direct descendant, that was. Effie also knew, though had not revealed, that there still existed a very powerful cousin.

Effie had many distinguished friends and an education better than most, till now had worked in some very high-ranking jobs. Betty was simple and losing her wits having lived her life as a hobo. Without arousing false expectations, Effie was hoping to validate her claim. The facts appeared to be black and white apart from one serious stumbling block. Betty's father, John Endecott, had not left a valid will and no one local had even known of her birth.

Violet's story was widely known, the terrible tragedy of her death having given rise to countless local legends. Fanned by the portrait in the pub, which always provided a talking point, all kinds of ghostly sightings had been reported over the years. She wouldn't rest, so the fantasists said, until the cause of the fire was known and the perpetrators, whoever they were, officially brought to justice. Which was all very well on the spectral front and did no harm to the

Three Crowns' trade but would not, alas, stand up in a court of law. The fact was Betty had no formal proof that she was entitled to anything. The fire had seen to that and, later, the war.

For decades the land had lain unclaimed until the development had begun. Swann Homes had swooped in with their cranes and mechanical diggers. No one appeared to have challenged them but only Betty had a vested right. Effie had been on a futile trail, trying to locate concrete proof that the frail old woman really was the last of the Endecotts. She had applied to the Land Registry for copies of the original deeds which had brought her, inevitably, back to the same dead end. Endecott Manor had been entailed to the family since such records were kept. Which, without proof of Betty's birth, landed her back at square one. She'd been born in Kenya. No records were extant here. Now even Effie was losing heart though had publicly vowed to move heaven and earth to find the missing parts of the jigsaw puzzle.

It was dark by the time they had finished tea but Betty needed no torch to guide her home. Back down the hill to the gates of the park then across the bridge to the narrow path that followed the river and led her into the woods. A friendly moon accompanied her; she never felt lonely knowing that someone up there was watching out for her.

*   *   *

The priest often came to sit with them. Father Domleo, she could see him now, his cassock over his riding clothes, the missal tucked into his boot. She had fancied herself in love with him but he had eyes only for Mama who, even in her state of decline, had always been the focus of male attention. She had lain all day with the shutters closed, eclipsing the brilliance from outside, on a day-bed draped with animal skins, listlessly fanning herself. The padre, hot from his afternoon ride, accepted iced tea from an unctuous servant and shifted closer in his rattan chair to catch Mama's languid whisper.

Which never amounted to very much. She was not a wit or even a flirt, merely a lonely frustrated woman whose life had ended along with her cherished dreams. She hated the endless African sun; it had not been her choice that they'd fled over here and her husband's ugly and premature death had blighted her life even more. And now the advent of Hitler's war meant she could not return to the green of Devon. All she had left were her memories and the child who had never lived up to her hopes, whom she hadn't been able to love because she was not the real thing.

The padre rose to take his leave, stooping to kiss the mother's hand. 'The Lord works in mysterious ways and some day, I promise, you'll see your loved ones again.'

'Let it be soon.' The whisper was faint and only her daughter heard it.

Effie still had a daring last card left to play which she was holding close to her chest. It was getting on for a year since she'd last held a seance. Though totally frowned upon by the Church (the vicar had made his position clear), Effie, due to her education, still remained open-minded. Having studied science at Girton College, her reading had been both eclectic and wide and had led to her studying a huge variety of cultures. Although respecting the laws of physics, what bothered her was the theosophical side. Science lacked an omnipotent presence deserving of worship. Curiosity and unease had led to her early affiliation with the British Society for Psychical Research, of which she remained a member. This society, for many years, had involved some extremely eminent thinkers: scientists and philosophers, even a former Prime Minister, Arthur Balfour. Effie attended its annual conference and occasionally wrote on the subject too. She took it all very seriously, though only within a small circle. Piers, though respecting her right to free thought, privately thought her nuts.

Now it was time for action, though, a final challenge to elusive fate. She summoned her small band of faithful believers to her cottage the following week.

A long shot, perhaps, but worth a go despite the fact that the last time they'd met they had all ended up being terrified out of their wits. It had seemed that a presence entered the room then left again when the thunderclap struck. By which time the vicar had gone, which was just as well. If the medium could be persuaded back they might progress further along that track. Effie was game though could not be too sure of the others.

There was, of course, always some element of risk. When summoning forces from the other side, you could never quite be certain what would come.

26

Erin was showering when the doorbell rang. She waited to see if they'd go away but, after a very short pause, it rang again. It was not the postman, of that she was sure, but could think of nobody else it might be. She dried herself then flung on a robe and took the stairs two at a time. She was not supposed to behave like this, to open the door without checking first, but she'd been here so long she had started to drop her guard. It was doubtless a neighbour on the scrounge, with luck the Commander to fix that drink. Anything had to be better than hanging around on her own in this dump. She was sick of these blank impersonal walls and watching the seasons gradually change. Even a salesman would be a relief, assuming one could get through those gates. It must be someone who had already got access. She undid the chain and opened the door to find herself face to face with a total stranger.

He was slight and boyish, with a megawatt grin which made Erin instantly drop her guard. 'Hi!' he said. 'I trust I didn't disturb you.'

'Not at all,' she said. 'I was in the shower.' The water was runnelling down her neck as she stood there, barefoot, in the doorway. At a cursory glance he appeared unarmed. He looked like someone, Tom Cruise perhaps, though, on closer inspection was not quite as young as she'd thought. When he removed the Ray-Bans she saw that he must be at least in his forties. Suntanned and fit and impeccably groomed; the shoes were lizard, the suit Savile Row. The car he had just stepped out of was primrose yellow. Which gave it away: she had figured it out before he even had time to produce his card.

He took her hand in a vice-like grip. 'Oliver Swann,' he told her. 'At your service.'

'I'm afraid I don't have a note of your name,' he added, running his eye down a list. 'It simply says here "unoccupied" which seems not to be the case.'

That smile again as he took his time, ignoring her state in a courteous way. Erin, her hair dripping round her face, was not sure how she should play it. She did have a special number to ring but only in an emergency which, faced with this affable stranger, seemed rather extreme.

'What exactly do you want?' From his name she

assumed he was management though hadn't seen anyone else of that ilk in the almost five months she had been here. Nor had she been notified that he might call.

'Nothing special, just checking things out. I thought I'd take this chance to make myself known.'

He appeared to be totally bona fide, the name was enough to convince her of that. And the clipboard he held looked very official. There was nothing remotely sinister about him.

'Do you want to come in?' she asked courteously.

'No thanks,' he said. 'Unless you need anything fixed. I'll be back with a working team for a couple of weeks.'

Erin, aware of her half-dressed state, was starting now to feel chilly. 'Thanks,' she said. 'I'll let you know if I need you.'

He didn't have a number for her so she gave him her mobile. She had no idea who owned the house and she didn't consider it her business. She only knew it had been arranged by Rod.

'May I ask your name?' His pen was poised when a sudden loud barking distracted them both. From somewhere offstage came hurtling a dog that wriggled and fawned at his feet. 'Jasper.' He sounded surprised and pleased and dropped to one knee to caress the dog that lavishly licked his face in whimpering joy.

It was cute to observe, brought a lump to her throat, till she heard brisk footsteps along the path.

'Jasper! Heel!' said Auriol, icy cold. 'I see you two have met,' she said to Erin, deliberately not acknowledging him. 'Take my advice and don't let him into your house.'

Oliver Swann, quite unperturbed, winked at Erin and rolled his eyes. 'I see', he said, 'that my reputation precedes me.' He checked his watch; it was time to go or else it was simply diplomacy.

'Nice to meet you.' He proffered his hand. 'I look forward to knowing you better.'

She couldn't fault him; he had natural charm and the brilliant smile appeared quite sincere. After giving Jasper a final pat, he vaulted into his car.

Auriol seethed as he drove away, almost too furious to speak. 'I told you he was loathsome,' she said through clenched teeth.

'I found him charming.' Which was the truth. Erin got out the dryer and dried her hair, then put on coffee to help to calm Auriol down. Just her expression warned her not to risk wisecracks.

'Charming, maybe, but the man's a shit. He would get his leg over and not bother to ask your name.'

'No need to worry,' said Erin calmly. 'He doesn't know who I am since I don't own the house.'

'What was the terrible thing he did?' she asked her

friend later, over a drink. Coffee not having done the trick, they had now moved on to the hard stuff.

'The usual thing.' She cradled her head, trying to claw back some dignity. 'I find it hard to say the words. The bastard dumped me for a younger model.'

Her eyes were slightly smudged with tears that, even now, she could not hold back. 'For twenty years I worked with the sod and made him what he's become today, a first-class prick without an iota of conscience.'

Of course there was more to it than that. Auriol wasn't faking.

'If you'll just allow me to dress,' Erin said, 'I'll treat you to lunch at the pub.'

Auriol filled Erin in, in the broadest of terms; her Sloane Street past and the way they had met, though she didn't divulge how bewitched she had been by the man right from the beginning. Which seemed unlikely meeting him now. To Erin the couple were worlds apart: she a woman of taste and class, he a charming chancer.

'Why is he here?' she was curious to know.

Auriol shrugged. 'He owns the place. Or did before he sold it off piece by piece.' She ground her teeth. 'What bugs me most is that he's okay and blithely getting on with his life, leaving me with the wreck of my career.' And an empty future.

Endecott Park, she now explained, had been her dream which he'd snatched from her and totally cheapened by turning it into a cut-price development.

'What went wrong?'

'I divorced him,' she said. 'The moment I found he was having it off with the bimbo.'

Erin raised an enquiring eyebrow. More dramatic than she had thought.

'Kimberley something, from Essex,' Auriol spat. 'Blonde and toothy. Taller than him. Exactly the age I was when we first hooked up.'

Now she attempted a rueful smile though the pain very clearly still went deep. Probably mainly pride; Erin sympathised.

'So why live here?'

'I have no choice. It was part of the crummy settlement. Believe me, as soon as I can I shall sell up and leave.'

It was never wise, Erin reflected later, to put your whole life in the hands of a man, especially one with whom you are totally smitten. The Rod situation suited her fine; she had his love but was not tied down. He had no control over what she did, except in his role of immediate boss, and the fact he was married worked both ways since it meant no one else could grab him. Commitment was a double-edged sword. Erin remained content with things as they were.

She missed him, though. It had been too long. It was almost six months she had been down here and apart from email and occasional calls, they'd had very little contact. She knew he was busy, had things on his mind, especially now they were part of a much larger set-up, but she sensed the old intimacy and trust were reducing. Once they had shared very similar ideals: the values her grandfather's group had upheld. They had put their lives on the line for Eire in the same way that Erin and like-minded writers were mounting such a valiant fight for Chechnya's independence. It was, by no means, a populist view as the recent assassinations proved, but one she still believed well worth fighting for.

If only she had more to do with her time. She needed some kind of new project to keep her sane.

27

Sylvia was doing her weekly shop, bemoaning the paucity of choice which was not in the league of Ashford or even Bromley. If Gerald allowed her to use his car she would drive to Okehampton where there was a Waitrose. He, however, begrudged her that. He needed the car most days, it seemed, despite the fact he was now retired, though he still remained cagey about what it was he was up to. He didn't mind dropping her off at times or picking her up in the Ring o'Bells but mainly she had to take the bus which only ran twice daily. Before, she'd had a car of her own, a nice little Polo she really loved, but that had been one of the things to go when they'd downsized and moved to the country.

'At least allow me to keep the car.' She was horrified when he broke the news. No other woman she knew had to wheedle lifts. But Gerald could be very stubborn at times (mean was the word that first came to mind) and said that he couldn't afford to run two now he was no longer working. So why had he stopped? He was fifty-seven and might have gone on for another ten years but Gerald flatly refused to discuss the matter.

Sylvia moaned. She did all the work, dragging herself to the shops every week then having to lug the groceries home instead of them being delivered. His answer was what else did she have to do?

Today she was planning a special meal, a rehearsal for her first stylish dinner party. She had watched the butcher disjoint the veal and then hand-selected the vegetables and had left both bags at the greengrocer's stall while she popped across to the dairy for cream. Where she opened her purse and found she had no cash.

'Don't worry, love. Next time will do.' In these country places they knew where you lived so credit was never a problem. Which was not the point; she was mortified and hated not to be seen as very well-off.

'I will just pop down to the cash machine.' There were other things she had thought of now: cheese and those special biscuits to go with the trifle. And coffee beans.

There was only one cashpoint in the village and at

this time of day, just before noon, there was already a small queue of people waiting. Tight-lipped, Sylvia took her place, hating to stand in the street like this, sincerely hoping that no one she knew would come by. Luck was against her; the district nurse pedalled up on her ancient bike, puffing and panting because of the very steep hill. Flustered, Sylvia moved away, pretending to be engrossed in the nearest shop window. How very demeaning.

'Don't wait for me, dearie. You go first.' The over-weight woman could barely speak. She bent at the waist and drew deep breaths; Sylvia feared she might have a stroke on the spot.

She took her place at the cash machine, furtively checking that no one could see, inserted her card and then punched in her PIN number. Nothing happened. It came up blank; there was zero cash, it said, in the account.

'That's ridiculous.' She tried it again. These country banks were all the same: run by a couple of idiots, semi-retired. Again that zero.

Good-humouredly the nurse looked on, interested now she had caught her breath. 'Been splashing out on the sales, have you, dear?' She winked.

Furious, Sylvia blanked her out, grabbed her cash card and stalked away. She didn't need money for the bus since she'd thought to buy a return.

*   *   *

'You have to do something about that bank. These country branches are total rubbish.' Sylvia was still fuming when she got home.

Gerald, lost in the City pages, silently gave her his basilisk stare. He was not amused which was more than usually apparent.

'What?' she said, flinging down her bag and spilling its contents all over the floor. 'Blast!' she added, stooping to pick it all up.

When he still didn't answer, she looked at him. Normally he would be over to help. He did have manners, or had done once, it was one of his few saving graces.

'What?' she repeated, nervous now. Something about him was scaring her. She froze as realisation gradually dawned.

He hadn't told her, he tried to explain, because he had hoped it would go away. It was only a question of cash flow, he reassured her. Soon to be sorted.

But what was she going to do? she shrieked. She had flowers to get and the cleaner to pay. And they didn't take credit cards in most of the shops.

'You will have to economise,' Gerald said. 'Do your own housework and wash your own hair.' They could grow their own vegetables too, if she'd only be bothered.

He was sick of being the one in charge, of always

having to make things work. He had slaved all his adult life just to keep her in hairdos and fancy clothes. He had loved her once for the way she looked: a gorgeous girl with a model's figure, porcelain skin and a traffic-stopping smile, who had chosen him. She couldn't type but what did he care; he treated her like a princess.

His daughters, too, when they came along, had both been the apple of his eye. They had grown up spoilt and petulant like their mother. Nothing was ever enough for them – the ballet classes, the pony club. And, as they grew older, the trips abroad with the school. He came from fairly humble stock and had worked very hard to get where he was, keeping them all in a style he could never afford. He had only survived this long, as it was, by being creative with company funds. Through sleight of hand and a very cool nerve he had kept the lid tight on the can of worms and succeeded in bluffing things through. Until the day of the unscheduled audit when the truth had finally come out.

He was fifty-six so they let him go with a clampdown on adverse publicity. The merchant bank was privately owned; they could not afford a scandal. Not even Sylvia ever guessed but she'd always had her head in the clouds. He acknowledged that it was mainly his fault for indulging her in her snobby ways and allowing her to live in a crazy dreamworld. His daughters, too: they were over-indulged which was why both marriages weren't that great. All three of his women demanded too much. It could only be his fault.

And now the proverbial had hit the fan and the bank refused to extend his credit. He hadn't had the courage to let Sylvia know. What he needed now was a private loan to see him through this unfortunate patch. If someone like the Commander came through, it was feasible that they would, after all, survive.

Not all of this did he share with her before leaving her shrieking, and going outside. She still didn't know the whole of it. He prayed devoutly that it would never emerge.

28

There was nothing more on the postman's death. From time to time Ned made it his business to check. The police investigation appeared to be closed. Out of curiosity, he called the station, to be met by a faintly frosty rebuff, the implication being it was none of his business. Ned, quite naturally, was put out. As a resident of Endecott Park, he needed to know his wife was safe alone there during the day. Until the killer was caught he would not rest easy.

Lisa, surprised that he cared at all, was secretly touched by this new concern, the more so since he had never even met Peter. That night she boldly moved closer to him in bed.

'What was he like, this postman chap?' he asked her quizzically over his book.

'Blond and gorgeous, like a Greek god.' She wondered if it was possible he was jealous.

'More gorgeous than me?'

Was he making a joke? It was worth the risk. 'No contest,' she said, sliding out of her nightie and into his arms.

When really aroused, her husband surprised her. It was Lisa's first experience of jungle sex. Wild-eyed and sweating, he pinned her down, rough to the point of hurting her but thrillingly passionate with it. She couldn't believe it. She wanted more but he rolled away, muttered something then fell asleep. Lisa was left to switch off the lights on her own.

Well, she pondered, as she lay there sleepless, shaming herself by her sudden desire, talk about still waters running deep.

She was up ahead of him next day, applying make-up before he woke and, instead of her sweatshirt and jeans, a negligee. She ran nervous fingers through her bird's-nest hair, decided it looked rather fetching untamed so, instead of tying it tightly back, left it loose and went down to start on the breakfast. Ned, when he followed, barely gave her a glance, just concentrated on tuning in Radio 3.

Lisa perkily poached his eggs. She always decided what he should eat, was keeping an eye on his general health as any caring wife should. The mornings were growing crisper now; he wore a heavier suit.

'Drop off your summer suits at the cleaners and I'll put them away for the winter,' she said. 'I will also get you some of those moth-proof bags.'

She liked a man to be well dressed and Ned cleaned up like the best of them. Today's shirt, though, she considered too pale, making him look anaemic. 'Pink would suit you.' She gave it some thought. 'Or hyacinth blue like the newsreaders wear.'

'Leave me alone,' he growled and flung down his fork.

Lisa watched him, open-mouthed, as he strode from the room and went up to clean his teeth. After last night's passion, she had hoped for more, a breakthrough in their relationship, but today he was like a bear with a sore head. She cleared the dishes thoughtfully. Perhaps she had somehow embarrassed him by flaunting her sexuality quite so boldly.

'What shall I get you for supper?' she asked, dazzling him with her sunniest smile. 'I feel we are both due a treat. Shall I book us a table?'

Ned merely grunted and picked up his case. 'I may be late home. It is up to you,' he said.

She sounded just like his mother at times. He reversed the car and headed off. Yap yap yap, about nothing at all. It was starting to drive him crazy. He slammed on the brakes; there was traffic ahead backed up, he would guess, for a mile or so. Something was blocking the road by the Sandy Park Inn. He heaved a deep sigh. Sitting there, tapping the steering wheel, impatiently waiting for things to move, he wondered if he had done the right thing by tying himself down in this way. Marriage, at times, could be palatable but only in very small doses.

He closed his eyes and thought back to the days before he'd met Lisa on that train and she'd come at him like a bull at a gate, knocking down all his defences. She could be sweet and she could be kind and most of the time he admired her looks. He didn't like her in trousers, though, or dressed like a trollop, the way she had been this morning. Women should not be provocative; it angered him when he lost control. His mother, whom he had loved and revered, had occasionally pushed him too far. He gripped the wheel just remembering and took some very deep breaths.

Someone behind him was sounding their horn. The traffic was on the move; he jerked into gear. He had to get going or else he'd be late and, in any case, such deliberations upset him. All that had been a long time ago. The worst of it was now over.

Lisa hesitated to tidy the room since Ned disliked her touching his things. She flung everything into the laundry bag and carried it down to the wash. The weather was breezy: a drying day. She was learning to do as the neighbours did. When she opened the doors to hang it all out, Erin was standing outside.

'Morning,' she said as Lisa emerged, wrestling with her new drying rack. 'I don't suppose you've seen Perseus? He's gone AWOL.'

'Sorry,' said Lisa. 'I see him about but he hasn't been in for a couple of days. My husband mentioned he's sometimes down in the woods.'

'It's amazing, isn't it?' Erin laughed. 'How adaptable animals can be. Perseus lived his whole life indoors until we moved down here.'

He was killing a lot and now eating them. She had stopped finding baby shrews under the bed. Having practised a bit, he had moved on to larger prey. Which reminded her what she had meant to ask.

'Has there been any further news on the murder front?'

'No,' said Lisa. 'It's all gone quiet. My husband checks but they don't want to know. Perhaps there's something they are covering up. I find it very disturbing.'

Erin agreed though didn't say why. She was finding it hard to settle at night. Because her windows had filmy drapes she was all too aware, when the lights were on, that she must be a sitting target for anyone passing. She tried not to think it but there it was. The fact that they lived behind locked gates did not automatically guarantee that they were safe. It hadn't, after all, protected the postman. She still didn't know why they'd want to kill him, perhaps the poor fellow was just in the way. What worried her most was that somewhere out there a ruthless killer had still not been apprehended.

She couldn't, however, tell Lisa that without betraying her own secret fears. The fact the police refused to talk might mean something but then might not. They weren't supposed to be guarding her. She found it all most frustrating.

Instead she put on her bravest smile. She wouldn't allow them to make her afraid. What was a Russian assassin against the power of her mighty pen? She called the cat. He failed to appear. She doubted a killer would go after him. In any case, Perseus was too fly to get caught.

'He'll come back when he's hungry,' Erin said.

Lisa stared at her worriedly and gave an uncertain smile.

The doorbell rang; Lisa rinsed her hands. She noticed a pale yellow car outside. Someone visiting Erin, perhaps. She looked like someone with an interesting private life. Lisa left on the chain when she opened the door; Ned had warned her to take no risks. A man she had never seen before stood there waiting. She wondered what he had come about; he looked far too smart to be a travelling salesman. He wore dark glasses and his hair was beautifully cut.

'Mrs Thornton?' He was checking a list.

Lisa nodded, enjoying her status. Being a wife still made her feel someone of note.

'Mind if I have a word?' he said, indicating that she should open the door.

She hesitated. It ought to be safe; she knew for a fact there were people about. If she shouted Erin was bound to hear. He would hardly arrive so flamboyantly if he were planning to kill her. Though you couldn't always be sure about these things.

'Just a minute.' She unslotted the chain and the man advanced with a dazzling smile.

'Allow me to introduce myself. Oliver Swann.'

Lisa stared blankly. The name rang no bells. His build was a bit like Ned's although he was shorter. Shorter but fit. He removed the shades and the twinkling eyes enhanced the smile. Against her better instincts, Lisa relaxed.

'May I come in? I'm your landlord,' he said. And, meek as a lamb, she ushered him into her house.

29

So the bastard was back. Auriol wasn't surprised, just that he had taken so long. It had always been only a matter of time before he'd be breathing down her neck, exulting over his victory and displaying the trophy bimbo. He would really hate the fact she had opted to go without a fight. Now she was sick of the thought of him, hated the house and the wreck of her dreams. As soon as she could, she planned to sell up and move on. But there were documents still to be signed and the tedious details that follow divorce. The one good thing she'd got out of the mess was Jasper. Who stood there hopefully wagging his tail, waiting for her to take him out. He would just have to bottle it till the coast was clear.

The yellow Lagonda was still outside, parked flamboyantly centre stage in the carport. She took a peek; he had disappeared. He must be trying to impress the neighbours with his oily manner and counterfeit charm. Had she known she'd have warned them to use a very long spoon. She only prayed he would not reveal her former role in the whole shebang, that the presence of wifey number three might teach him a bit of tact. Auriol hated the thought of it coming out, having gone to such extremes to keep it secret. She wondered what someone like Gerald would think if he found out she wasn't at all what she seemed, that her haughty manner belied the fact that she hadn't been widowed but ignominiously dumped. Sylvia, she was pretty sure, would be exultant.

Jasper shoved his nose in her hand and whined beseechingly in his throat.

'Not yet,' she told him. 'You'll have to wait.' Then ran upstairs to get a better look.

She was still obsessed by Peter's death, could not get the images out of her head. Sudden death was bad enough but the way that poor boy had been hacked about was sickeningly repulsive. Anyone able to act like that was more deranged than Oliver Swann, who might be a sociopath but never a killer. In those shady dealings she knew about, he had kept himself carefully out of the frame, was far too fly to jeopardise his reputation.

So who had done it? Somebody had and was, presumably, still at large. She wondered why the police had gone so quiet. There was movement below, she could hear his voice and there he was, striding back to his car, while out in the forecourt, waving, was Lisa Thornton. Auriol grinned; he was at it again. It gave her a quite perverse kick to watch her ex reel in another victim. Lisa should be easy game, she was highly strung and unsure of herself. Auriol watched as he drove away, zapping the gates to let himself out. She wasn't sure he should still be allowed such access. Now that the houses were all sold, such privileges should be exclusive to the owners. At least, now he'd finally gone, she could go for that walk.

This time she met the Commander head-on. He was standing outside his house with his dog at his side. Both dogs barked but their owners reined them in.

'Good day,' he said, with a cheerful smile, displaying teeth that were definitely his. Now that she saw him closer he looked younger. His eyes were periwinkle blue and his face agreeably lightly tanned. He strode across to shake her hand and introduce himself.

'We meet at last.' He looked at her with approval.

They chatted briefly; he knew her name and that she lived at number one. She asked how long he had owned his house; he told her most of his life.

'I inherited it from my mother,' he said. 'But only after she passed away. She spent the last ten years of her life in a home.'

Which explained a lot. 'You're an Endecott?'

'On the distaff side, hence the house,' he said. 'She rented it out for many years while we were living abroad.'

'And now you are back for good?' she said, secretly hoping.

'In theory, yes, but I travel a lot so can't get down as often as I would like.'

She turned to go, would have loved to stay on. Longed to chat more but played by the rules. Never ask questions and leave all the running to him. But, she thought as she ducked through the hedge, she now knew something her ex did not. If Piers Compayne was an Endecott he must surely know who rightfully owned the land. It was strange that, since he was here, he had not brought that up.

Fascinating. Her step was brisk. He had given her something to think about. The searches they'd made had been superficial because the land had lain fallow so long. Had they persevered they would doubtless have found that the plot they'd purloined was still held in trust. It was unlikely it didn't belong to someone.

But Oliver never took notice of rules; when he wanted something he went for it. Because she had fallen in love with the house, he had simply taken it over. In the time it took to draw up the plans, she had never seen the Commander around. The gatehouse, though obviously cared for, had always stood empty. And when they had their big falling-out and she had insisted upon divorce, he had simply abandoned the dream house and bulldozed the land. Realisation gradually dawned. Revenge was a dish that was best served cold. Without her having to do a thing, Oliver Swann might soon get his comeuppance. And that was something that really made her smile.

'But where does that leave the rest of them?' Like Auriol, Erin could not care less but everyone else had paid through the nose for their houses. Their permanent homes.

'You want to know something? I don't give a damn.' Auriol was getting off on it. She loathed her house in any case, would be only too glad to move out. And she couldn't lose; he owed her big because of the settlement. 'That'll teach him to play around.' She loved the idea that he might get caught. If it weren't for the split, she'd have made quite sure that things were on the level.

But why didn't Piers Compayne intervene? Erin was a journalist, accustomed to digging deep for facts and checking them over and over. It made no sense that he'd live down here and watch the travesty of the land that must belong to his family, if not to him. Why did he let it happen? she wondered. What possibly could be in it for him? The first thing she'd do when she got back home (they were in the village having tea and scones) would be Google him. She still had a feeling she'd heard that name before.

Auriol stood on the patio watching the sunset, the most spectacular she had seen. The sky was ablaze like the burning of Atlanta. She sipped her Coke and felt more at peace with herself than she had in months. Her demons were all being laid to rest though certainly not before time. Hatred was a destructive force, the more so when it emerged from the embers of love. Twenty years had been a long ride but now she was finally shot of him. Let him wallow in his murky affairs, she had a bright new future.

The larches stood out inky black against the furnace of the dying sun. Tomorrow she might have a crack at painting a night scene. Something moved on the croquet lawn. She crossed to the steps for a closer look. Black against black in the velvet dark, she sensed more than saw an alien presence, heard a faint stirring of the bracken denoting a stealthy tread. She froze on the spot and checked that the dog was safely shut up inside the house. Instinct told her real danger was very near. She stood quite still for several seconds, aware of something passing by.

In the final rays of the dying sun she glimpsed its sinewy outline.

Then Jasper barked and the movement ceased. For just one flicker, time stood still. Then she saw a pair of enormous eyes staring at her from the edge of the wood. Eyes unblinking and showing no fear, too large and too widely spaced to be human. She stood there, frozen, locked in their gaze.

Then they'd gone.

30

Betty woke to the sound of birds, still hungry from the previous night and cold because the rags she wore failed to stave off the chill of an autumn morning. Painfully she pulled on her shoes and wrapped herself in her rug before opening the door. Outside the glade was a pearly grey with a dusting of early frost on the grass. Big bold footprints led to the foot of her steps. He had not let her down. His latest kill awaited her; she shuffled down, relieved, to examine the bounty.

An animal's head with startled eyes, the ears extended as though in fright. A baby deer: he had tracked it down and slaughtered it in mid-flight. This was his latest offering to her, the rest he would have consumed himself. It would make a stew with a bunch of herbs and wild mushrooms gathered from the wood. She had known he would come; he had never yet let her down. Lucifer would be out there too, watching her safely from a tree. They worked as a team and acted as her guardians.

She collected sticks and dead leaves for the fire and hauled out the pot from beneath the van. The stream was just fifteen yards away; she had chosen her camp-site well. The venison stew should last her at least a week.

Her only human friend was Effie now that dear Marigold had gone, the last of her family ties that Betty knew of. They had taken her off many years ago and her house had stood empty ever since though some-times, lately, Betty had noticed lights. Effie was taking care of things and reassured her all would be well. Meanwhile she lived a contented life in the woods with her animal friends.

Or had done until that young man's distressing murder.

'You can't be serious.' Effie was shocked. Piers rubbing shoulders with charlatans. He'd invited the cowboy builder for a day's shooting. She couldn't imagine where they had met and what they could possibly have in common. Apart from the minor fact, of course, of owning adjacent land.

Piers was amused. 'Relax,' he said. He loved the way she still went at things, as fiery as in their shared days at MI5. She didn't alter and never would, an eccentric to her fingertips though still very much a force to be reckoned with. He was often dazzled.

'The fact is, he invited himself. Was hanging around, smarming up to the neighbours and caught me standing outside with my gun. Said he wanted to take up country pursuits.'

His grin expanded. Though Swann was no fool, this time he had taken on more than he knew. The Commander's sights had been on him for years. He had simply walked into his trap. Effie beamed. Well, that was all right. She had guessed that Piers would be one step ahead. She was only in this at all because of Betty who was, as it happened, his first cousin. Though the poor old thing was now so confused, Effie couldn't even be sure she would still remember.

'I assume,' said Effie, 'that's why you are here.'

'One of the reasons,' he said.

It was a blindingly beautiful day, perfect for rambling on the moor. Such opportunities would grow rarer once winter got into its stride. Jasper was certainly up for it; Auriol invited Erin too. She, reduced to cleaning the fridge, was delighted.

'We'll drive up to Fernworthy Reservoir and then walk over the moor from there. There's a terrific pub at the very top with a fire that never goes out.'

Which was where they were when the hunters came,

their shotguns cocked and their dogs in tow, dressed in their fancy schmancy suits, ready to massacre. 'Best put Jasper back on his lead,' advised Erin.

She surveyed the group with mild distaste, with their braying voices and tailored tweeds. They looked like a bunch of hedge-fund boys out on a company freebie. Why they'd waste money slaughtering birds was something she simply could not comprehend. She'd have thought they'd have bigger priorities: Porsches to run and wives to keep clothed, spoilt little kids to send to expensive schools. She was turning away when Auriol quietly nudged her.

'Look,' she muttered through gritted teeth, indicating a man at the rear. 'My beloved ex and his fancy friends. Talk about pretentious.'

But Erin's attention was otherwise caught by the man at the front who seemed to be host, currently deep in discussion with the beaters. 'Isn't that the Commander?' she said, at which point he saw them and cheerfully beckoned them over.

Fairly reluctantly they complied, Auriol lagging behind with the dog. She hated being this close to her former husband.

'Ladies.' Piers swept off his cap, welcoming them with unfeigned joy. 'What brings you up to the moor today? Apart, of course, from the weather?'

'Just walking the dog.' Auriol glanced around. The

hedge-fund boys started closing in. Hoof beats sounded (thank God for that). A horse appeared in the distance, heading their way. 'It's Kasia,' said Auriol, frantically waving, glad to be off the hook.

The Polish girl circled them very fast, then pulled back her steed to walking pace and finally came to a graceful halt beside them. On horseback she certainly looked the part, immaculately kitted out like landed gentry.

'Fancy seeing you,' said Erin. The shooting party was moving off: Auriol succeeding, to her delight, in totally blanking her ex.

'I like to ride on my afternoons off,' said Kasia in her fractured English. 'Is good. The reason for being here.' She indicated the moor.

'Then we won't hold you up.' They continued their walk and Kasia cantered off in pursuit of the hunters.

'I'm amazed she can afford a horse on the sort of money she must earn. I wonder where it came from,' said Auriol.

'Probably exercising it for a farmer.'

'That was no farm horse. That was pure class.' Auriol came from county stock and knew a thoroughbred hunter when she saw one.

'There's something about her that doesn't quite fit,' said Erin thoughtfully, watching her ride. She sat so comfortably in the saddle it didn't entirely add up.

Now, in the distance, Kasia had stopped and was deep in conversation with the Commander. Which didn't add up either; how come she knew him?

'Well, it takes all sorts.' This was village life. Auriol remembered last night's confrontation. Great yellow eyes staring out of the dark, apparently disembodied.

'You are sure it wasn't the Endecott Ghost?' The subject always made Erin grin.

'It wasn't poor Violet, if that's what you mean.' Now Auriol was grinning too. 'Or, if it was, she wasn't wearing her cloak.'

'How could you tell if all you saw were the eyes?'

Point taken. They laughed and wisecracked a bit though fundamentally Auriol had been pretty scared. Something unknown had come in from the moor. It had moved through the bushes with stealthy tread and shown no sign of being afraid. She wouldn't have liked to have met it further from home.

'Could it have been a fox, perhaps?'

'Larger than that with a much broader face.' From what she had seen it was more the size of a tiger.

'Wow,' said Erin, believing her and not even asking how much she had drunk. Scary stuff in an outpost like this. Could be they both spent too much time on their own and heard too many pub stories. 'Where was Jasper? Why didn't he see it off?'

'Indoors,' said Auriol. 'I made sure of that.' It scared

her more now than it had done then; last night she had been too startled to have a reaction. At first she had thought it might be a deer but those eyes had been dangerously feline.

All of a sudden the mist came down, like a heavy blizzard eclipsing all views. Here and there a dark obstacle revealed itself as a pony or sheep. Walkers got sucked into bogs in conditions like this.

'Guess it's time to be turning back.' It was also considerably colder.

Ahead of them they heard random shots. They shouldn't be shooting in weather like this, though every now and again the sun broke through. Jasper refused to come to heel, was too wound up by the goings on. He was racing around dementedly, barking and having the time of his life, hurtling through the swirling mist like a mad thing. Auriol was struck by a terrible thought; somewhere out there was that psychopath, Oliver Swann. With a loaded gun.

'I'd better get him. It isn't safe.' She called and whistled, to no avail. The dog was quite crazy enough to seek out its master.

Erin immediately understood. 'I'll try and round him up,' she said. 'You head back to the car and maybe he'll follow.'

She moved towards him in a crouching run, unsure

where he was but still hearing him bark. He was making a fool of her; she could wring his neck.

'Here, boy!' Erin called but his bark grew fainter. She sensed he was moving away at considerable speed.

Then, all of a sudden, the mist was gone. She could now see the hunters and also the dog and what was probably Kasia's horse, grazing alone in a patch of succulent grass. There was no sign of either Kasia or the Commander.

'Jasper!' she shouted, but he was still racing in circles.

She ran towards him then heard a shot and dropped instinctively to the ground, covering her head and rolling out of range. A very close shave indeed, she was trembling with fear. With pounding heart she raised her head and then heard Auriol's terrible scream.

Jasper was lying motionless having caught the bullet head-on.

Winter

31

Erin was headed for Exeter. There were books she needed and DVDs, some warmer clothing, perhaps even boots since she still didn't know how long she was going to be here. Plus a really expensive lunch; she was due a treat. Mostly though, more than anything, she needed to get away from the house. It was driving her mad with its blank white walls and the dismal landscape of skeletal trees. The wind came howling down from the moor and rattled the ill-fitting windows. She was sick of not having enough to do, needed something specific to fill her time; missed being in the centre of things and the strictures of working to very tight deadlines. Also she had to erase from her mind the images of the dog.

The sight of him with a hole through his head and those trusting, rapidly glazing eyes now filled her every waking moment since she had seen him killed.

It returned whenever she tried to doze, the slow-motion roll as the bullet struck home split seconds after she dived for cover herself. That bullet, she hadn't the slightest doubt, had been intended for her alone. Poor Jasper had inadvertently saved her life.

Auriol though, demented with grief, was blaming it all on her much-loathed ex, certain it had been done just in order to spite her. Swann hated her for not caring enough, for letting him go without more of a fight, for not sinking down to his levels of petty warfare. He had taken the one thing she had left, that she cared about more than anything else, and casually destroyed it to make her suffer. Even though Jasper had once been his pet, brought home expressly against her wish and doted on for a couple of years, he had been cold-blooded enough to casually shoot him. He had done so without a second's thought in front of her, in a public place, in order to make a point and exert his control. Indisputably psychopathic behaviour.

Erin suspected Auriol was wrong, that a Russian assassin had been on her trail, that it could now only be a matter of time. Poor old Jasper had got in the way, something Erin would always regret, but it proved that Rod's concern had been justified. When they'd ordered her off into isolation she had thought they were making too much of a fuss but now it was only too clear the threat had been real. She wished she dared talk to Auriol but still didn't know whom she could trust. She also suspected her neighbour was back on the booze.

The question was, who had fired the shot? She did not believe it was Oliver Swann since, apart from anything else, he lacked any motive. She had only met him that one brief time and found him to be the essence of charm. He might be a crook but not, she was sure, a paid killer. Others that day had been carrying guns apart from him and the hedge-fund boys: a handful of hunters not known to them plus, of course, the Commander.

Which focused her mind on one very strange thought that had nagged at her for a couple of days. Where precisely did Polish Kasia fit in?

She wasn't your average immigrant, turning her hand to whatever it took in order to eke out a living by doing odd jobs. She ran the deli superbly well, doing most of the cooking herself, and had been a star turn at Sylvia's cocktail party. She was chic and savvy and ultra cool, overqualified for such jobs, so what could be her reason for living down here? She had fudged the answer when Erin enquired and then appeared on that thoroughbred horse, confident and entirely at ease, holding her own with the hedge-fund boys and, it appeared, on chatty terms with the Commander.

It didn't take long for the penny to drop. Erin was not in this mess because she lacked brains. Kasia claimed to be Polish by birth but her accent and Slavic features might also be Russian. Unless she was totally paranoid, it seemed to be more than coincidence. She would bet Kasia wasn't at all what she seemed but had an ulterior motive. In which case, how did she come to know the Commander?

She urgently needed to talk to Rod. If Kasia was an assassin, she must be stopped. Before she could pull the trigger again and cause more damage, not only to her at whom she had fired at in front of a group of armed men. Perhaps she should call the emergency number, there for precisely this kind of thing. She had no idea who was guarding her; whoever they were they were very discreet. But neither had she heard from Rod in a while. Of course he must have a lot on his plate but her safety should surely take precedence. Because she was all the things she was, she hated to waste his time. In no way was she the clingy sort, not even when she was on the frontline or when, like now, she knew her life was in danger. It was something Rod said he liked about her, her brave independent spirit. And she, in return, respected his privacy. This was no time, though, for faffing around. The danger was real; she could well have been killed. The proof was poor Jasper, who had taken the bullet. And now the assassin had shown her hand she was hardly going to stay around. Rod should either allow Erin home, to share the risks with the rest of them, or be alert to the probable consequences.

He only called her occasionally now, never with time to talk for long. He blamed it on strict security; it was hard to tell if the line was tapped and, since she was a prime target, he had to be careful. She felt they were rapidly drifting apart which was, she accepted, inevitable. Once she'd been able to make him laugh but now he seemed always preoccupied. She understood: they had separate lives and he was busy while she was not. Added to which he was a married man.

She longed for him, especially at night, with no one but Perseus in her bed to whom she could snuggle up and pour out her feelings. Being undercover was lonely work; she could almost sympathise with the assassin.

Even Amy seemed equally rushed; the reasons she gave were the same as Rod's. She was having to do two jobs at once because they were so understaffed. These days she called only at Rod's request and, even then, always kept it short. She never had time any more for a good old gossip. Which did make sense; she was smart and keen and great at holding the fort in Erin's absence. But it didn't help Erin feel better to know she had now become obsolete.

Which was why she was desperate for something to do to prevent her mind being atrophied. All the walking was keeping her fit but not doing much for her brain-cells. She was making rough notes for a future book which, all going well, she would never write, on how to survive on her own in a village like this. It mostly resembled a 'How To' book: to forage, to hunt, to keep boredom at bay. To manage without a car in the middle of nowhere. To make new friends (she was good at that) and survive in a soulless development with only a tinny transistor and a cat. The cat was the vital ingredient. Without his wise and unflagging support by now she might well have packed it all in and gone home to face the assassins.

What she had in mind, after serious thought, was a slice of social history based on the small community she was now part of. Its ancient roots, its inhabitants, its former role as a stannary town. From habit, she always carried a notebook for jotting down random thoughts. It was slowly starting to fire her up. Soon she really would pay the long-delayed visit to Miss Willcox.

All this was whirling through Erin's head as she walked through the farm to catch the bus. She kept an eye open for danger but saw only cows. Yet bad things constantly happened here: the postman, the dog, Auriol's spectral eyes. All that was yet to show was the Endecott Ghost.

The Exeter bus ran twice a day, connecting villages on that route: Drewsteignton, Castle Drogo and Tedburn St Mary. Though due at ten it was often late and Erin was used to a lengthy wait; through some mysterious alchemy, however, the driver always managed to make up time. She sat on the bench across from the pub and watched the traffic filtering by. It only took one piece of farm equipment to bring things to a halt.

It was chilly now; she wished she had gloves, had not expected to be still here, had hoped by now to be safely back in Wapping. It was winter already; she'd arrived in June with just her laptop, a couple of bags and good old Perseus in his travelling box. Two months at the most was what they had said when they'd dropped her off at the dead of night and left her to sweat it out alone while they stabilised the Russians. Nothing was happening on that front except for two very suspicious deaths, in London, described in the press as accidental.

The bus arrived and she climbed aboard, settling herself in a seat at the rear. Travelling by bus was conducive to thought. She no longer missed having a car.

She thought about the Endecott Ghost and the fact so many people she'd met truly believed it existed. Poor tragic Violet, so full of life, who had died on the night of her coming-out ball and now still roamed her family's land and tended her own lonely grave. Her parents had abandoned her and fled abroad when the house burnt down. No one knew what had happened to them. Small wonder she couldn't rest.

She might make the basis for a book. Erin jerked suddenly fully awake. A colourful slice of local life based on a recent legend.

The bus returned by a different route, via the turnpike and Whiddon Down, which meant it conveniently passed by Endecott Park. Since she had done this trip before, Erin now understood how such things worked. A friendly word in the driver's ear and he would drop her as close as he could though, because of a major bend in the road, it meant walking the last fifty yards.

The last bus home was at 5.15 and Erin was there in plenty of time. She hadn't remembered the clocks had gone back or else she might have thought to bring a torch. By the time they reached her stop it was fully dark.

'Goodnight!' she called as she climbed down the steps, clutching her books and DVDs, then watched the bus pull away into total blackness.

No street lights, no pavements, no houses at all: she had never encountered darkness this dense. Along this stretch, which ran through the woods, she couldn't even catch a glimpse of the stars. Erin was paralysed by fear. All she could see were the lights of hurtling motorists who couldn't see her. But she'd lived through worse in the course of her work, manoeuvring mine-fields and dodging enemy fire. Gritting her teeth, she hugged the hedge and, inch by inch, worked her way along until at last she could dimly make out the tall iron gates of the park.

Taking her life in her hands, she crossed and, once inside, heaved a sigh of relief. No more traffic but still a very long drive to negotiate in solid darkness. Way in the distance, through the trees, she could now make out small pinpricks of light which meant that some of her neighbours must be home. She would switch on the lights, the TV and the fire then pour herself a very strong drink. After which she would soak in a leisurely bath and recover.

Close in the darkness, something moved; she sensed it rather than heard it. She stopped in her tracks and listened but heard no more. Only the sighing wind in the trees and the thunderous beating of her own heart. Cautiously she moved forward – and felt it move too. Whatever it was must be tracking her. She fancied now she could hear it breathe. For a moment she fumbled for her phone but didn't know who she could call. And if she spoke she might activate something far worse.

So she clutched her belongings and blindly ran towards the nearest light she could see and, when it turned out it was number four, she shouted loudly for help.

Phil, the doctor, was standing outside, unloading something from his car, when an ashen-faced Erin came out of the dark and almost fell into his arms.

'What?' he cried, grabbing hold of her and swinging her round in a rapid reflex while urgently fumbling for something in his belt.

'There is someone out there in the darkness,' she said. 'I don't know who but it came very close.' She was shaking so much she dropped all her things on the ground.

The door to his house stood open. He shoved her inside. 'Bolt the door behind me,' he said. 'And don't open up till I tell you to. Stay away from the windows whatever you do.'

Erin, still in a daze of shock, silently complied.

Shortly afterwards Jenny came home. Erin saw the lights as the van drew up and after a muffled conversation, Jenny yelled to her to open up. 'It's okay,' she said, coming in with a smile. 'Whatever it was has cleared off.'

'How can you know that?'

'We do,' she said and very soon after, Phil came in too.

'You were right to be scared', he said, 'in an outpost like this.'

'It wasn't the dark per se,' Erin said, feeling now a bit of a fool. 'There was definitely something there though I don't know what.'

'Always feel free to bang on our door,' he said, 'if it happens again.' He had warm brown eyes and a lovely smile. He was hunky, athletic and comforting. His patients must all adore him, Erin was sure.

They offered her coffee but she declined. Her pulse rate was back to normal now and Perseus would be waiting next door for his food.

'You must both come in for a drink one night,' Erin said as he watched while she unlocked her door. 'I can't think where all the time has gone. I haven't achieved very much.'

He didn't ask what it was she did which, later, she found slightly curious. She had been around so long they must surely have wondered.

32

Finally faced with admitting the truth, Gerald seated Sylvia down and put a strong drink in her hand. Not sherry this time but the harder stuff. It threatened to be a bumpy ride and he wasn't at all certain how she would react.

'Now listen to me.' His face was grave and he loosened the knot of his RAC tie. No more posing or fudging issues, the time had come for the truth. Not all of it, though, if it could be avoided. He planned to hold certain things back.

He had left the job at the bank's request due to discrepancies in the accounts. Their affluent lifestyle had been topped up by occasional furtive dipping into the funds. He hadn't discussed it with her before because he had known how upset she would be. He had kept on hoping to straighten things out but had not succeeded in time. Looking now at Sylvia's face he knew his decision had been right. What she hadn't known had not worried her in the least.

'The car,' she said.

'It had to go. I told you all along that we didn't need two.'

'But I have to be able to get around.'

'Stick to buses,' he said.

She didn't listen, she never had. She still wasn't properly taking it in. 'Why can't you get another job?'

He laughed. She had no idea.

It wasn't her fault. She had never been bright. He had married her for her stupendous looks but now the years had started to take their toll. All he saw when he looked at her was a caricature of the glorious creature he'd married. She had put on weight and dressed far too young. Her thighs were pitted with cellulite and her upper arms, when she let them show, were flabby. She soaked in the sun which had damaged her skin and her face was becoming jowly. From the rear she looked like the much older woman she was. But he couldn't tell her, not even now, and eliminate the trust in her eyes. She believed she had hardly aged at all. He couldn't destroy that illusion.

'I can't get another job,' he said, pouring himself another stiff scotch. 'Because they won't give me a reference.' As simple as that. He didn't add there was still a chance they might sue. Apart from which he was now too old. It had been a gamble that hadn't paid off. He'd been milking them steadily over the years and the reason it had gone wrong was due to his greed. Her greed, rather; he was all right. His expectations had not been so high. He'd been satisfied, more or less, with the lifestyle they had. He had gambled a little and usually won. Ploughed it straight back into stocks and shares. Had been canny enough not to dig himself in too deep.

But Sylvia hadn't been satisfied. She wanted the lot and she wanted it now: the latest fashions, a fancier car, a Mediterranean cruise. She had chipped away at him night and day until he began taking larger risks. He had borrowed sums in increasing chunks, still meaning to pay it all back. He couldn't really blame it on her, should have put his foot down years ago. He simply couldn't face up to the fact he had failed.

The truth was they never discussed such things; she still remained vague about what he did. 'My husband works in a merchant bank,' she would trill when the subject arose. She had no idea how he spent his time, had never worked in an office herself except for that year in the typing pool from which he had rescued her. Money was something not talked about. That was very vulgar, her mother said. He had promised the day they married to care for her always.

And care for her was what he had done, with an ever-increasing salary and increments. She was proud of his progress and let it show. The problem was their expenses were rising too. Both the girls went to ballet class, even though Lucy was not that keen. They needed it, Sylvia said, to improve their deportment. Later they both had speech coaching too and private piano lessons, though neither ever showed much aptitude. They grew up like their mother: spoilt, shrill and demanding and not very nice. They viewed him with the same empty detachment that she did.

She was staring now with accusing eyes, a mottled flush rising up her neck, eyes bulging like a goldfish out of water. What did he plan to do, she demanded, to get their finances back on course? Which was a hard one. He had no idea. He'd been hoping to make a killing down here but so far none of his plans were amounting to much.

The telephone rang. No doubt one of the girls. 'Tell her I'm out,' he said.

The barmaid down at the Rose and Crown was fit and frisky and up for it. Lorelei she now styled herself, though her parents had christened her Myrtle. She was thirty-nine though looked a lot less with her low-cut tank tops and throaty laugh. Gerald and she had a good thing going, the nights he could get away. Sylvia thought he was working late and kept a meal for him warm in the oven, not knowing that he was downing pints and spending too much on the horses.

It had started off as a bit of a laugh, an antidote to his gruelling day, and built him up in the eyes of his fellow imbibers. The pub was far enough off from home for word not to reach the ears of his wife. When he came in complaining he'd had a bad day she believed him. Poor old Gerald, he worked so hard but, then, he had an important job. She bragged about him to everyone, especially her daughters. And they, accordingly, took what he gave them for granted.

He drove a Jaguar and took up golf, at weekends spent much of his time at the club. Sylvia grumbled but grew to enjoy their ever-improving lifestyle. Double-glazing, a three-piece suite: whatever she asked for he let her have. What started off as infatuation morphed into laissez-faire. As the years went by and her looks declined he was forced to face up to one glaring fact. The beauty queen who had caught his eye was a shrill, demanding airhead. She only ever read magazines (which she always referred to as books) and had no interests beyond herself and doing things to the house. She wasn't even much fun in bed any more.

They bought The Firs when he joined the board and Sylvia's avarice rapidly grew. Now she needed a car of her own and a cleaner three times a week. She had no hobbies or interests, just tango lessons to keep herself trim and coffee mornings to show off her house to her friends and drop a few names. She shopped a lot which meant regular trips up to town.

Francesca and Lucy had grown up spoilt with a cool, superior attitude. They looked down on their hard-working father, considered his utterings naff. They mocked the way he took care of his clothes and for mispronouncing occasional words which they only knew since he'd paid for their education. Both, like their mother, had married young to hardworking dullards to keep up their standard of living. But they still came bleating back to their dad when Kevin or Terry failed to deliver the goods. Which was how his secret liaison had come about.

Lorelei was a barrel of laughs, bright and sparky and generous too. She wasn't in it for what she could get but purely because she liked him. Loved him, even. Their riotous nights sent him back to his wife a much happier man. She found him attractive, laughed at his jokes, occasionally helped him to pick out a tie and was never so tired or headachy as to refuse him. Sylvia, cocooned in her own selfish world, continued to be unaware.

Until their relocation down here, since when he seemed to be always slightly off colour.

Shattered by what he had done to her, deprived of life's little luxuries that had rapidly grown into being essentials, Sylvia collapsed on the sofa in a heap. It was unbelievable how he'd behaved, caught red-handed in a petty crime, allowing himself to be strong-armed out of his job. How could she hold up her head again or start a new social life down here without an income in line with the one she was used to? There were things she needed, standards to keep, a public persona she must maintain. She had cut back as far as she could when they'd sold The Firs.

She stuffed her handkerchief into her mouth to stifle the cries that she dared not utter. These walls were thin; she feared what the neighbours would say. The dinner party she'd been preparing, a practice run for the real thing, would have to be cancelled now. She would say she was ill. The guests were of no real consequence, acquaintances rather than proper friends, a cousin of one of their neighbours in Kent who had recently moved to Taunton. She must cancel the wine and the canapés, must ring that girl at the deli first thing.

Distraught, she tottered across the room and poured another strong drink.

Gerald, down at the Ring o'Bells, was wistfully thinking of Lorelei. It was over a year since he'd been in touch though he thought of her constantly. Longed for her and her throaty laugh, her sensuous body with generous curves which she offered to him willingly purely out of affection. They had had some great times in his affluent days, trips to the Derby and down to the coast while Sylvia thought he was slogging away in the office. His eyes grew moist.

Never again. He was now a marked man, condemned to a life of near penury under the eye of a scold who would never forgive him. They were bolted together with bands of steel more restrictive even than their wedding rings, reduced to living within his retirement income. The thought appalled him. He ordered a scotch. Sylvia's conversation would rot his mind. All she ever talked about were her soaps and how hard up they now were.

Back to his plan. He would not give in, was still determined to make that elusive fast buck. Which brought him back to his neighbour at the gatehouse. What was that all about? He still didn't know, had been ushered out before he could ask any questions. Since when he sensed he was being held at arm's length. The fireworks party had not come off; the weather was bad and the neighbours weren't keen and Sylvia was damned if she'd let them tramp mud through her house. The Commander had gone away for a while with still no explanation of what he did. Whatever it was, though, it must be very high-powered.

Gerald, more than ever before, was determined to know the answer.

33

Lisa was dazzled by Oliver Swann, overwhelmed by his affable charm. She found it hard to get him out of her mind. She had meekly shown him around the house while he made professional-sounding noises, all the while scribbling notes on his business-like clipboard. He had complimented her on her taste: classy understatement with accents of colour. What she had done showed remarkable flair; he asked if she did it professionally and when she said no, gave her his card and told her to ring if she felt like taking things further. Swann Homes, he said, could always use talent like hers.

When she pointed out the things that were wrong – the cracked lintel over the terrace doors, the water seepage in two of the bathrooms and the dishwasher drawer that always stuck – he laughed and said he'd be back.

'Other than that you love it, yeah?' His dark eyes sparkled with merriment. He really was very appealing. Lisa softened.

But when she reported all this to Ned, she was unprepared for his terrible rage. The man had no right, he thundered, to call unannounced.

'He should make an appointment. Tell him next time. I don't want him coming here while I am out. I am the householder. He should be talking to me.'

Lisa stared at him, open-mouthed. What was he talking about? she said. The house was in both their names. They were equal partners. Besides which, she was the one at home during the day. But Ned was no longer listening, having stormed out. She still wasn't used to these unexpected flare-ups.

Something occurred, she never knew what, that made him suddenly lose his temper. He went off like a thunderclap though was normally mild and reserved. It had to do with his earlier life; she couldn't forget how he'd ripped up his mother's picture.

There'd been no more sex of the jungle kind; Lisa was secretly disappointed. They were back to quick pecks and half-hearted hugs and occasional after-dark congress. She wished there was someone to whom she could talk who could throw some light on his volatile side but he had no family nor friends outside his work. She suggested he invite colleagues home, she would love to meet them and also their wives, but he said they all lived too far away. Besides, she had nothing remotely in common with them.

There was nothing to do in the garden in winter so, encouraged by Oliver Swann, Lisa turned her attention back to the house. She bought silk cushions to go on the beds and matching chairs for the guest rooms, plus bedside lamps with contrasting floral shades. They never had any visitors but if they should she liked to think they'd approve of what she had done. It looked very enticing. Flower prints next, to go on the walls; she was keeping an eye on the village shop and might take a trip into Exeter for a browse round.

She broached the subject of weekend guests: a couple of people she'd known from work, even her two half-sisters who lived in London. Although they had very little in common, they had shared a father and were her kin. If only because of him, they should stay in touch. Ned, however, did not agree. She barely knew them, he pointed out, and they hadn't put themselves out for her since her marriage. He had no interest in knowing them, was not a sociable man.

She ought to be pleased, in a way she was. She liked the feeling of being special, the one with whom he had chosen to share his life. But now the evenings were drawing in and the weather was stormy and nippy at night, she felt less the urge to be out of doors instead of huddled inside by the fire with a book. She considered joining some sort of a class to help fill the empty afternoons but could think of nothing she really wanted to learn.

They'd been married now almost seven months and the novelty was wearing thin. They had settled into a civil routine that lacked an element of oomph. She was still not forty, with time on her hands and a sudden desire to take life by the throat. So when Oliver Swann strolled into her life, Lisa was an accident waiting to happen.

He was back again the following week with a gang of men and a Portaloo that they placed discreetly out of sight of the houses. They came in a truck bearing ladders and things that they dumped in the carport along with their tools. Lisa watched him from the study window, strutting around like a bantam cock in his trademark Ray-Bans, and experienced a visceral thrill. She automatically checked her hair and wondered whether to hop in the shower. She had found him so persuasive last time, she couldn't refuse him access. She was, after all, in control of her life and would do as she jolly well pleased.

She waited for the doorbell to ring, having brushed out her hair (no time for a shower) and quickly applied some make-up. She ran the Hoover around down-stairs and checked that the cloakroom had clean towels. Then she made fresh coffee and perched herself at a vantage point to keep an eye on proceedings. She hadn't felt this keyed up in weeks, not since before Peter's death.

In the event, nothing happened at all. They carried the ladders round to the back and then seemed to disappear. When she opened the door and ventured outside they were gone. Later she heard the truck start up and saw it was him, heading back to the gates. Disappointing. Though he'd come again, she had his promise on that. And then she would pin him down to a definite time.

She liked the idea of working with him, earning money doing something she really enjoyed. It would make her less dependent on Ned and the office was in Exeter which was handy. Swann Homes appeared to be growing fast, she saw their ads all over the place, featured also on the Internet. Luxury homes in rural surroundings, making the most of natural assets. Endecott Park drew largely on its history and social cachet. There were sketches of how the manor had looked in its glory days before the fire. Tasteful town houses built as a terrace, the flashy advertisements said.

Tasteful houses. She looked around at the water damage and leaking taps, at the light fittings that were so badly wired they came away in your hand. That, however, was superficial and, bit by bit, she would get it all fixed. It meant she would be in regular touch with him. She bought an armful of magazines, *House & Garden* and *Country Life* and also a subscription to *World of Interiors*. Oliver Swann had pointed the way towards a new career for her. Ned might disapprove but it wasn't his life.

All had gone quiet on the postman's death; no one mentioned it any more. Even the local paper carried no news. Ned, who occasionally checked it out, seemed inexplicably grumpy. Lisa was touched by his concern. It seemed he must love her more than he liked to show.

'There have to be things they're not letting us know.' He flicked out his napkin and sampled the wine as Lisa was ladling the stew. He had tried to speak to the man in charge but came up against the usual brick wall. Nobody seemed to want to discuss it with him. Though they wouldn't say why.

'Poor boy,' said Lisa. 'I miss him a lot.' That cheerful smile and those dazzling looks and the irrepressibly sunny smile. 'His mother must miss him too.' She had meant to go to the funeral, he had always been very kind to her, but understood that the body had not been released. She wondered what they were waiting for. From the little she knew, it seemed like a one-off crime.

'They owe it to us, the residents,' said Ned, 'to keep us informed.'

Lisa agreed. It was private land for which they were paying over the odds. No outsider should have easy access, especially not to commit such atrocities. She beamed at him in the candlelight, enjoying the cosiness they shared. They rubbed along very well in the main. Their marriage, despite a few hiccups, seemed to be working.

Ned was silently considering, the candlelight glinting off his lenses concealing his expression. The hint of a smile hovered round his mouth; Lisa waited for him to speak. He sliced the bread and passed it over to her.

'Mind you, a pansy like that,' he said, 'probably mixed with all kinds of low-life. I wouldn't waste too much sympathy on him.'

Lisa stared at him, thunderstruck. Peter a pansy? No way was that true. He was fit and athletic, a regular sports-mad jock. 'Where did you get that idea?' she asked, appalled he should ever think such a thing let alone express it. What a bigot!

Ned stared at her blandly, unperturbed, and helped himself to more of the stew. 'The necklace,' he said. 'I just assumed as much.'

'It wasn't a necklace, just shells,' she said, biting back her sudden rage. 'It is simply part of the surfing culture. Most surfers wear them,' she said.

She carried her dish across to the sink and held it under the running tap, trying to stop herself shaking with disbelief.

'How did you know?' she suddenly asked. 'About Peter's necklet? You never met.' Ned always left two hours before Peter came.

Ned looked vague then picked up the paper. 'You must have told me,' he said.

Oliver Swann returned the next day, back in the yellow Lagonda this time, wearing a well-cut suit of Italian design. He fished his clipboard from under the seat, removed the Ray-Bans and checked his breath. Then vaulted out of the car and rang Lisa's doorbell.

'Ah,' he said when she opened the door, hair freshly washed and her make-up on. 'Mind if I come in and take a look round?'

'Please,' said Lisa, stepping aside and showing him into the living room. 'I was just about to make coffee. How do you like it?'

34

Jasper was dead but life went on. Auriol's anger was manifold though not exclusively aimed at her former husband. She took a long hard look in the mirror then emptied the gin bottle down the sink. It was time to get a grip on herself and move on. She arranged for the vet to dispose of the body. What was done was done, she would shed no more tears. She refused to allow that bastard to win but fighting him head-on would be counterproductive. Her future mattered more than revenge; she would leave it to the Commander to sort him out. Meanwhile she had the rest of her life before her.

She was pleased with the progress she had made. Her boxroom was gradually filling up with canvases and watercolours executed during her sojourn here. Some of them she had hung on the wall, others were propped around the room: mostly landscapes of the moor in all its varying moods. Erin, seriously impressed, was urging her to exhibit them. The village gallery might be the place to start. They had excellent taste.

'I'll certainly buy one,' Erin said. 'As a souvenir of my time spent here. More than one, providing I can afford them.' She had plenty of room in the Clerkenwell loft with all that empty wallspace still to be covered.

'Don't be daft. I'll give you one. I wouldn't dream of letting you pay.' It was the very least she could do as a token of their new friendship. But Auriol's ambitions were more pronounced; she still had excellent contacts in the metropolitan art world. At the risk of putting her neck on the line, she was planning to get a dealer down for an educated opinion.

She hadn't intended to act this fast but Jasper's death had spurred her on. She had no more time to waste in prevarication. Jonathan Kyle was a long-time friend whose Cork Street Gallery had wooed her once. Then she had chosen the property world as a faster route to success. Now, however, she needed him and still had a couple of favours to call. She invited him for a country weekend before the weather got worse. Exeter was just under three hours from London, she offered to meet him off the train to save him the tedious journey down. She need not have worried. He couldn't have been more delighted. A breath of country air and a pub sounded just the ticket to him.

So the die was cast. She stocked up the fridge and ordered in some expensive wines. She promised herself she would hear what he said. And steeled herself for the verdict.

Erin admired her tenacity. Whatever Auriol wanted she went for. In similar circumstances she'd do the same. They were much alike.

'Would you consider painting full-time?' Erin asked.

'If Jonathan thinks I could make it pay.' She was neither a fool nor a fantasist but still had some money put by. And whatever she did for the next thirty years would have no bearing at all on the property world. That was one decision she wouldn't change.

Erin told her about Monday night, the terrible fear she'd experienced. A presence close to her in the dark, there but not tangible. Which brought them back to Auriol's fright, those huge unblinking eyes.

'Do you think we are both going potty?' she said.

'It is possible, stuck on the moor like this.'

Both missed the bright lights of the city and traffic noise. Which reminded Erin of Phil next door and how he had rescued her from the dark. 'He was wonderfully down to earth,' she said, 'when I leapt upon him, crying.'

Nice man, they both agreed, the doctor. Or was he? They still weren't quite sure.

Jonathan Kyle was fifty-two, elegant in well-cut tweeds and soft suede shoes that had never had contact with mud. He sported a Barbour. Auriol, meeting him off the train, waved with a genuine sense of relief. She trusted his judgement implicitly. He would tell her what she should do. She ran towards him and they embraced. He smelled of tobacco and lime cologne. Relieved, she linked her arm through his and led him back to the car. A breath of nostalgia from the past; she knew she was going to be all right. Just having a man around again made her feel heaps better.

He loved her paintings, or so he said. Waxed lyrical with enough reserve for her to be fairly sure he wasn't lying. He admired her technique but criticised aspects of her use of the actual paint. In places she layered it on too thick but was at her most effective when dealing with light. He stood in silence in front of one depicting moonlight over the moor. Then turned to her with a glint in his eye she recognised as endorsement.

'My darling,' he said, 'I can truthfully say you've got what it takes. I will gladly take you on.'

Whoops all round and a drink for him though Auriol stuck with mineral water. They settled down by the fire to discuss her future. She was feeling great;

as her confidence grew her former beauty surfaced again. She looked up and caught the look on his face of genuine admiration.

'What did you do with that creep?' he asked. 'Who was never near good enough for you.'

Auriol laughed. 'That's another story. Which I'll keep for some other occasion.'

Because she couldn't be bothered to cook – she gave up those skills when she moved down here – they headed down to the village for an early supper. First she thought of the Ring o'Bells but that was inclined to be noisy at night so she parked by the church and settled for the Three Crowns.

The fire was blazing, the bar was snug. What in summer could be oppressive was cosy and warm. A handful of locals were having a drink but keeping their voices to a minimal burr. The bar menu looked acceptable so they stayed. It was private in the inglenook which effectively cut them off from the rest of the throng.

Auriol went to freshen up. One of her contact lenses had slipped and she needed a moment's privacy to exult in Jonathan's verdict. He liked her work, it was saleable. There was room right now for these moody paintings. Town dwellers still had a yen for the great outdoors. He'd suggested an exhibition in March which would give her time to fill a few gaps. A handful of small ones would not go amiss among the larger set pieces. She fixed her lens and touched up her eyes, then ran a brush through her thick tawny hair. She grinned at herself in the glass. Things were working out.

Jonathan seemed to be transfixed and hardly noticed when she reappeared. He was mesmerised by the portrait over the bar. Auriol hadn't seen it before; she never normally drank in this pub, was only here tonight because of the parking. She fidgeted and reread the menu. The barman wandered over and stood. Both were waiting for Jonathan, absorbed in a world of his own.

At last he emerged from his reverie. 'Who is the painter?' he wanted to know. 'It looks very much like a Strickland to me. Very big in the years between the wars.'

He looked at the barman who shook his head. 'Don't know, sir. No good asking me. All I know is it hung in the manor before the place burnt down.'

All of them stared then Jonathan rose, pulled out a magnifying glass and went round the bar to take a closer look. 'It is a Strickland. I was right. 1935, it says. Who, may I ask, is the very beguiling sitter?'

'That I do know,' the barman said. 'Violet Endecott, bless her heart. Painted for her eighteenth birthday which was also her coming-out ball.'

Jonathan studied it long and hard. 'Well,' he said after a lengthy pause, 'she was certainly a looker. What's the story?'

Quickly the barman filled him in then Auriol took up the rest of the tale including the spooky bits from the Brennans' party. 'They say when the wind's in a certain direction . . . ' The barman chuckled and left her to it. The bar was filling; he had a job to do.

'But why,' asked Jonathan, 'is it here? A Strickland is quite a collection piece. This one, I'd guess, is worth a few bob. It should be in a gallery, somewhere safe.'

'Search me,' said Auriol. 'All I know is the daughter died in the fire and shortly after the parents went abroad. And never returned.' A very odd story indeed, now she thought about it.

She filled him in. How she'd seen the ruin one late afternoon when the sun was setting and conceived her happy-ever-after dream on the spot.

'Manderley?'

'Something like that,' she agreed. 'It looked so romantic I had to have it.'

'So you left it to Prince Charming to fix . . .'

'Instead of which he fixed me.'

They stared at each other and then they laughed and Jonathan grabbed her hand and kissed it. 'Come on,' he said, picking up the bill. 'We could both use an early night.'

35

In the moonlight the churchyard was bright as day as Betty knelt beside Violet's grave, doing as much as she could to pretty it up. The grass was frozen and the weeds were dead but she polished the granite with linseed oil, all the while softly crooning under her breath. The task was a self-imposed labour of love which she did whenever the moon was full, which meant she could see to remove every atom of dirt. The violets lay in a tidy bunch ready for placing once she was done, silk instead of real ones because it was winter.

'Violet, dear.' She sat back on her heels and addressed the long-dead sister she'd never known. 'I am having a spot of bother. Perhaps you can help.'

They needed to find the murderer of the nice young postman who'd meant no harm. She had also heard that the friendly dog was dead too. It was very distressing. There were forces of evil out there on the moor that not even Satan and Lucifer could control. She was growing feebler with each new season and, increasingly, starting to fear for her life. Her pets would always be there for her and Satan provided her with fresh meat but not even he could cope with a man with a gun or a knife.

She knew the vicar and Effie Willcox were still conspiring to put her away, just as they'd dealt with poor Marigold close to the end. And she wouldn't have it; she liked this life, even in winter when things were so grim. Her freedom was all she had left and must be clung on to. She talked to Violet whenever she came and, though she never received a reply, felt confident she was listening and giving it thought. Lying there quietly beneath the stars, Violet had all the time in the world to think and bring what had once been her worldly knowledge to bear on her sister's plight. Violet had danced with the future king; had she not died he might have held on to the throne.

She needed proof that the land was hers in order to drive the invaders away and to barricade herself against killers and robbers. Violet had always been here on the spot and must know exactly how things should be. She had been sole heir to the Endecott land so that Betty, not even conceived when she died, should by right of birth step into her shoes. There were no more contenders she knew of. All she'd ever wanted was peace and quiet and sanctuary for her remaining years along with her wildlife friends.

There went that blasted cockerel again; it was time to get moving before the dawn broke. She gathered her tools and positioned the flowers then kissed the stone as she always did.

'Goodnight, my precious. Sweet dreams,' she said. 'I know you would help if you could.'

Effie knew more than she ever let on. MI5 had trained her for that. It stood her in excellent stead when it came to other people's secrets. Also being a librarian played its part. To Piers she was always a useful source; they had played together in nursery school and reconnected over the years whenever their paths collided. Recently he had found out a lot about the village that neither had known and had shared this new knowledge with Effie, which made them both stronger.

She had known his mother was an Endecott, a younger half-sibling by a second wife to the one whose daughter had died in that terrible fire. What she hadn't known until recently were facts that Piers had himself just turned up and was keeping under wraps till he'd checked them out. These facts he had lately divulged to her with the request that she not pass them on.

Both had only one focused aim: to restore the Endecott land to its rightful owner.

It wasn't, however, as simple as that. The story was complex and fairly far-fetched. Piers had only come by the truth when he executed his mother's estate after her long, drawn-out illness and subsequent death. There were still a number of complications to be sorted. He was also treading with utmost care since the crux of the matter lay, it turned out, uncomfortably close to home.

His mother had married very young a feckless charmer with an agile brain which he had handed down to his only son. The marriage, due to the outbreak of war, was short. He had joined the air force as soon as he could and covered himself with glory as a fearless flying ace. He had died in action the year his son was born.

Later Marigold married again and the family moved to Canada where Piers had stayed until adulthood when his stepfather died and his mother came home to live in the house she'd inherited from her own father. The rest, being land, all went to her brother whose only child perished when the manor burnt down.

All of which Effie already knew. The sad, gaunt ruin had stood there for years, dominating the Endecott acres, a grim reminder of what had happened that night. The grief-stricken parents had turned their backs, unable to cope with the terrible truth, and run away to the African sun from where they had never returned. Gossip and rumour had gradually paled, the Second World War had come and gone and no one had known for sure who the legal heir was.

Except for Effie, who had known for years since, as a child, she had first befriended a strange pale girl who emerged from nowhere with a cardboard suitcase containing all she owned. Betty had no proof that she was who she said. She was awkward, tongue-tied and insecure. Her parents were dead; no one knew of her existence. But Effie believed her and took her in hand, brought her food, found her somewhere to stay and to this day, more than fifty years later, remained her only real friend.

She stood now listening, enthralled, to Piers, her long face sagging, her mouth agape, unable to take in what she had just been told.

'You can't be serious. It's monstrous,' she said, covering her mouth to hide the incredulous grin.

'I'm deadly serious,' he said with similar mirth. Then added, bringing things back to earth, 'Please don't breathe a word till I have written proof.'

Effie, who knew how to hold her tongue but was also a conscientious carer, waited till Friday, Betty's library day. She watched her slow progress across the square; the poor old joints must be seizing up. Her distinctive hobble was visibly worse. Effie wondered how many more winters she could survive in the woods. In her strange attire, wrapped in a rug with a rancher-style hat balanced on her head, Betty looked what she was: a refugee from an exotic time warp.

Effie made coffee to warm them both up since the temperature had dropped by several degrees. She insisted that Betty relax for a while until she'd begun to thaw from the wind-chill factor. She steered the conversation to the past; Betty was always more fluent when looking back.

'How old were you when your father died?'

Betty considered. 'Thirteen,' she said. 'It was always claimed that he died of a broken heart.'

'All those years later?'

'That's what they said. My mother too, she just wasted away. Though she had this massive crush on a priest that kept her going for years.' Effie glimpsed in the faded eyes a glint of mischievous malice.

'And would you say you were close to him?'

Without having to think, Betty shook her head. 'He only had one daughter,' she said, 'who died before I was born.'

How unutterably sad. Effie bled for her. What cruelty families could inflict. The mother, too, for

302

being so deeply selfish. And then they had died, leaving Betty alone in a foreign land with no heritage. It was only because she had guts she had found her way home. Home, though, to what? She had no stake here except for the one she had claimed for herself: a decaying caravan deep in the heart of the woods.

But now it was winter and she was old, too old to have to be living this way. Effie's resolution strengthened; she would solve the mystery once and for all if it were the last thing she ever did.

'Tell me more about your pa. How did he pass his time out there?'

Again Betty didn't hesitate. 'At his club,' she said. 'Every afternoon. Drinking and playing poker.' He had drunk and gambled his fortune away which was why she now had to live as she did. Not that she held it against him after so long.

'Indeed,' said Effie, restraining herself. She turned her attention back to the books. Shortly she'd wander down to the pub and hope to run into Piers.

36

Erin was on her way to see Effie when the two of them met at the library door. The older woman was heading out. 'Come', she said, 'and join me for lunch, my dear.'

Erin, here to pick her brains, happily fell into step beside her. The Three Crowns was the handiest pub, only two doorways away. A huge fire roared – it was very cold – so they took possession of the inglenook and Effie ordered mulled wine to suit the occasion.

'It was her I wanted to see you about,' said Erin, nodding at Violet's portrait. Effie, with similar things on her mind, readily acquiesced.

It wasn't easy to know where to start. Erin explained she was a journalist.

Here for an indefinite stay, prompted Effie who never forgot a thing.

Erin laughed, feeling more relaxed, liking Effie's

forthrightness. 'You were going to tell me about the fire,' she said.

'I was, indeed, and poor Violet's death.' Both paused for a second's unspoken respect. 'Well,' said Effie, flexing her hands, 'why don't we start by ordering lunch? I eat here a lot and can recommend the Ploughman's.'

She was into her story when Piers walked in and hailed them both with sincere delight. 'Great,' he said. 'I was very much hoping to find you.'

He removed his sheepskin and rubbed his hands, ordered a whisky and pulled up a chair.

'I was telling Erin about the manor,' said Effie, holding his gaze.

'Then let me not interrupt,' he said. 'Though I hope you'll allow me to join you.'

As Effie continued her narrative, Erin studied them both at close hand. Two forceful, highly intelligent people, clearly at ease with each other. They even occasionally prompted the other's stories.

'You've known each other a long time,' she said.

'From kindergarten,' said Piers with a grin. 'Though for most of the intervening time we lived in different countries.'

She was dying to ask what it was he did but felt she should wait till he volunteered. He was older than her by quite a bit and by waiting she usually got a more accurate story. But he had been present when Jasper was shot, along with Kasia and the rest of the group, so she had to find out who he thought was responsible.

He looked surprised and, indeed, concerned. The first about it he'd heard, he said. He had left his companions up on the moor to go to an urgent meeting.

'What a terrible thing,' he said. 'I am truly sorry.'

Effie needed a private word with Piers so, once they had eaten, Erin withdrew. Erin thanked her profusely for her time and Effie said she was always there. She very much liked her idea for a book. Piers too.

'Do you know how long you'll be here?' Effie asked.

Erin said no, it was out of her hands.

'We must fix for you to come by for that drink,' said Piers as he walked her to the door. 'I would like to talk to you further.' He took her number.

She couldn't be bothered to wait for the bus. There was only one and it went via Moretonhampstead. It was cold but she was well wrapped up so she took the familiar river walk which led eventually to the path through the woods. The sky was leaden; it looked like snow. A gale was driving down sleet from the moor. The sooner she was out of this place and back to the civilisation of London, the better.

She had thought a lot about Piers Compayne, finding him charming and very urbane, yet although his name still rang distant bells she had no clear idea who he was. Except that he seemed on familiar terms with Kasia. She had tried several times to get through to Rod and had asked him to call, though he hadn't as yet. She must update him on Kasia and the Commander. She must also tell him about her fright and how the doctor next door had come to the rescue. It was reassuring to know there was help so near.

She reached the weir and entered the woods, picking her way with care on the frozen ground. There was no one about that she could see though she still had the feeling of being followed. From time to time she stopped to check but nothing stirred among the silent trees. She felt herself growing paranoid; she had been on her own for far too long. When she reached the farm track she made the decision to take the more circuitous route and avoid the lower meadow where Peter had died. It meant facing the traffic for fifty yards but it wasn't yet dark and she still felt safer that way. The eerie feeling of being watched continued.

Once through the gates, she could relax and walked more slowly along the drive. A van was parked by the Portaloo; the workmen were still around. One of them, Gregory, nodded to her, he was slouched by her railings having a smoke. They never appeared to be working, these Poles, and were starting to give her the creeps. Though it wasn't her business how long they took to complete the final snagging.

Once she'd fed the cat and warmed her hands, checked the headlines and also her email, Erin thought it was time for a catch up with Rod. Not only because she missed his voice and wanted to know what was going on but mainly because she was now getting really nervous. It was all very well having Phil next door to comfort her when she felt slightly spooked but he was a doctor and not much use when it came to the serious stuff. She was hiding because they were hunting her down and already two lives had been violently lost – first the postman and then the dog. She needed some reassurance.

She chopped up vegetables for a stew and left them on a very low heat, then poured a vodka with plenty of ice and curled up on the sofa. It was almost seven; he should still be at work. With luck he'd have time to talk.

Her luck was in. He was and he had: sounding slightly less rushed than he had of late, also less concerned about the line being tapped. She imagined him leaning back in his chair with his view of the river at Tower Bridge, his jacket off and his sleeves rolled up, his desk lamp accentuating his thinning hair. Erin softened. She loved the man; the sound of his voice immediately made her feel better.

He asked how she was bearing up and said how much he was missing her. He filled her in on some of his day-to-day problems. On the Russian front things had quietened down. There had been a recent change of regime that still had to demonstrate if it was working. Dissenters' voices so far were few though the *Globe* had stuck to its policy of down-pedalling adverse commentary from its writers. Now was not the time to be making waves.

'How are you, babe? I miss you,' he said and she felt the old familiar ache. If only he weren't so far away; she longed to be in his arms.

For one split second she wondered if she should bother him with her minor fears which might very well just be paranoia. But he knew her enough to pick up on her hesitation.

'What is it?' he asked on a sharper note. 'Is there anything you're not telling me? I need to know even the smallest thing so as I can protect you.'

'It's not much more than instinct,' she said, reluctant to feel she was wasting his time yet also suddenly keen to unburden herself. She told him about the Polish girl who seemed to pop up wherever she went and had been on the scene the day she was sure she'd been shot at. 'I could be wrong but am starting to think she is Russian.'

Rod was instantly on the alert, firing questions and

making notes, demanding every detail she could remember. This was precisely what he had feared: a Russian operative on her trail, masquerading as a Polish waitress. She asked if perhaps she should ring the security number.

He hesitated, as if in thought. For a moment it seemed they had been cut off, then he told her not to do anything yet but wait.

'It's complicated,' was all he would say. 'I need to check that everything's still in position.'

So then she told him about the Commander, about whom she also had serious doubts. Very charming, almost too much so. She thought he might be in league with the Pole; he always seemed to be carrying a gun and had also been on the spot when the dog was killed.

'He is said to be a diplomat, working on his memoirs,' she said. 'Yet something about him doesn't entirely ring true.'

She felt his interest begin to wane; he had the attention span of a flea. There were voices now in the background, interrupting.

'Tell me his name.' At any second she expected him to say he must go.

She spelled it out. 'He goes by the rank of Commander.'

For a moment she thought they had lost the connection. There was total silence, the voices stopped. Then, 'I have to go,' he said. 'I'll call you back.'

Erin looked at the cat and sighed. That was the downside of dating a married man.

Effie Willcox was on the phone, having taken Erin's number when they had lunch. 'Look,' she said, 'I've been thinking, my dear, about your splendid idea for a book. It occurs to me that I may be able to help you.'

'Great,' said Erin. She'd expected this. Women like Effie Willcox could not resist meddling. She was clearly highly intelligent as well as grossly under-employed. And since she had lived here most of her life, she was an invaluable information source. The only thing troubling Erin was her conscience. She might not have time to write this book but Effie need never know that.

'I am hosting a small gathering soon,' Effie continued, 'of like-minded souls. I think you might find, if you'd care to join us, the proceedings . . . illuminating.'

'Thanks,' said Erin, sincerely pleased. She needed something to fill up her time. Especially now the evenings had really closed in.

37

Gerald was still obsessively bent on finding out what it was that went on in the private room at the rear of the Ring o'Bells every Thursday night. At a certain point, when the ale was flowing and closing time still an hour or two off, a ripple would pass round the favoured few, an eyebrow raised, a complicit nod, and surreptitiously, one by one, they would slide like conspirators into the inner sanctum. Trays of drinks were carried in, after which the door would be firmly closed and none of them would emerge for the rest of the evening. Gerald would linger on in the bar, very often the last to leave, straining his ears for any clue as to what was going on behind that closed door. The landlord blanked his questioning and would pointedly wait for him to leave before wishing him goodnight and bolting the door. As he walked frustratedly to his car, Gerald would hear occasional bursts of laughter.

Whatever it was, he wanted in and would not rest until he had been accepted. He had lived in this village for eighteen months and should, by now, be inner circle. They never baulked at letting him pay for a round. On one occasion, unable to sleep, he had sat by his window in the dark until the dog barking in the gatehouse announced that his neighbour was home. He checked the time; it was after one though the pub officially closed its doors at eleven.

The Commander remained his charming self if ever their paths should happen to cross which was not, to Gerald's annoyance, very often. The bonfire night party had not come off due to particularly stormy weather and Gerald himself had kyboshed Sylvia's plans for a dinner party. Put in the plainest terms, they hadn't the cash. He must do something, they were sinking fast; his dwindling funds were almost gone. He thought of selling the house but they had to live somewhere. He desperately needed some sort of financial boost.

Sylvia grizzled, which didn't help, and both the girls relentlessly nagged until he felt they'd be better off without him. At least if he went they would know the score and have to learn to survive by themselves. He took an illicit two days off and, on the pretext of seeking work, drove back to Lorelei and the Rose and Crown. She made him feel like a man again and he unloaded some of his woes which, over a series of Scotches, seemed slightly less dire.

'Why don't we run away,' he said. 'And start all over again in Spain.' They could buy a bar on the coast and run it together.

Lorelei laughed but did not recoil. She was now forty but in very good nick. He could do a lot worse, he theorised, with her as his second wife. The problem, though, was ever the same: how to dispose of the first.

Oliver Swann paid a call on Sylvia while Gerald was off on his secret skive. He flashed his irrepressible smile upon which Sylvia melted. He took her through his clipboard routine and asked if she had any special gripes. She offered to show him round the house if, first, he'd remove his shoes. She had a list as long as her arm: swollen woodwork, patches of damp and a constantly dripping tap. A smoke alarm that went off on its own, a musty smell in the downstairs loo. Creaking floorboards, a washing machine that left the clothes still damp. Oliver reeled. He hadn't bargained for this.

But he came inside and had a look round, admired her decor and buttered her up. He had always been a dab hand with the ladies, especially once they had passed their first flush of youth. The spotlight treatment caused Sylvia to bloom; she made him tea and carried it through on a silver tray set with an antique lace doily. She slipped on a Michael Bublé CD, her latest fave in the pin-up stakes; even in her fifties she was a flirt. And then she made a fatal mistake and started to brag about money.

She mentioned her husband's prestigious job, how much the bank had begged him to stay when he'd chosen early retirement to pander to her. The house in Kent had been far too large, two acres and a tennis court, she'd hardly seen him all week he worked such long hours. Their daughters, too, had both married well with husbands in very lucrative jobs. She preened as she told him how close-knit the family was.

She smiled at him beguilingly, perched on a chair to show off her legs, and when she leaned forward to pour the tea, he could see almost down to her navel. A pathetic woman, lonely too, who must have been, in her youth, a real head-turner. Oliver mouthed some platitudes and scribbled meaningless notes on his pad. He would send round his team to do superficial repairs. She had, however unwittingly, planted a seed in his crafty unscrupulous mind. Gerald Brennan, cards played right, should make a profitable target.

'What does your husband do to relax?' he enquired.

This and that, she had said at first, annoyed to find that his interest had shifted. She altered her pose and fluffed up her hair, swapped the disc for an Eartha

Kitt and asked in a provocative tone if he would care for more tea. Oliver Swann seemed preoccupied, had capped his gold pen and put it away, was glancing now at her china dogs as if assessing their worth. Golf, she added, and sometimes bridge. A speculative gleam came into his eye.

He checked the time and said he must go. His foreman would be in touch about the repairs. He hurried away and she watched him stride, short but supremely confident in his well-cut suit and designer shades, to ring the bell of number six next door. After a pause Lisa let him in, her hair brushed loose instead of scragged back, wearing a dress instead of her usual jeans. As well as no shoes.

Sylvia watched and pursed her lips. She had seen him go in there before, a couple of times. Once, like today, should have been enough since all he was doing was checking things out. She would hang around and see how long he stayed. Lisa Thornton seemed very uptight: small, intense and not very friendly. Despite the fact they had come to the party, she had not yet invited them back.

The husband, Ned, seemed a decent sort, conscientious and social-minded. He had been very helpful with the police inquiry. He worked as some kind of architect though Sylvia thought he looked more academic. He always wore a suit and was very well-groomed. She hovered close to the kitchen window. She wondered how he'd react if he knew that his wife was playing around.

Gerald came whistling home at six, suddenly full of the joys of spring even though it was still the middle of winter. His confidence was fully restored; he felt like the conquering hero again. Lorelei had this effect on him. He was secretly making plans. All he needed now was a stroke of luck, a financial windfall to clear his debts and get him up and running again and the world would be his oyster. He wasn't a man to give in without a fight.

He parked beside the yellow Lagonda that lately had been around a lot. Sylvia said it belonged to Oliver Swann. Gerald was pleased; it was long overdue that the lazy builders got off their butts and completed the snagging list. Their workmanship was not of the highest order.

Perfect timing. As he grabbed his bag the man himself emerged from the house next door.

'Mr Brennan? What a piece of luck.' Gerald ignored the outstretched hand. 'Oliver Swann at your service.' The smile was corrosive.

There were loads of complaints Gerald wanted to air but now was not an appropriate time. He had been on the road all afternoon and was gasping for a drink.

He was also in too good a mood right now for what might well turn into a fight. Let him come back at another time and go through the list in detail.

The builder, however, seemed unperturbed. 'I was going to phone you in any case. Your lady wife informs me you like to play cards.'

Gerald, totally unprepared, took a mental step backwards and stared. What had Sylvia been blabbing about? She just couldn't learn when to button her bloody mouth.

Oliver Swann had his diary out and his gold pen poised as he flicked through the pages. 'I wonder if you would care to join us for our regular poker game', he said, 'on Thursday nights at the Ring o'Bells? We could use another recruit.'

The Ring o'Bells. On Thursday night.

'In the room at the back,' he heard himself say.

Oliver beamed. 'Correct,' he said. 'Your neighbour, Piers Compayne, is one of our number.'

'What?' asked Sylvia suspiciously, seeing his grin when she opened the door. Something had happened, she didn't know what, but she hadn't seen him this cheerful in a while.

He put down his bag and pecked her cheek. 'I think this calls for a drink,' he said. Instinct told him that, finally, his luck was about to change.

38

Lisa was in an emotional spin. What had recently happened had knocked her for six. She knew she was playing with fire but couldn't resist it. Oliver Swann wouldn't mess about. He was, she could tell, a real go-getter, accustomed to snatching whatever he liked and later, just as ruthlessly, dumping it. She had few illusions. She was no longer an ingénue but a married woman of thirty-nine. Time was fast running out; she was not getting younger. Ned had induced a hunger in her that he wasn't able to satisfy. He aroused her passion but failed to follow through. What Oliver offered was what she craved: raunchy sex with no strings attached. The thought of a mindless fuck brought her out in a sweat of anticipation.

He had flirted with her outrageously and she had given as good as she got. She liked his style and that brazen stare that seemed to undress her on the spot.

She had known, in no uncertain terms, what the outcome was likely to be. He excited her so she went for it, was tired of feeling dissatisfied as well as slightly cheap, as she did with Ned.

The first time he'd called she had still been shy, had found his approach resistible until he had made a grab for her and she'd melted into his arms. Their copulation was short and sharp and left her crying aloud for more. He had done it again on the stairs and then in the kitchen. After which he had looked at his watch and said he really must go. He had a fairly new bride at home who was also still at the needy stage. He apologised and said he'd be back. For once he had kept his word.

The second time she was gagging for it, opened the door with no underwear on and surprised him with the intensity of her fervour. Oliver Swann had wiped his face and begged for mercy while he caught his breath. She had poured him an ice cold beer then they'd done it again.

'Whoa,' he had cried at last. 'Give me strength. I am not as fit as I used to be.' He would have to go home very soon and service the bimbo.

She watched him dress in his ultra sharp suit and wished that her husband was more like him. Oliver revelled in sex while Ned was embarrassed.

'You will come back?'

'I promise,' he said. Then grabbed his phone and made a fast getaway.

Ned noticed nothing when he came home except that Lisa seemed feverish which he put down to the time of the month, about which he knew very little. She mentioned Oliver Swann had called. Both the Brennans had witnessed that and she dared not run the risk of it getting back, as it certainly would.

'What did he want?' He was scanning the newspaper headlines.

'Oh, just another quick look around. He is sending his men to sort things out. I said you'd prefer to deal with them but they have to come during the working day and aren't around at weekends.'

Ned merely grunted. He'd had his say and reminded her who was boss round here. As long as she didn't forget that, he wasn't much bothered. He went upstairs to change his clothes and noticed one of the towels was damp. It seemed an unusual time to have taken a shower.

'I was feeling cold,' Lisa quickly explained.

It was certainly very nippy outside, with gale-force winds blowing down from the moor and the steps from the carport slicked with a thin glaze of ice. From this point on, it would grow consistently grimmer.

'Park yourself by the fire,' Lisa said. 'And I'll call when supper is ready.'

She had got away with it. Just as well. She purred with delight as she stirred the bolognese sauce. Ned hadn't noticed a thing which didn't surprise her. He wasn't tactile or highly sexed though his temper tantrums could be alarming. She'd been seriously scared the first time he blew his top. Now, though, she had things under control and just went quiet when he started to yell. His mother had clearly not slapped him enough as a child. That made her smile as she went about the business of making his supper.

'Nice day, dear?'

He was very bland and their conversation reflected it. He gave her a résumé of the traffic conditions.

Silently, as she spooned out the sauce, Lisa exulted about her day. If Ned had an inkling of what she'd been up to she thought he would probably faint. Would he, though? How much did he care? She hardly knew him well enough yet to be certain of his affection. Well, she told herself, smugly secure, what he didn't know couldn't hurt him.

That night, as he was sorting the rubbish, Ned noticed the beer bottle under the sink. When he pulled it out, Lisa's heart nearly missed a beat.

'Drinking beer?' He seemed slightly surprised especially now it had turned so cold.

'I used it to rinse my hair,' she said, thinking fast. Such small details might give her away. She must learn to be extra careful.

The following night was crystal clear, the full moon bathing the countryside in its white ethereal light. The blustering gale had suddenly ceased and the frozen larches stood to attention like soldiers. Ned stepped outside for a breath of air, his scarf wrapped tightly round his neck, blowing hard on his fingers and stamping his feet. Next door's cat went scurrying past, carrying a rabbit in its mouth, silver against the even more silvery background. Ned watched it carefully dissect its prey. Killing was clearly a natural instinct to this cat that had spent its whole life indoors yet had adapted instantly to the wild. Ned clicked to it but it didn't respond, was scratching now at its own terrace door, what remained of its prey now discarded. Erin O'Leary opened the door then recoiled when she saw what was lying there.

'Oh, for God's sake,' he heard her exclaim. 'Go away. You can't bring that dead thing in here.'

The cat, a city sophisticate, hesitated then went inside, leaving the rabbit for some other predator. It would not be there long; the night was alive with creatures preying on one another. A fox, a badger or something larger would soon be along to claim it.

Moonlight was magic and called to Ned. He popped back inside for his heaviest coat. 'I am going for a walk,' he said to Lisa.

Lisa, scraping the dishes, looked up. It would have been nice if he'd offered to help.

'Isn't it rather cold?' she said.

'That's the way I like it,' he said. 'Don't wait up.'

He took the path down the edge of the woods that led into the lower meadow where that postman fellow had come to a sticky end. In winter the ferns were sere and dry, frozen now by a virulent frost. There'd be no more hiding places until the spring. His feet crunched over the frosty grass and the moon rode high like a satellite, keeping a watchful eye on all beneath it. First the postman and then the dog, now the rabbit at Erin's door. Death was most active on nights like this. Ned began to hum.

He still wasn't back but she wasn't tired, was restless and couldn't settle. It was ten o'clock so she watched the news but switched it off when the sport came on. Neither had any interest in things like that. She stood at the window looking out at the rimy trees and the endless moor. In other seasons the deer came by but what had become of them now? The croquet lawn was bathed in white light right to the edge of the dark silent woods. In winter even the burbling stream froze up.

All was still. No movement at all. The wind had miraculously gone away. She thought about Oliver Swann and felt molten inside. She wondered when he would come again; the thought of his fingers on her skin made her dissolve with longing. Sex with Ned was never like that though he had, that one time, allowed himself to be aroused. She wondered what was needed to make him more virile.

Which was when she saw it, as clear as day, a figure walking along the path, looking neither to left nor right, obviously going somewhere. Lisa pressed her face to the glass, ready to wave if it looked around, but whoever it was appeared to be in a hurry. Man or woman? She couldn't tell. It was wearing some kind of shapeless robe that in the sharp hard light had no visible colour. Lisa's breath caught in her throat as a dawning realisation struck. Weird as it was, could this be the ghost who only appeared by moonlight?

Ned was still out but she wasn't scared – excited, rather, and feeling bold. On a sudden impulse she grabbed her coat and stepped out on to the terrace. If it was a ghost, what had she to lose? It was nothing more than a memory condemned, for eternity, to this endless circuit. She would follow and see if it disappeared and, if it did not, then perhaps she'd find out who it was. At the very worst, she risked making a fool of herself.

It remained in view, still walking fast, so she opened the gate and speeded up. It swung away from the houses, towards the woods. Her teeth were chattering now with the cold, she wished she'd remembered to pick up her gloves, but determination drove her on. She was still feeling quite elated. She hurried as fast as she could on the slippery grass.

Down the path to the gate that opened into the lower meadow beyond which lay the farm and the nearest pub. A motionless figure was standing there, dark and still in the bright white light, now not moving at all, as if waiting for something. She couldn't see details of the face because of the enveloping hood; man or woman, she still couldn't quite decide. She slowed her pace, feeling suddenly scared. Why was it standing so totally still? And then it suddenly moved again and headed into the woods. Should she follow? She wasn't quite sure, suddenly feeling less confident. But the challenge remained. If she didn't move fast, she would never find out who it was.

It was waiting silently under the trees though looked slightly different and more at ease. Now she suddenly saw the face with a mixture of relief and disappointment.

'Oh,' she said, feeling a bit of a fool. 'I thought I

was following somebody else.' And laughed for one split second before it struck.

The knife went in again and again and the creature laughed like a thing deranged and Lisa screamed as she fought for her life and struggled to break free. It showed no mercy, just slashed away, and she held up her arms to protect her face, remembering as her blood ran cold the fate of poor Peter the postman.

'They'll catch you this time and put you away,' she threatened as she slid to her knees, seeing her lifeblood flow into the frozen bracken.

39

News of Lisa Thornton's death spread like wild-fire through Endecott Park after her stricken husband called the police. He had been for a walk on the moor on his own and found her missing on his return, the lights still on and the doors not locked even though she had taken her coat. He'd been out of his mind, so the story went, and was now under heavy sedation.

Auriol wasn't at all surprised. The poor bugger had only been married seven months and she was still pretty shaky from losing her dog. This threw a nastier light on things; whoever the perpetrator was appeared to be closing in and not killing at random. The police came round, as they had before, and asked the same mainly routine questions. The MO would seem identical to the murder of the postman. This time, however, it was far worse. Lisa's body had forty-nine stab wounds and, in addition, her head was completely severed. They had found it placed on her chest like a Halloween pumpkin.

Even Auriol cracked no jokes, not even to Erin when she filled her in. Only somebody barking mad could have done something that macabre.

'I didn't exactly warm to her,' she said to Erin, though not to them. 'But she certainly didn't deserve such a gruesome death.'

The question now on everyone's lips was, inevitably, how did the killer get in? They were, after all, protected by electronic gates.

'They probably came through the woods,' Erin said. Without a car that would not be hard. The gates were really only a deterrent.

The main question was, why Lisa Thornton? She had seemed an insignificant little thing, always polite but never with much to say. And lacking in warmth.

'Ah,' said Auriol. 'It's always the quiet ones, you know.'

Ned was apparently out of it, hospitalised for a day or so, with a twenty-four-hour police guard just in case.

'You think they might be after him too?' The possibilities grew more shocking.

Erin, the journalist, merely shrugged. Until they

established a motive, there weren't any leads. Though she did have a secret terror she wasn't divulging.

Auriol, apart from this latest horror, was currently riding on top of the world. Jonathan Kyle had opened up new frontiers. His total approval of her work, combined with his personal admiration, was doing wonders for her self-esteem. She leapt out of bed at an earlier hour, lived on a healthy organic diet and drank only water or juice that was freshly squeezed. She looked amazing. Life was suddenly treating her well. As soon as she could she would sell up here and move back to central London. The rural life was most definitely not for her.

Except that her paintings were Dartmoor inspired: abstracts and landscapes that harnessed the light and threw up glowing colours she'd not used before. Keep them coming was what he had said; he could unload them to the super rich who were inflating the property market even in a recession. The exhibition was underway. Two of his colleagues were coming down soon to see the canvases in situ and then decide how to hang them. If it weren't for missing Jasper so much, Auriol hadn't a cloud in her sky. Apart, of course, from this latest murder and the fact that her slimy ex was still hanging around.

His car was frequently parked in the drive, the

yellow eyesore she so much disliked, a perpetual reminder to her of his presence. His workmen, too, and their Portaloo, seemed to be always in evidence though what they were actually up to she couldn't have said. She saw them smoking and drinking tea, slumped outside every house in turn, fixing gutters and touching up paint with a minimum of effort. She loathed the way he upkept this place in the sloppiest, most cack-handed way and shuddered to think what her house would be worth by the time it went on the market.

Though that didn't matter, the way she felt now. Provided he kept his distance.

The police had erected another tent on the spot where Lisa's body was found, only yards from Peter's last resting place. It was all very spooky. The same tired team were back on the scene with Sergeant Hollis in charge of it all, though a couple of guys in suits had been poking round too. Not to mention the press. They were camped outside, beyond the gates, not just the local newspaper but a clutch of London reporters, too, the *Sun* and the *Daily Mail*. Lisa, though not a big hitter in life, was finally making her mark.

It was Sylvia, of course, who let it slip that Oliver Swann had been calling on her. Not only was his car parked outside but she had seen him with her own eyes coming out of her door on several occasions. 'I thought it strange at the time', she said, 'that he seemed to have more to do in her house than in ours.'

Trust Sylvia Brennan to stir things up. Deep down she was not a nice woman at all, full of bile and envy and resentment. Still, Auriol was fascinated to learn he'd been playing around again so soon. It didn't bode well for his marriage, she said with a grin.

Erin enjoyed Auriol's caustic humour which stopped her worrying about herself. What she was curious to find out now was where the Commander fitted in.

Auriol met him out walking his dog and he stopped and was pleasantly courteous to her. 'Nasty business,' he commented, nodding towards the police cars.

Nasty indeed. She asked him how much he knew.

Something about him inspired respect. He looked like being a leader of men. But on this occasion she drew a blank. He was discreet to the point of being evasive.

'I'll keep you posted on what I find out.' He flashed her a knowing smile and went on his way.

Now Jonathan Kyle was back on the scene and Auriol was working so hard on her art, it seemed only gracious to step aside and let Erin take her chances with the Commander. She said as much but Erin only laughed.

'Thanks,' she said, 'but I think he's too old for me.' Not that she didn't prefer them that way, just wasn't about to say so. 'In any case,' she added, 'I'll be out of here soon.'

'You think so?' Auriol was curious; her friend was still holding back a lot. Though she knew that, in time, she was likely to spill the beans if she didn't ask questions. 'Anyhow, for what it's worth, I think he's too good to let slip.'

Though chilly at night, the weather was great with a blazing sun and a swathe of snow that looked like the nursery slopes in a ski resort. It would make a great picture. Auriol muffled herself up well and took her canvas and easel outside. She could fit in a couple of hours before it grew dark. In front of her was the blue and white tent that covered the area where Lisa had died where a group of men in boiler suits were still working. A grim reminder but, what the hell, she had a tight deadline and life must go on. Since it wasn't a photograph she was taking, she would simply leave them out.

The air was so pure and the light so clear, she set to work with tremendous zeal though having to squint against the powerful sun. All of a sudden the peaceful scene was rent asunder by a horrible noise and a cloud of terrified birds rose into the air.

Bloody hell. Auriol looked all round, expecting an RAF jet to fly past. At the height of summer they were a pest with their noisy low-flying manoeuvres. This was no jet though; a minute black dot appeared like an eagle high in the sky, circled twice then quickly descended to land in the lower meadow. A small two-seater with an open cockpit and a pilot who looked like a wartime flying ace gracefully taxied to stop by the blue and white tent.

Auriol, intrigued, laid down her brush and wiped her hands on a rag soaked in turps, then strolled across the croquet lawn to see what was going on. She assumed the noisy intruder was part of the team.

Not a bit of it; as she approached she recognised the goggled invader who was standing on the wing, about to jump down. Too late – he had seen her and vigorously waved.

'Over here!' shouted Oliver Swann. All the policemen scowled in her direction.

If she'd had more guts she'd have turned on her heel but hated to look like a coward retreating. She continued to stroll at a nonchalant pace until she reached where they stood.

'My wife,' he said, introducing her, grinning and slipping his arm round her waist.

'He can't land here,' said the cop in charge. 'There's important police work underway.'

'Move your bloody plane,' she said. 'And get the hell out of my garden, too. If you wouldn't mind, I am trying to paint in peace.'

In any case, he shouldn't be flying. She doubted he had a licence.

She left them arguing and turned away though Oliver tried very hard to stop her. He wanted to know what was going on though she sensed he already knew. She had heard the rumour that Sylvia had spread, was weary of having to bail him out. If he wanted to screw up his life, that was up to him.

'Wait,' he shouted. 'I'll give you a ride. There is room for two in my little machine.'

Auriol didn't even turn her head. Just shouted to him to piss off.

40

Recent events had unhinged Betty. She sat on her steps in the heart of the wood with Lucifer perched on his usual branch and Satan somewhere nearby, undoubtedly sleeping. Here was the place she felt most secure although winter's bite was taking its toll and her old cracked hands were swollen with open sores. Wrapped in her rug with her hat pulled down low, she whistled a tune from her debutante days, one she had somehow imbued through a form of osmosis. As she reached the end of her natural life she was drawn more and more to her dead sister's world and remembered things that had happened before she was born.

Violet Elizabeth Endecott. They shared the same name and astral sign, one conceived purely to replicate the other. The more time she spent at the other one's grave, the greater the insight she had into what had occurred. Violet's death had been accidental though less so than people had realised. By closing her eyes and concentrating, Betty was having visions.

Elfrieda Willcox remained her friend, the only one, apart from her boys, on whom she could always depend. Elfrieda had only her interests at heart though was somewhat misguided and apt to interfere. Betty was frail now yet still independent, having developed over the years an indestructible will. There was no one at all she would permit to take complete charge of her life.

Violet's portrait hung in the pub and occasionally Betty sneaked into the bar to gain inspiration from those knowing eyes. Her sister had been quite a character; had she survived, might have conquered worlds. As it was, even dead, she made a lasting impression.

On Thursday nights the Ring o'Bells was usually packed to overflowing. Just round the corner, not far away, Effie Willcox also had company tonight. Her low-ceilinged cottage was packed with people who had travelled some distance to be at her seance. Word had got out since the previous time and luminaries from the psychical world had gathered to witness first hand what was going on. Erin was there, her notebook concealed along with a small recording device, agog to discover what Effie had hinted at. It sounded great fun.

Only tea was served at this stage. The social part would follow the spooky business. The wood-stove blazed and the dogs were locked up. Outside in the street the temperatures dropped. Gale-force winds had risen again; the whole of the cottage creaked. Effie, dressed in her usual tweeds with a ribboned monocle round her neck, ushered in the guest of honour and settled her on the settee.

'Some of you already know Mrs Collins. She has come from Bovey Tracey to join us tonight.'

The audience nodded and some of them clapped. They were keen to get down to the matter in hand and wanted to waste no more time. The medium, flaccid and middle-aged, adjusted the cushions around her and lay back. Effie lit candles and switched off the lamps, semi-darkness being conducive to the trance state.

Erin was dying to jot down notes but didn't want to cause any offence or draw undue attention to her presence. Later, perhaps, if things worked out she would interview the participants. If nothing else, it might make a piece for the *Globe*. They looked a fairly motley crew, all at least ten years older than her, some well into their sixties or even more. A few looked distinctly like academics with parchment skin and intelligent frowns. One, sitting close to her, smelled distinctly of mothballs. Where was the vicar?

No sign of him yet; Effie had mentioned he might turn up, also that he disapproved of the proceedings. But Mrs Collins had closed her eyes and was visibly sinking into a trance. The onlookers sat up straight, conversation ceased.

This time she held, slightly curiously, a pack of worn old playing cards which she shuffled nervously as she withdrew from this world. Erin, remembering Madame Hortense whose tent they had passed at the village show, had to control herself and suppress a smile. Village high jinks in darkest Devon. Wait till she told her London friends about this.

The woman's breathing had audibly changed. It sounded slower, rougher as well.

Effie leaned closer. 'Is there anyone there?' she asked.

Indistinct mutterings, whispering as well as though there was more than one person in touch. The cards continued to flip through her listless fingers.

'Can you hear me?' Effie asked, lightly tapping the antique table.

Rustlings and murmurings, then a distinctly male voice that startled them all.

'Where the hell am I? What time is it? Where's that girl with my blasted drink?' The manly baritone issued from the female medium's throat.

What the . . . ? All were electrified, Erin possibly more than the rest. She felt her scalp prickle, incredulous, though logically knew it had to be a trick. But if Mrs Collins were a fraud, she was certainly very convincing.

'Ask him something,' an onlooker hissed.

'Will you tell us your name?' said Effie. 'And, if you can, where you're speaking from.'

A longish pause. 'I don't really know,' said the disembodied voice.

People murmured and looked around. An academic scribbled a note. Erin resisted the urge to switch on her recorder.

Effie continued. 'Who are you?' she said.

'John Endecott. Of Endecott Manor. It was all my fault that the place burnt down.' A choking cry that might be a sob issued from the medium's throat, causing further consternation.

'What do you mean?' Effie urged her on. The medium's hands still shuffled the cards but a couple of genuine tears now shone on her cheeks.

'The fire,' she said. 'It was all a mistake. I hadn't intended to go so far. Just to scare them a little . . . oh God. My darling, darling child.'

She had to be faking. It couldn't be real. But the baritone voice with its plummy tones was chilling and very effective. Mrs Collins struggled to sit and Effie leapt forward to help her up. She looked round the group with triumph writ large on her face.

'Be calm, my dear. You are safe', she said, 'here with

friends who wish you no harm. Turn on the lights,' she ordered. 'And I'll make tea.'

Erin didn't know what to believe. She knew there was no way it wasn't a con and yet it was hard to see how it could have been fixed. The medium, now looking pale and ill, was being assisted to her feet by two of the members of the psychical crowd. How had that very rich voice emerged? Maybe she was a ventriloquist. Whatever the truth, she certainly had Erin fooled.

'Not conclusive,' she heard them say. 'We still need tangible proof for authentication.'

Effie, though, looked positively smug and beamed as though she had all the proof she required. 'Don't go,' she whispered as Erin rose. 'Piers will be joining us soon from the pub. I believe there is something he wants to discuss with you.'

He was stamping off snow as he came through the door and shaking it off his Burberry cap. His hair shone silver in the lamplight and the hand he extended to Erin was icy cold.

'Winter's here,' he announced to the room whose occupants now were all starting to leave. 'When that wind blows down from the Arctic we are in trouble.'

'Sit,' said Effie, having seen them all out, producing glasses and a very good Scotch. She let the dogs back into the room and slumped into an armchair. 'Would you like me to leave?' she asked Piers, who shook his head.

For a long time he sat staring into the fire without any hint of why he was there. Erin, baffled, waited for him to speak. At last he gave her a long hard look and his blue eyes twinkled with genuine warmth.

'There is something I think you should know,' he said, 'which may come as a bit of a shock.'

41

Where to begin? It was complicated. Piers sipped his drink and stared at the flames.

To begin with, he said, he was not what he seemed. The memoirs bit was a subterfuge to allow him to work undercover without any questions. He owned the gatehouse, that much was true. His mother had left it to him when she died in a Totnes nursing home several years before. It was hers by birthright; her father (and John's) had been Thomas Endecott, owner of the estate.

'They were brother and sister?'

'Half,' prompted Effie. 'Marigold's mother was the second wife.'

So Violet and Piers were cousins. So much, so clear.

And, due to the right of primogeniture, all the land had been left to the son though the gatehouse had been a personal gift from father to much-loved daughter.

'My own father died in the war,' said Piers. 'And my mother remarried when I was still very young. Effie and I were childhood friends but my mother's new husband was not from these parts. When I was six we relocated to Canada where he was from.'

Something was stirring in Erin's brain, that vital elusive missing link. She stared at him as realisation dawned. Piers Compayne. Of course, that was it. Newspaper baron and plutocrat. Owner of A.N.I., their new corporate bosses. The name had been nagging away in her mind all this time.

'You recently bought the *Globe*,' she said.

'Among other things,' added Effie.

A long, long silence as Erin digested this startling new piece of information.

'Also,' said Effie helpfully, 'the house you are living in.'

Erin, bewildered, stared at Piers who silently nodded in affirmation. 'The story is quite complex,' he said. 'I am only just starting to get at the truth myself.'

Which was why he'd decided at last to fill Erin in.

'I know how good at your job you are,' he told her with a complicit smile. 'And since I've been paying you all this time, I figure the least you can do is help me out.'

It all boiled down to one man, he said. Rod Stirling.

He waited for her to compose herself, could see how flustered she had become. Rose to his feet and crossed the room and came back with the bottle.

'Effie and I worked for MI5,' he said. 'Which explains where she fits in. She has been my spy in these parts for a very long time.' He topped up their glasses.

Effie was chuckling now, loving it all. 'I only wish you could see your face,' she said to Erin. 'It's a picture.'

As indeed it must be. Erin was flabbergasted. 'But what about Rod? I don't understand.' Could this be why he had lately been so elusive?

'All in good time,' said Piers who seemed very calm.

Rod had been a political firebrand since his campaigning days at RTE. For a very long time Piers had studied him from a distance. He admired his commitment and recklessness, his fearlessness in the face of fire. He was a man who, time and again, would put his whole career on the line, never for reasons of personal gain, purely for sound, though occasionally cranky, ideals. He had always been a passionate idealist but lately his fervour was blinding him. He threw himself into causes without enough thought.

'For instance, our current position with Russia. The Russians are not our enemies. They simply sometimes have varying goals. And go about things in a slightly different way.'

Erin listened in silent awe, stunned and confused, her thoughts all over the place. 'But the Russian assassins?' she said.

'We are checking them out.'

'Which means?' She couldn't quite follow his thread. She had nailed her colours to the Chechnyan cause, backed – she had always assumed – by the man she loved. Who was also her boss. She had risked her own life to get at the truth while men of great courage were losing theirs, had been at her most articulate on their behalf.

Piers leaned forward and jiggled the fire. Outside the gale was gathering force and rattling the windows throughout the ancient cottage.

'Don't worry,' he said, catching Erin's glance. 'I will drive you home. We are, after all, near neighbours. Putin and I are acquaintances who have known each other a very long time. I am not suggesting I approve of him but we do have an understanding. And, believe me, killing journalists isn't his style. Apart from anything else, he's too arrogant.'

'So why then . . . ?'

'That we have yet to find out. It is why I need your help.'

Baffled Erin stared at the fire and put down her glass which was still untouched. Nothing Piers said quite added up. She couldn't see where this was leading.

'Why then', she continued, 'am I here?' Six months wasted and all for what?

Piers looked grave; the twinkle had gone.

'That', he said, 'is what I aim to find out.'

It was snowing hard by the time they left. Erin was grateful for the lift. Piers drove the Range Rover fast but with utmost control. She felt totally safe. She was very confused by what she had heard; her thoughts were whirling around in her brain. The axis of her world had shifted in view of this new information. He reached the park and opened the gates. The snow was almost a blizzard now.

'I'll drive you right to your door,' he said. 'I insist.'

Which reminded Erin. 'You own my house? I didn't know that. They never said, just that it was a safe house and very secure.'

Piers laughed. 'I bought it when it was built, for private reasons, via one of my holdings. When Stirling asked for a bolthole for you, no questions were asked, he was given the keys.'

'Which is why you are here?'

'Certainly one of the reasons.'

'And police protection?'

'It couldn't be closer,' said Piers.

The door to number four was ajar, the light spilling out on the falling snow. Phil, in wellingtons, stood outside, flashlight in hand. He seemed a bit startled when Piers drew up and saluted him in a tentative

347

way as though not entirely sure how he ought to greet him.

'Good evening, sir,' said Phil as Piers opened his door. 'Well,' he said, as Erin emerged, tracking his flashlight round her feet. 'I think I've discovered what scared you the other night.'

All three looked at the marks in the snow, animal pawprints the size of his hand circling Erin's front door and freshly made.

'Well I never,' said Piers, impressed. 'That is no ordinary fox or cat. I haven't seen prints that size since I hunted in Kenya.'

Erin, keyed up, laughed nervously. 'The Hound of the Baskervilles,' she quipped. Not, after all, the Endecott Ghost. In a way she was disappointed.

Both men waited to see her safely inside.

'If I were you,' the Commander said, 'I would not let your cat out after dark.'

'Don't worry,' she said as she bade them goodnight. 'I won't.'

All night long Erin tossed and turned, trying to cope with what Piers had said. The death threat she had been hiding from had come from the man in whom she had put her trust. Rod had deliberately lied to her, had been on the opposite side all the time, not a Chechnyan defender but their oppressor. The story she'd written, one of her best, explaining their cause and defending it he had deliberately spiked out of deference to Putin. He had then cold-bloodedly sent her away, pin-pointing her as an easy target rather than using his power to save her life. It hadn't been 'them' but simply him though she sensed the Commander knew more than he said. Gradually, through that long dark night, the missing pieces started to slot into place. Once, their ideals had been the same. Now, she suddenly saw, they had widely diverged.

A couple of times she picked up the phone but it wasn't fair to involve the wife. Even in the heat of her rage, Erin retained her honour. She ran their whole history through her head: the initial click on the radio show, the way she had thought they were so much in tune, their turbulent love affair. All these years she had trusted him, respecting his integrity as well as the fact he was married. Her career came first in the order of things but he had long been her guiding star as well as, she had thought, her trusted protector.

So that even when he had silenced her after winning the very prestigious award, the highest that Fleet Street had to bestow, she had gone without question into immediate exile. She'd invented a story and lied to her friends, careful not to implicate them because of the hostile power that was stalking her. She had been here six months when it should have been two, guilelessly doing as she was told, when all the while no such threat had ever existed. At least not from them.

So what were his reasons for this deceit? She believed he loved her and always had, had been too involved in her own career to question the fact that he would not walk out of his marriage. Her Catholic roots went deep and had seen to that. It was not an issue. So what then? She hadn't a clue to his motivation.

Until the next morning when she made the call and a woman answered his mobile who wasn't his wife. Which was when the penny finally dropped and Erin saw what a fool she had been not to have guessed what was going on.

Rod and Amy.

42

Lisa's murder had shattered them all but Gerald had other things on his mind. It was Thursday. Tonight was his date at the Ring o'Bells. Sylvia whined, as she so often did, but he hadn't got time for her petty complaints. He was buffing up his blazer buttons, preparing to make hay while the sun still shone. It was now or never to make his mark with the coterie that mattered.

Much was happening at number six with a trickle of men wearing boiler suits in and out of the empty house all day. Ned was still in the hospital, though due to be discharged very soon. The police were waiting to talk to him once he was compos mentis. It was inconceivable what he'd been through. The village was buzzing with all kinds of rumours. Two violent murders in just a few months was causing a media frenzy. Not to mention the shooting of Auriol's dog, though that still could have been accidental.

'If you've nothing better to do,' Gerald said, 'you could pop next door and find out more. Offer to do some shopping, perhaps. The poor sod will come home to an empty house.' Not to mention an empty love-nest after only seven brief months of marriage.

Sylvia, though, simply pursed her lips. The slut had been openly playing around so had probably had it coming. Who would have thought it; she had seemed such a mouse though the flash builder's car had been outside her house more than once.

Sergeant Hollis was still on the job, making inquiries from door to door. Erin, now that her cover was blown, was taking a more active interest. As a star reporter for a national newspaper, the very least she could do was her job.

'I can't believe it,' Auriol said, 'that all these months you have been undercover. You might have tipped me the wink, you rat. Who was I going to tell?'

'Sorry,' said Erin. 'It wasn't allowed.' She was feeling a fool at having been gulled. At present it hurt too much to discuss, even with such a sympathetic friend. She still hadn't had it out with Rod, there was now no point since she knew the full score. She doubted, in any case, he would take her call.

Someone, however, was still on the loose, slaughtering

the locals one by one. Which wasn't a joke in such a sheltered enclave.

At seven Gerald went down to the pub. At eight they welcomed him into the inner sanctum. The Commander was seated by the fire, his dog at his feet and a pint in his hand, and he greeted Gerald with his customary courtesy. There was also an assortment of others, most of them known to Gerald by sight: a couple of gentleman farmers and the owner of the village general stores. Drinks were offered; he ordered beer. Tonight he needed to keep his wits about him.

He was more keyed up than he'd been in months, since the bank had uncovered his dubious dealings. Then he had managed to bluff his way out of disaster. But dicing with death was what Gerald enjoyed. He hadn't felt this alive since he'd left the bank. He was willing to gamble all he had left on the chance of changing his fortunes tonight. This could very well be his ultimate fling.

Oliver Swann came swaggering in, flashing his phoney self-satisfied grin. It was clear to Gerald that none of the others could stand him. He approached the Commander. 'Piers,' he said, clapping him matily on the shoulder. The Commander saw him off with a frosty stare.

Gerald was starting to relax. He had the measure

of all these men and a gambling habit second to none which nobody here was aware of. Poker had always been his game; when he mentioned bridge to his gullible wife, he lied. He missed his regular London sessions as well as the back-room boys at the Rose and Crown. He was out of practice but not so much that he wasn't likely to make a killing tonight in amateursville. They all knew each other. The stakes were high. But Gerald Brennan was back in fighting form.

Oliver Swann was the one to watch. Gerald prided himself on his powers of observation. He studied the way he shuffled the cards and the glint in his eye as he laid them down. The builder was so in love with himself he wanted the world to know it. He was loud and flashy and nouveau riche and he raised his bets with such nonchalance as if he were playing cards with a bunch of cub scouts. Look at me, his stance proclaimed, I am the king of the castle.

The shopkeeper played his cards close to his chest, the farmers at differing levels of skill. The Commander was so deadpan he barely flickered. Gerald, having been to his house, assumed that he had no financial restraints though he still hadn't figured out what it was the man did. And the suave controlled Commander gave nothing away.

They played several hands before raising the stakes. Each time Gerald came out on top. These country bumpkins were no kind of match for a man of his expertise. He was well and truly into his stride and hoping it might go on all night. He offered to buy them drinks all round but was told that in here it was on the house. He loosened his tie and savoured the old familiar adrenalin rush.

Sylvia stood at the window and snooped, something she'd always been prone to do. An ambulance had arrived next door and a fragile figure, wrapped in a rug, was being assisted out by two uniformed figures. Poor Ned Thornton, home at last. How would he manage without his wife? Tomorrow she'd pop down to Annie's and check out the gossip. This was now her main currency since her profligate spending had come to a halt. Gerald had cut up her credit cards, even the cleaner had had to go. Soon she would even have to give up her hairdos.

There was something about Ned Thornton she liked, his perfect manners and classic good looks and the rimless glasses that gave him the air of a scholar. She shuddered to think about Lisa's death – hacked to pieces with her head chopped off – right on the edge of their woods where Peter had died. Something dreadful was going on; the country idyll, she now saw, had only ever been a romantic myth. She had never felt this nervous back in Kent.

Gerald was out with the boys tonight, had told her not to wait up for him. There was something afoot, she didn't know what, nor did she very much care. Like most men, he lived by rules of his own; it was all very well for her to scrimp but nothing would keep him away from the pub and a night of bridge with his cronies. He had warned her not to open the door should anyone call without phoning first. There was serious danger lurking out there on the moor.

The room was fuggy with heat and smoke. Even though it was almost one, the game was still going strong. Gerald had several times scooped the pot, had removed his blazer and rolled up his sleeves. The drinks kept coming; he had switched to Scotch. One of the gentleman farmers had quit and gone home.

Oliver Swann kept raising the odds, a manic gleam in his scheming eyes. Gerald, with nerves of steel, recalled the ancient adage about a fool and his money. Also the builder was hitting the booze in a rather intemperate way. The Commander, observing them wordlessly, maintained an inscrutable vigilance. He had thrown in his hand and resumed his seat by the fire. It crossed Gerald's mind to wonder why he stayed.

Someone suggested enough was enough; outside,

in the bar, the landlord was visibly pacing. But Gerald, still on his winning streak, was not yet ready to call it a day. Before him, on the table, his winnings were stacked. He thought of all he had just been through: the humiliation of having been caught, the downsizing of his affluent lifestyle, Sylvia's look of disbelief when the cashpoint rejected her card. He wasn't prepared to live that way; one of society's rejects. He had lived his whole life on his wits and would not stop now.

The builder dealt. There were just two hands which they laid on the table for all to see. Gerald had a full house. He sighed with relief. Oliver, though, had four of a kind which he tossed on the table with jubilant glee.

'The best man wins,' he said and scooped the pot.

A deathly silence. Gerald lost. He sat there, stunned, unable to take it in. All he possessed had gone in that one final flourish. The landlord, with relief, called time and Oliver Swann swept up his winnings.

'I can't stop now,' pleaded Gerald. 'One final hand.'

Oliver shrugged. 'Your call,' he said. 'What are you offering as your stake?'

Gerald thought fast. 'The deeds to my house.' He scribbled a promissory note.

'Are you quite sure?' the Commander said, rising now and coming to watch. It was very late, both men had been drinking all night.

357

'I am,' said Gerald and dealt the cards, face down, while everyone held their breath.

Gerald turned over three of a kind. Oliver Swann slapped down a royal flush.

'Bad luck, old chap,' he said as he rose. 'I will call you in the morning.'

43

One by one they visited Ned to commiserate with what he'd been through. They found him always immaculately groomed though with no intention yet of returning to work. A policeman stood outside, it wasn't clear why.

'What are they guarding him from?' someone asked.

'More of the same, I suppose.' The Endecott woods were now swarming with armed policemen.

All the papers were full of it and the TV cameras were back on the scene though still not allowed to enter the gated park. Jenny and Phil were in evidence, having shed their cover as plain clothes cops. Now they were both back in uniform and keeping a regular vigil.

'I thought you were both too outdoorsy to be doctors,' Erin remarked. Now that she, too, was back on the job she was quietly digging into everyone's past.

There was no further reason for her to stay but Piers had requested it as a personal favour.

'Since you know all the inhabitants here you start with a huge advantage,' he said. He also guessed she was not yet ready to face her colleagues in Wapping.

Rod was under investigation, suspended indefinitely from the job. The case against him was very bad and growing worse since they'd picked up Gregory, the builder.

'Or Grigor, which is his Russian name,' said Phil when he came to bring Erin the news. 'He was armed to the teeth in those overalls. You are truly lucky to be alive.'

Nobody even thought to ask what had happened to Amy.

So Erin grasped the bull by the horns and rang the doorbell at number six. She'd rejected the thought of phoning first in case he gave her the brush off. Which, had it been the case, she'd have understood. Poor man, he'd suffered enough as it was without inquisitors butting in. The last thing he needed right now were impertinent questions. But better her than the *Daily Mail*; at least the *Globe* knew where to draw the line. And she had a slight advantage by being his neighbour.

She waited till noon when he ought to be up and

boldly arrived on his step with her arms full of flowers. She felt that was better than chicken soup as he wasn't exactly an invalid. Ned opened the door looking strained but alert in pale grey trousers and a plain white shirt. The light glinted off his tinted lenses so she couldn't look into his eyes.

'Oh,' he said uncertainly. 'That's nice of you. Come in.' That easy: she followed him through and into the kitchen. 'Just stick them in the sink,' he said. 'I'll sort out something later.'

'Why don't I just find a vase?' Erin said, wishing she'd already thought of that. She burrowed in and found one under the sink.

It gave her something to do with her hands without having to look at him while she talked. 'Tell me how you are,' she said. 'And how are you bearing up?'

'As well as can be expected,' he said with a savagely hollow laugh.

'I'm sorry', she said, 'for intruding like this. I probably shouldn't have come.'

'No,' said Ned more humanly, running one hand across his face. 'I could really do with some company, else I'll go mad.'

The flowers were done. She carried them into his sparse though tasteful living room and put them carefully on the glass-topped table.

'Nice,' she said approvingly, looking round. Everything

was in its place; it looked as if no one had ever really lived there. She saw what could be done with a little flair. And now that she knew, amazingly, that her own place belonged to Piers Compayne . . . She still hadn't quite got to grips with that. There were so many pieces missing from the puzzle.

Ned was hovering. She offered to leave but he asked if she would stay awhile so she made coffee and then they sat, like the strangers they still were, politely talking. She wasn't sure how far she dared go. There was no way, though, she could fudge the issue. The police inquiry was well underway and even now, from where they sat, they could see the crime squad in action.

'So,' she said, 'tell me about yourself.' And coaxed him into opening up a little.

He liked his work in Newton Abbot. It was not too stressful and the drive there and back was a joy. When the roads were clear he could do it in forty minutes.

'Is that why you moved down here?' Erin asked.

That and the fact they had seen the sign for the new development and bought it on an impulse.

'Lisa's idea,' he said with a smile. 'She was always springing new things on me. I'm afraid I have always been somewhat set in my ways.' His mood became pensive.

'How did you meet?'

'At work,' he said. 'We were both employed by the council then. I designed public amenities, Lisa was shifting papers.' He smiled. 'Looking back, the job was godawful. I can't believe I stuck it so long.'

When he relaxed his looks improved and took on a wistful boyish expression that knocked ten years off his age and made him appealing. The eyes, she now saw, were a silvery grey, fringed with lashes as long as a girl's. He rarely smiled but when he did the teeth he revealed were perfect. A nice-looking man just a few years older than her, she would guess. Early forties. What a tragedy to have lost his wife so young and in such a manner. This she conveyed discreetly and he nodded.

'Lisa was a wonderful girl. Totally transformed my life. This house was entirely her inspiration. Those little feminine touches she handled so well.'

'Before that where did you live?' Erin asked. Fishing like this was how she'd been trained though it had been years since she'd been a straightforward reporter.

'Purley,' he said. 'In the family home. My father died a long time ago so for years it was me and my mum, who worked from home.' He lapsed into silence.

'And your mother?'

'She died. Very suddenly.' His eyes clouded over. He looked away.

Erin held her breath and tried not to intrude.

'Anyhow', he took a deep breath, pushing the painful memory away, 'I had to go away for a while which was when I lost touch with Lisa.'

Erin waited expectantly. There was something, she sensed, that was troubling him. 'How did you come to marry her then?' she asked.

Ned suddenly smiled and his face lit up. 'We met on a train,' he said.

Erin had run out of questions to ask. He wasn't exactly telling her much. Soon she would have to make her excuses and leave, which would be frustrating. She needed to get a fix on him and also to try and help him in his grief. She felt a sudden urge to give him a hug.

Instead she walked to the window and stood looking out. The patio was immaculate though, at this time of year, all the plants were dead. She had often seen Lisa outside with her trowel and trug.

'What will you do with the house?' she asked. 'Will you continue to live here alone? Forgive me,' she added, 'I am sure it's too soon to decide. And it's none of my business.'

He rose and came to stand by her. He was slightly built, about five foot nine with a grace of movement that went with his classic good looks. He should not find it hard, she thought, to find himself another wife especially in the circumstances, the childless widower. Then she chided herself for jumping the gun so fast.

'I'm not sure,' he said reflectively. 'I'd be sorry to leave the moor so soon though also cannot imagine life here without her.'

In the far distance, beyond the lawn, a fingertip search was still going on, a dreadful reminder of what had happened to Lisa. She ought to go and leave him alone, must already have stayed far too long. By now he must be fed up with her superficial chatter.

Right then the silence was split by a sound and in the sky she saw a black dot. A police helicopter, she thought at first, but as it approached she saw it was a two-seater Mustang, seeking to land, with Oliver Swann at the controls. Ned's expression tightened like a fist. He opened the terrace doors and strode out, glaring ineffectively into the sky.

'How dare he hang around here?' he said. 'He has done enough damage as it is.'

Erin, startled, looked at him. 'What are you suggesting?'

'Just that the bastard was sniffing round my wife.'

'I can't believe that.' She was adamant. Such a rumour had never reached her and she did, after all, have the confidence of his ex-wife. He might be a bit

of a Casanova but Lisa Thornton? Surely not. Apart
from anything else, he had just remarried.

Ned, however, was black in the face and his jaw
was clenching enough to crack his teeth. 'He had better
stay clear of me,' he said, stalking back into the house.

44

He was buzzing around in that dratted plane, constantly swooping in from the skies, startling the birds and causing the sheep to stampede. Oliver Swann had never grown up; what had once seemed sexy and devil-may-care now seriously got under Auriol's skin and sent her blood pressure soaring. Boys with their toys; if it wasn't the plane it was the bloody Lagonda.

She still believed he had shot the dog as a gesture of petty gratuitous spite though she had no proof and he swore he'd been nowhere nearby.

'But Jasper was following you,' she had said. 'I watched him with my own eyes.'

Erin agreed. Though she hadn't at first she had now come round to Auriol's way of thinking. A lot had occurred in the past few days that they still had not had the time to catch up on. Erin, for instance, had been in to talk to poor Ned.

Carol Smith

'And what's the story?' asked Auriol, who had never much warmed to him or his wife though his loss, she had to concede, was far greater than hers.

'I'll tell you later when I know more. The poor guy is still in shock, as you would expect.'

She might have to go back to London, she said, was being mysterious but busy at last, working all hours on whatever it was she was writing. Which suited Auriol who was hard at it too, painting as fast as she could for the exhibition.

'It is great to have a tangible goal,' she said when they met for a quick glass of wine. Country living was easier to take when she didn't have time on her hands. Though she missed poor Jasper almost more than she could bear.

Lisa Thornton had been stabbed to death, viciously butchered and her head cut off and left, like a sacrificial offering, on her chest for the world to see. What kind of maniac could do such a thing? Apart from the horror of the crime, it had to have taken considerable strength, especially the last part. Public opinion was veering one way but Auriol still had serious doubts. It seemed likely whoever had done the deed must have murdered the postman too; her former husband, whatever his faults, did not have it in him to act in such a way. He might have criminal tendencies though not,

368

she was certain, of the murderous kind. Even if he had shot the dog, it would only have been out of spite.

She was quietly painting and thinking things through when footsteps came crunching along the path and Piers Compayne and his dog appeared and hailed her from the gateway.

'Mind if I have a word?' he called and Auriol put down her brush and beckoned him in.

He left his dog and his gun outside and gratefully accepted a cup of tea. It was freezing cold in the woods, he said, though the full police contingent was still on the job. He admired her work, had a clearly discerning eye.

'I shan't keep you long.' He came straight to the point. 'I understand you were married to Swann and worked as his business partner for many years.'

'Correct,' she said.

'Without breaking any confidences, do you recall when he bought this land? Were you, in fact, an accessory to the sale? Did you witness the deal?'

That was a hard one: the answer was yes, she was an accessory to the sale, though he had done all of the paperwork in her absence. She was the one with the vision while he made the deals. The Commander cradled his cup of tea and looked at her with appraising eyes.

'Tell me the honest truth,' he said. 'Which one of you has the deeds?'

'He must do, I suppose,' she said. 'He took care of the business side. I have the deeds to this house in the bank but, as far as I am aware, he kept the rest.' It was one of the main things they'd fought about, the clinching point in their bitter divorce. What they'd bought to fulfil her long-time dream had ended up in the pot with the rest of their assets. 'Why are you asking me this?' she said. 'Why not just ask him yourself?'

The Commander smiled. 'Don't worry,' he said. 'I intend to do just that very soon. I have a small matter that needs urgent sorting. Just wanted to check out the facts.'

Auriol looked at him candidly. 'I wouldn't trust him an inch,' she said. 'For the record, though you didn't ask, I don't believe him capable of murder.'

The Commander looked at her long and hard. 'I shall take that into account', he said, 'when talking to the police.'

45

A fire was burning in the library grate when Oliver Swann was ushered in by the housekeeper at the gatehouse. The Commander was seated behind his desk, Rufus, as always, at his feet while in a winged armchair beside the fire sat Miss Elfrieda Willcox, village librarian. The builder stopped mid-stride, slightly taken aback.

'Do come in and sit down,' said the Commander.

Oliver Swann looked round the room with blatantly covetous eyes. He'd been trying to see inside this house for more years than he could remember. 'Nice place you've got here,' he said with a nod. 'If you ever want to sell . . .'

'Quite,' said the Commander. 'Now, down to business.' He wore half-moon glasses upon his nose and now looked over them slightly sternly like a magistrate or public school headmaster. 'I won't waste your

371

time. I'll come straight to the point. About the business of Brennan's deeds. I watched you win them in that poker game and would now like to have them back.'

Oliver Swann just stared at him, his cocky assurance for once on hold. 'What the fuck are you on about?' he asked, ignoring Elfrieda.

'The deeds, as I said, to the Brennans' house. They don't, nor ever will, belong to you.'

The Commander played with his paper-knife and Elfrieda stared peacefully into the fire. Outside a gale was blowing and rattling the windows. The dog on the floor gave a great fat sigh and rolled over.

'You are talking rubbish.' Swann leapt to his feet and urgently strode round the wood-panelled room, a short man in an expensive suit, full of bluster and inflated self-importance. 'I won those deeds, as you know full well, quite fairly.'

The Commander pondered. 'Well,' he said, 'let me now put it another way. What proof do you have of your ownership of the land? I mean Endecott Park.'

Oliver Swann was stopped in his tracks; it was clear he had not seen this one coming. 'The deeds are with my lawyers in London,' he said. 'If it's any of your business.'

The Commander continued to play with the knife. A fistful of snow spattered into the grate. Effie appeared to be nodding off. The dog was now peacefully snoring.

'I hesitate to correct you on that.' The Commander pulled open the drawer of his desk and produced a manila envelope from which he withdrew a thick wadge of yellowing paper. 'These are the title deeds', he said, 'to what was once the estate of Endecott Manor.'

Silence fell. Effie opened her eyes and watched the exchange with birdlike attention. A burning log rolled out of the grate which the Commander retrieved.

'What do you say about that?' he asked of Oliver Swann, who seemed to have been struck dumb.

'That's preposterous,' he eventually said. 'You have no idea what you're talking about. Swann Homes controls the entire estate. I have the papers to prove it.'

'I don't think so,' said the Commander, smiling. 'If you want to examine them, be my guest.' He offered the papers to Oliver Swann who suddenly seemed to have lost the use of his hands.

After a lengthy and pregnant pause, the Commander showed his visitor out. 'You'll be hearing from my lawyers,' he said. 'In the morning.'

'Perfect,' said Effie, clapping her hands as Piers poured them both a triumphal drink. 'Idiotic little man not to have seen that coming.' She dragged up her chair and roasted her hands. The wind was now howling and shaking the eaves. The gatehouse, built these three hundred years, was perfectly able to cope. Less so the slipshod creations of Swann Homes.

'What do you suppose he will do?'

'If he has any sense he will disappear. Though a rogue like that, I would guess, will put up a fight.'

'How did he get away with it?'

'Natural cunning,' Piers replied. 'He saw a loophole and grabbed it. The house was a ruin. The owners had fled. As far as the locals knew, there were no natural heirs. The land had stood fallow for sixty years. If I hadn't chanced to have business here who's to say what else he might have done.'

'The murders too?' She was very astute.

'No,' said Piers. 'I truly don't think so. Oliver Swann is an opportunist. Whoever killed like that must be seriously mad.'

The weather was brutal. A Dartmoor winter was not something to be lightly undertaken. Arctic winds snarled through the streets and the ground was treacherous and frozen hard. The few people out and about were heavily muffled.

Effie's cottage was bright and warm, the wood-stove stacked and the kettle just boiled. Piers stamped his feet then removed his boots, not to tramp snow inside.

He had left the dog at home today out of deference to her two.

'Not here yet?' He looked around.

'Betty lives by a law of her own. She will turn up when she is good and ready. Meantime I'll make us some tea.'

She settled back in her rocking chair and Piers took his place on the window seat from where he had a good view of the village square. This meeting he'd called had momentous meaning. He hoped that at last she'd be satisfied. Her life so far had been one long disappointment.

They knew she was coming because of the dogs who rushed to the door and stood there waiting, heralding the arrival of someone they knew. Effie leapt up and went to greet her. Betty was still ill at ease in company. She came in timidly, wrapped in her rug, her face protruding like a mouse from a hole, shapeless boots on her feet, her hands swathed in rags. The dogs sniffed round her and wagged their tails and she bent with great effort to pat their heads.

'I expect they smell Satan and Lucifer,' she said in a little girl's voice.

Piers sat quietly watching her. This was the first time they had met and he instantly saw the resemblance to the dead sister. The faded eyes in the weathered face had once been a much more brilliant blue and the wild mass of hair had probably once been jet black. But the true resemblance was in the chin: spirited and defiant. He recognised the Endecott spirit that had helped her survive all these years through such odds. This was his cousin John Endecott's child, born in a vain attempt to replace her dead sister.

He had deliberately kept away until he had news he could share with her. Her life had been hard enough as it was without arousing false hopes. Now he rose and offered his hand. 'Delighted to meet you at last,' he said.

Effie leapt forward to do the honours. 'May I present your cousin, Piers Compayne.'

She was not as simple as people said; the life she had lived had made her fey though that might also be due to her odd upbringing. She showed all the signs of a life lived outdoors, the calloused fingers and rotting teeth, but her spirit remained indomitable he could tell from her spirited eyes. And when she smiled, apart from the teeth, her face assumed an expression of innocent sweetness.

'Violet Elizabeth.' He held her close, feeling her heart beat fast like a frightened rabbit. 'You have lived too long in the wilderness. I am here to bring you home.'

It was quite straightforward. Piers presented her with the keys to number five Endecott Park. Miss O'Leary, the tenant, was soon moving out so, from this point on, it was hers to do as she liked with. And one day the rest would be hers as well, once they'd been through the tedious legal process. He privately hoped she would live to see it settled.

'What would I do with a house?' she said, once Effie had taken her through all the details. 'To start with, I don't think my boys would like it at all.'

Startled, Piers looked across at Effie who shrugged and smiled and opened her hands. Betty's life was still an enigma and who she cared to associate with remained her private business. She was fully adult, almost seventy-two, and could do whatever she liked with her life.

'We just thought', said Effie practically, 'that you'd find it warmer in winter.'

Betty turned to stare at Piers and considered him with a level gaze. 'Are you saying you own the Endecott land?' she asked.

'I am,' he said. 'But it should be yours. And now I want you to take it back. The house is only the start of it. The rest will take slightly longer for us to settle.'

'But how did that come about?' asked Betty.

'I hate to admit it,' said Piers with a grin, 'but my father won it from yours in a poker game.'

377

46

'Hang on,' said Erin. 'Let's get this straight. Exactly what kind of a poker game?' She was in the gate-house, interviewing the Commander.

'A regular one in the Ring o'Bells,' said Piers. 'As it happens, on a Thursday night. Even in those days it was a regular fixture, I have discovered.'

'And who exactly was your dad?' She was sitting across from him, scribbling notes, totally absorbed in his family history. Violet Endecott might be dead but her story was leaping alive from the page. At this rate she'd need another year off from the paper in order to write it.

Piers laughed. He found her very engaging, with her reddish-gold hair and vibrant looks plus just enough Irish in her voice to add a sultry appeal. She was brightening up his life no end with her energy and instinct for a good story. If he wasn't already employing her, he would find himself offering her a job.

'My real father was Jude Brackenberry,' he said. 'A local boy who married my mother when they were still barely out of their teens. A bit of a wild card and roisterer, so I've been told. He joined the air force as soon as he could and was shot down in 1944 a couple of months before I was born, so he never lived to see me.'

He watched the mental arithmetic; good for his age, he could see her thinking. Well, better (he might have replied) than a two-timing shit.

'And then?' she asked him, pen still poised.

'She remarried a few years later. Another airman. Canadian. The rest you already know.'

'And the poker game?'

'Well, he won the lot. Including the manor and all its land. I think they must have been pissed at the time. In no way was it responsible behaviour.'

Food for thought. Erin curled up and accepted the wine he handed her, her mind still back in those frivolous days directly preceding the war. The world had changed. Life was not the same, nor would ever be like that again. She told him about her grandfather, Seamus O'Leary, whom she still so much missed. Piers, who had fleetingly known him too, was impressed. Now he could understand her more, this passionate woman who never relaxed. She had, without doubt, been born to the job, a dedicated reporter. He liked the way her eyelashes curled, also the way her nose crinkled up when she laughed, which she did very often.

But the poker game. She didn't give up. 'And then what happened?' she wanted to know.

'The manor burnt down soon after. The night of the ball.'

They stared at each other with the same thought. Could it be it had not been an accident at all?

The rest was simply a matter of facts which Erin industriously jotted down. Violet's parents had fled the scene and spent the rest of their lives abroad while Marigold, now Compayne, had moved to Toronto. The burnt-out ruin and its acres of land had remained unclaimed for six decades. Nobody still remembered the family connection. It was perfect fodder for a man like Swann who had chanced upon it fortuitously and quickly found out its provenance was unknown. He had moved straight in and staked his claim, relying no doubt upon squatters' rights, and might have got away with it had not Marigold finally died.

'She moved back here when my stepfather went and lived in the gatehouse alone for some years until she needed nursing care so we placed her in a home.

I lived abroad and was far too busy to bother myself with domestic things. I came back after her death to sort out her estate.'

By which time he needed to slack off a bit so took advantage of her bequest, renovated the gatehouse and then moved in. Only then, with more time on his hands, did the thought of inheritance ever occur. The new Swann houses were selling fast; on impulse, he bought the last one. There was something fishy about the sale which nobody local appeared to have thought about.

'So,' said Piers, 'I at last got stuck in and did something I should have done years before. Got my mother's papers out of the bank and discovered the deeds to the manor.'

'So how do you know about the poker game?'

'I have John Endecott's handwritten pledge,' he said.

Soon Erin would have to return to real life, especially now she must leave the house, but she had one more thing to do in order to settle her conscience. Her talk with Ned Thornton had cut very deep. There were certain facts she was keen to check that would involve a flying visit to Wapping. But when she mentioned this to Piers he laughed and said she'd be wasting her time. He led her into the room at the rear from which the heart of his newspaper empire functioned.

Carol Smith

Erin stood in the doorway stunned, as overwhelmed as Gerald had been. She'd had no idea that the 'diplomat' was so hands-on in running his newspaper empire.

'Be my guest,' said Piers. 'Just help yourself. There is nothing up there that you can't find from here.' He also gave her the name of someone who would help her out at head office.

He admired the thoroughness of her work. She had done enough on the foreign front. Piers already had plans in hand for a major promotion for Erin. In addition to which, he wanted to keep her near him.

'I said he was dishy,' Auriol said. 'He may be older but he's very fit. How do you feel now about the other guy?'

Erin sighed. 'I don't really know. I believed him to be the love of my life but then I also believed he truly loved me.'

'In his own way, he probably did. Men have a different view of such things, are able to compartmentalise in a way most women can't.'

'Sorry,' said Erin, 'that just won't wash. I put up for years with him having a wife. Never made any demands on him or let her know I existed.' Now that she came to think of it, perhaps that was one of the things she'd done wrong. Maybe she should have tried harder to prove that she loved him. Too late now. He was out of her life and, although it still hurt, she was already learning to cope. The one thing she'd never forgive him for, though, was such total and mindless deception.

When she thought of how alarmed she had been – the midnight flit and the lies she had told, the constant fear that her life was in danger – she couldn't believe he had done it to her. And all because of his loony ideas. And Amy.

Piers could never behave like that. He was a gentleman through and through. The more time they spent together, the more she liked him. He treated her with a proper respect and took serious notice of what she said. The fact he was her ultimate boss was ceasing to be quite so scary. The *Globe* was only one of his things; his newspaper empire spread throughout the world and Piers moved around on a regular basis between his different homes. It was early days yet. She need not feel pressured. But she hoped very much to be always part of his life.

47

Gerald's world had fallen apart although the Commander advised him to wait before he even thought about telling his wife.

'I cannot go into details,' he'd said. 'But this situation should soon be resolved. Trust me. It's not quite as bad as he let you believe.'

It was bad enough. All his money had gone and now their only home as well. He had gambled everything he possessed and lost the lot to the builder.

Sylvia moaned and moped around, spying on neighbours through half-closed drapes. Though, now it was winter and the weather severe, none of them ventured out very much. She passed her time checking up on the police.

They were still hard at it in the woods, crawling across the frozen ground, often in driving sleet, seeking evidence. The violent killer, having now struck twice, had left no clues to his whereabouts. All they could do was a minute search and hope that perhaps if he struck again he would make a mistake. Thinking perhaps not politically sound, but by now they were growing desperate. The world was waiting outside the gates; they had to provide some answers.

Poor Ned Thornton, pale and wan, stood shivering by his terrace doors or sometimes pulled on sturdy boots and strode across to the woods to check their progress. They treated him always with courtesy: look what the poor guy had just been through. Though when Gerald attempted to quiz them too he was met with a chilly rebuff.

'Perhaps they think it was me,' he said, warming his hands on the radiator. These houses were fitted with fake gas-fires, quite useless in bitter weather.

'Don't make jokes.' Sylvia was not amused, just wished the sordid proceedings would cease. The rest of the year had been bad enough but now the nights closed in before four and they were left sitting with nothing at all to discuss.

Lately Gerald seemed hardly himself. She had no idea what was bothering him but he hung around in the house all day and no longer went down to the pub. His face was gaunt, he had dropped some weight, and his flashes of humour were very rare. When the girls rang up he usually told her to say he was out or busy. Yet still he refused to confide in her. Sylvia worried which also made her nag.

Meanwhile her daughters were nagging too; life was one long appeal for funds. Having been deprived of Disneyland (Gerald had come up with some excuse) they now felt the need to go skiing in France *en famille*, like the rest of their friends.

'Dad can afford it. Cough up,' they said. 'After all, he can't take it with him.'

Ha ha ha. If only they knew the truth.

When he did go out, Gerald drove to South Zeal and drank alone in a pub where nobody knew him. He had little cash so just stuck to beer. Soon he would be reduced to not buying his round. He talked to Lorelei frequently and expanded his dream of escaping to Spain. She had no idea what dire straits he was in, just that he longed to make a new start to which, to his surprise, she had not said no.

She was the lifeline that kept him sane. If he could survive this major blip, he reckoned there was nothing he could not do. And Oliver Swann had gone suddenly quiet, had not been in touch since the night of the game which did seem odd in view of the situation. He had seen no sign of the yellow car; even the workmen had disappeared, though leaving their tools and the Portaloo as if they were coming back.

The cloakroom had now sprung a leak and they hadn't fixed most of the items on Sylvia's list. Talk about cowboy builders; these were the worst.

Sylvia now had to take the bus which stopped outside at twelve minutes past twelve and got her into the village in fifteen minutes, depending on traffic. The return bus left at twenty to three which gave her time to pick up some food, eat a sandwich and drop into Annie's for a bit of cheering up. She had little cash, just what Gerald doled out from a pension fund that had not yet matured and on which, the odds were, they might have to depend to support them for the rest of their lives. Since Gerald was not yet sixty, this seemed very grim. The one good thing was they owned their home. Without that they would be sunk.

Warm-hearted Annie, who knew what was what and had heard enough rumours to work out the rest, welcomed her now like a genuine friend and part of her tight little circle. No more sniping or sending her up. It was plain that Sylvia was in serious trouble and Annie was always the first to offer support. She made her coffee on the house and allowed her to stay there as long as she liked, warming her hands and catching up on the gossip. She even cut her hair for nothing on the pretext that she was trying out a new style.

Sylvia felt humbled and very contrite. She saw

herself now as a snooty bitch who had turned up her nose at village life as though she were Lady Muck. She felt ashamed of her arrogance as well as her futile social climbing. She was one beat away from asking Annie for work.

And then one day the Commander called and asked for a word with Gerald.

Gerald was making his get-away plans; he had no money but might beg a loan after which he was bound for the Costa Brava on a one-way ticket. Whining Sylvia could cope on her own. He had sacrificed thirty-five years to her and was left with nothing but thanklessness from all three women for whom he had sweated and toiled. Talk about scheming malcontents. It seemed his only role in their lives was to cough up the requisite readies.

Lovely Lorelei was coming too. She had money saved up for a rainy day, enough to rent them a water-side bar until they were back on their feet. They would work together as man and wife and build back their fortunes through sheer hard slog. She was learning Spanish; Gerald would too. New horizons beckoned.

Sylvia had two sons-in-law, both with prospects and steady jobs. She could move in with each in turn as resident granny. And then the Commander rang the bell and Sylvia led him into the room. She hovered as though she wanted to stay but Gerald dispatched her with one freezing look.

The Commander said, 'Things are looking good. It's unlikely that you will lose your home though the situation remains unclear. We still have a lot of legal stuff to get through.'

He outlined the basic situation: that Oliver Swann didn't own the land, had never had any right to build, had simply moved in as a squatter.

Gerald absorbed this with dawning hope. 'But the deeds to my house . . . ' he said.

'Are not worth the paper they're written on,' said the Commander.

He refused a sherry. He had to go. He was up to his neck in the legal side but had wanted to put Gerald's mind at rest as soon as he possibly could.

'So what happens next?' It was hard to take in.

'That,' replied the Commander, 'remains to be seen.'

48

Edward Thornton stood at the window staring out over the snowbound moor. Policemen, heavily clad in stout boots, still laboured away in the falling snow. It was early afternoon but the light was fading. Most of the press corps had gone away, discouraged by Dartmoor and its harsh conditions, though he didn't doubt they'd be back in a flash should anything tangible emerge. This was the place where his Lisa had died; he thought of her now with a softening inside he hadn't always been able to raise in her life-time. He missed her now she was gone for good though her constant presence had got on his nerves. If he had the chance to bring her back he would try again a lot harder.

He crossed the dark landing to his study, to which the door was always kept shut. From here he had a clear view across the carport. The hated Lagonda had gone away. He hoped that bastard would never return. The thought of him daring to dally with Lisa made acid rise in his throat. He stuffed his knuckles into his mouth to stop himself screaming aloud.

A figure emerged from the house next door, carrying rubbish across to the fenced-in enclosure. Her cat walked daintily in her steps, picking his way through the melting slush, so pale he was almost invisible in this weather. She reappeared and he followed her back, as stalwartly faithful as a dog. Ned, who had never had a pet, felt the need of one now.

He heard the bang as her front door closed and experienced an unbearable urge to go round there and see her again. Though he found conversing with women hard, Erin had touched a deep chord in his heart that time she had come to call. He thought of his mother, so brave and strong, who had been the focal point of his life until her horrible death four years ago. Erin reminded him of her: no fuss, no nonsense, entirely sane, mainly concerned with the job in hand, unwilling to be deflected. None of the silly girly stuff that had so much annoyed him in Lisa.

He could hear Erin's footsteps climbing the stairs, the walls in these houses were wafer-thin. It gave him a visceral stirring to think that her bed must be just through the wall. Unless she slept on the floor above. It didn't seem very likely he'd ever find out.

He longed to be able to talk to her, to ring her bell and invite himself in. She had told him to call any time he felt the need. She was a writer, so he believed, here for reasons he didn't know. Working on a book, he remembered her saying. A woman like that, who had a career that encompassed her, would suit him well. His mother had made him stay out of the way while she was busy with patients.

Lisa had too much time on her hands and wittered so much that it drove him mad. She had been a good wife but had wanted to be his mother. He dug through the drawer where he kept the files containing his more artistic work. He had kept it locked since the day he caught Lisa snooping. He spread them out, the drawings he'd done of the saintly woman who had given him birth. What wouldn't he give to be able to turn back the clock.

There were voices below and a car door slammed. A man and a woman in uniform; more of the tiresome invasion of the police. He had told them all they could possibly need, they were doubtless on to the neighbours now. This investigation was taking too long, he wished they would all go away. And then his doorbell rang and he suddenly froze.

Out of courtesy he invited them in. The wind was chill, it was snowing again and they said they wouldn't take much of his time but had a few more questions they'd like him to answer. He wanted to tell them to take off their shoes – Lisa was fussy about such things – but felt he should not, the occasion was far too formal. They came inside and he led them through to the room he hardly used any more. He ought to offer them tea but had no milk.

'Edward Thornton,' Sergeant Hollis said, producing a notebook through which he flicked. He looked very serious; Ned was alarmed. They knew all they needed to know. 'About your mother. In Purley,' he said and something inside Ned died.

Outside there was a terrible noise. All three crossed to the terrace doors to see what was going on. That damned two-seater private plane was circling over the meadow. Ned went wild; that man again. He opened the doors and ran outside then, despite the fact he was still in his slippers, down the steps and across the lawn, waving and screaming abuse. The officers followed him in concern; he could hear their voices summoning help and saw the ones in the distance stop and stare back in his direction.

But Ned only cared about Oliver Swann who he now knew had sullied his wife. If he'd had a gun he'd have loaded it. Instead all he had was a knife.

* * *

The plane was taxiing over the snow, close to the spot where the police squad worked. They pointed towards the 'Keep Out' sign but the pilot just kept on coming.

'I'll have you know that I own this land,' he bellowed at them through a megaphone.

'Back off!' they shouted, waving their arms, but the pilot refused to stop.

They dropped their shovels and then linked arms, approaching the plane in a solid phalanx, but Oliver Swann was belligerent and exercising his rights. Meanwhile, behind them, Ned just kept on running.

'Mr Thornton!' A whistle blew but Ned was taking no notice of them. His life might be on the line but he no longer cared. She had nagged at him and driven him mad and flaunted herself at the local men. First the postman and now this creep, coming here in his fancy plane like a conquering hero. The phalanx had now diverted to him but they couldn't stop him, he ran too fast. Knife in hand, he leapt at the plane, taxiing straight towards him.

The propeller, still turning, caught him full on and he spattered in pieces all over the snow. What was left of his head had been cleanly sliced, one of his eyes, like Peter's, dangling. His rimless glasses flew into the air and landed, undamaged, on the wing.

Along the terrace, curtains twitched as the neighbours peered out to see what was going on. A squad car came ploughing over the grass, its siren going and its headlights flashing and the running policemen stopped in shock, then removed their headgear out of respect. A young one, stopping to take a look, fainted into the snow.

'Case closed,' muttered Sergeant Hollis, shutting his notebook.

As darkness fell and the ambulance came, those left outside started wandering back in. The cold was cruel. There was nothing further to see.

'Was it my fault?' Erin wanted to know, now safely installed by the gatehouse fire with a double brandy against the shock as she tried to expunge the image from her brain.

'You were only doing your job,' Piers said. The one he had given her access to do. Sooner or later the mother's death would have come to light as a matter of course. All they had done was accelerate the process.

They had, for the moment, forgotten the plane. The police were too sickened to think that one through. What they had seen they would never forget, however many more years they spent in the force.

So the opportunist, Oliver Swann, who had come to gloat but had now changed his mind, revved up his engine and flew off into the night.

49

'So he got away with it, just like that?'

'It wasn't his fault. Ned ran into the plane. I think he was making a statement of his own. The poor devil was bonkers.'

'Pretty nasty from what you say.'

'Trust me, you really don't want to know.' It would be months before Erin could sleep through the night.

They were having coffee at Fingle Bridge, sitting outside in their scarves and gloves. It was mid-December. The shallow waters were partly frozen over. Soon they would both be returning to town. Erin's exile was finally up and Auriol had her exhibition to prepare for. The fate of her house and the rest of the land was in the hands of the lawyers.

Erin blamed herself for Ned's death though it must have been only a matter of time before the legal system caught up with him too. He had killed his mother in a frenzied attack purely because she nagged him too much. What would finally have nailed him were the similarities to the murders of Peter and Lisa.

Based on what Ned had said to her, Erin had gone in search of his past using the latest technology, courtesy of the Commander. The trail had started with St Pancras Council and taken her back to his earliest roots: a childhood in Purley, south London, with a distinguished Jungian therapist mother.

He had been a lonely little boy. She had talked to neighbours who told her that. Through his early years his mother had found him an irritating encumbrance. But she'd raised him well, with perfect manners, and publicly they seemed to hit it off. Her brutal murder, hacked to death, had been attributed to a random intruder. Ned, who found the body, had fallen apart.

'So they put him away for a couple of years in a psychiatric institute. For the first eighteen months he was out of it but gradually he recovered. Lately he claimed to have no recollection at all. His mind was a blank.'

Auriol snorted. 'As if,' she said. 'How is it possible that they didn't suspect him?'

'I wondered that,' said Erin. 'And raised the question. It all has to do with the public sector. Somehow it seems he slipped through the cracks. Also he changed location on meeting Lisa.'

Both sat and pondered and stared at the river, thinking about the bouncing dog that neither would ever forget.

'Would you ever have another pet?' asked Erin. She knew she'd be lost without Perseus.

'Impractical,' said Auriol, who had never wanted Jasper in the first place. Which brought them back to Oliver Swann and how her ex had got clean away instead of facing a court of law for theft and mis-appropriation. The charges against him were many, some of them serious.

'I do give him marks for trying,' said Erin. 'In a village like this he might even have won.'

'Had it not been for your valiant friend, the Commander,' Auriol smirked.

Her life had changed immeasurably in the several months since she'd come down here sad, embittered and grieving for her lost marriage. Now her future was bright again with a fresh career and great expectations. Jonathan Kyle, the new rock in her life, was already more than a friend. She looked far better than she had: was slimmer, fitter and off the booze. Her caustic humour was back in spades. For months she had felt little more than an ageing reject. A lot of the way she was feeling now was due to her friendship with Erin.

'We will stay in touch?'

'We most certainly will.' That was understood, they had so much in common. The same warped humour and take on life, the same determination and ambition.

Erin's prospects were rosy too. Her job promotion meant travelling more though she hoped to spend Christmas in the Clerkenwell loft. The Rod thing still hurt and would do for a while. He'd been part of her life for a very long time and she still found it hard to accept how he'd cheated on her. Amy, too; that was almost as bad after all the time she'd devoted to her. She had looked upon her almost as a kid sister.

That, however, was behind her now. It was time to move on. She had few regrets. Though she couldn't wait to get back to the smoke, she would still retain some lasting memories of Dartmoor.

'Will you ever come back?' Auriol asked.

'I doubt it,' she said. She was, and always had been, a city girl.

They finished their coffee and rose to go. Auriol stood squinting into the sky. Somewhere up there, who knows, was her errant ex-husband.

'Well, at least I won't ever see him again.'

'I wouldn't bank on that,' said Erin, laughing.

50

December the twelfth. Another full moon. On Sunday, thank God, she'd be back in the loft with plenty of time to sort herself out and get on with the business of Christmas. Piers was driving her up himself, had said it was the least he could do since she was moving out to make room for Betty.

'Nonsense,' said Erin. 'It is long overdue that I got back to real life.'

She was suddenly dying to get away, back to the noise and the bustle of town, to catch up with friends and let them know the truth about what she'd been doing. Some she had emailed already, of course. The rest she felt deserved a more personal explanation.

Her bags were packed and she'd cleaned the house from top to bottom as well as she could. A cleaner from the village would come to give it a final once over. Not that Betty would notice, of course. It was decades since she had lived in a house, not since her somewhat neglected childhood in Kenya. Effie didn't believe she'd move so was already negotiating to bring the caravan too. Piers had said it could stand in his lower paddock.

Tonight there were drinks in the Ring o'Bells, a last farewell to the friends she had made. There were some people here she would truly miss and intended to stay in touch with. Kasia, for instance, the Polish girl who had turned out to be what she'd said she was: an upwardly mobile immigrant who liked riding. It was funny, now that she knew the truth, the way she had worried about being shot. She well remembered her first night here, being terrified by the storm.

Perseus was asking to be let out but she wasn't sure she should risk it tonight in case he took it into his head to go missing. Cats were like that, with minds of their own, they always seemed to know in advance what changes were being made. He mewed again and rattled the door, his topaz eyes expressive with pleading.

'Go on then,' said Erin. 'If you must.' Their relationship was based on mutual trust. After tomorrow he'd have to revert to being a totally indoors cat, though they did have a modest terrace in Clerkenwell. She opened the door and watched him streak off to the woods.

Auriol arrived. It was time that they got going.

*   *   *

Piers had his vintage Rolls outside. Tonight they were doing the journey in style.

'I almost feel it's cheating,' said Erin. 'And that I should be walking one final time.'

'Not in this freezing cold,' he said. 'And also not at this time of night.' The danger lurking out on the moor had gone but it paid to be careful. She liked his proprietary concern to which she thought she could well get used. No one before had treated her like a lady. She would do one final walk though, before she left, just for old times' sake.

The moon was so bright it was clear as day. The Brennans were getting into their car and shouted to say they would lead the way. Lately both had seemed slightly more relaxed. Sylvia had lost her permanent scowl and somehow seemed subtly humanised. Something seemed to have changed, Erin sensed, since the showdown with Oliver Swann. She wondered what he was up to now, whether or not he would ever return to face the music over the mess he had made. She thought probably not.

Number six, where the Thorntons had lived, was fully lit with every light on. The same police team was in there now, giving it a scrupulous working over. Erin felt sad about Lisa and Ned. In a way they had been victims of each other.

Gerald had opened the gates ahead; the Rolls

swiftly followed him into the road. It was seven o'clock so the homecoming traffic was already thinning out. It brought back the night she had been so scared and the strange encounter so close to her door. If it had been the fabled panther, she was fortunate to have survived. Jenny and Phil had now packed up and gone their separate ways, she back home to the Tavistock force, he to London and Special Branch. Erin was still impressed by the show they'd put on of being a couple.

It was crafty Rod who'd arranged all that in order to make her feel more insecure. She couldn't think how he had managed it but her new awareness of his deviousness was helping her through the pain. A man who could act in such a way to a person he supposedly loved was not the one she had thought she knew and dedicated her life to.

They bowled along past the Sandy Park Inn and the house where Evelyn Waugh once stayed, then took the right fork down the road where she'd first met Effie. She was seeing Effie before she left. The pair of them would, she believed, remain friends. She admired Effie's sharp intelligence and original outlook on life. She had asked her to stay whenever she liked. With Rod off the scene, there would always be plenty of room. Since the night of the seance the two had become close friends.

What was all that about? Erin now wondered. She still hadn't figured things out in her mind but must visit Violet one last time before she left. If that really had been John Endecott's voice expressing his guilt from beyond the grave, then perhaps the Endecott Ghost was not who they thought.

Being Friday night, the pub was packed. The room at the back was reserved for them. The whole of the village seemed clustered there just to see Erin off. She was overwhelmed by the kindness shown and the way the message had been passed round. Even Annie was there with her team of helpers.

Corks were popping, the wine just flowed; the Christmas spirit was alive and well. Everyone gave her a final hug; she would, they said, be very much missed in the village. Somebody popped outside for a smoke and came straight back, extremely concerned. There was, he reported, a bright red glow in the sky. Over Endecott Park.

They raced up there in a convoy of cars but the fire was already so well underway that the terrace of new houses was fully ablaze. Because of the police presence on the site, the fire brigade had arrived in record time. All they could do was stand and stare, the heat from the furnace was too great for anyone to approach beyond the main gates.

'Perseus!' screamed Erin, agonised; at least she had listened to him and let him out. With luck, he was still safe in the depths of the woods.

'Don't worry,' said Auriol, squeezing her arm. 'Cats are natural survivors.'

Not so the houses, though, which were burning like tinder.

Auriol thanked her lucky stars that the bulk of her paintings had been removed. Only that morning Jonathan Kyle had come down from London and picked them up. Sylvia, though, looked pretty distraught. All they owned had been in the house. Gerald seemed more anaesthetised, was hovering around with the hint of a smile; probably just numb with shock. The rest of the houses, fortunately, had already been closed for winter so no one was there.

It was just like the last time, an old man said who lived nearby and had been on the scene the terrible night the manor burnt down in the thirties. Only that time thirty-seven young people had died.

The gatehouse, situated some way off, remained unscathed as it had before. Once the flames were under control and the fire brigade said it was safe to return, Piers invited the homeless few back to his place for the rest of the night. He had plenty of room, he lived alone; it was, he said, the least he could do. Gerald and Sylvia leapt at the chance. Even in her current dazed state, Sylvia's pushiness prevailed. Erin, however, was concentrating on searching the grounds for her cat.

'Please don't worry. He will come home.' Auriol knew about such things and that particular cat was almost preternaturally bright.

Later they sat in the gatehouse kitchen with mugs of cocoa that Erin had made and wondered what possibly could have sparked off the fire. The police had luckily been on the spot or things could have turned out considerably worse. Faulty wiring or simply poor workmanship? No one had ever conclusively proved exactly what had happened before but that was seventy years ago. Any human perpetrator would be a long time dead.

Perseus walked in the next morning, unscathed, though he smelled of smoke when Erin convulsively clutched him. She shut him for safety's sake in the kitchen where he would stay till she left the next day. Rufus didn't appear to mind; it was clear they had met before. Her few bits of luggage had gone up in flames but little that mattered, she travelled light, except for her laptop; there went her notes for the book.

Later she had a date with Effie who hadn't been able to come to the pub. They met for tea in the cottage at five o'clock. The dogs were baking in front of the stove, exhausted by their afternoon walk. Effie produced an elegant sherry to go with the cherry cake. They sat and gossiped and reminisced until it was time for Erin to go.

'I can easily drop you off home,' said Effie, reaching for her car keys.

Erin insisted that wasn't the point. She wanted that final river walk. It epitomised the entire six months she had spent here.

'It's very cold.'

'I am well wrapped up.' She had learnt to layer her clothes like a local.

'Well, if you are sure.'

'I am.' She gave Effie a hug.

Down the hill and across the bridge where a medieval battle was fought, then a sharp right along the sign-posted path she had walked so many Sundays throughout the summer. The moon rode high in a cloudless sky, sailing above the skeletal trees: white and frozen with branches as fragile as glass. The air was so cold it hurt her lungs and her breath hung around her like vapour. Absolute silence; no one was out. All she could hear was the crunch of her boots as she strode along the path that was rimed with frost.

The moon was reflected in the water that stirred so

little it looked like ice. Before her was the first of the kissing-gates. This was the place where she'd first met Piers, striding along with his dog and his gun, masquerading as a country squire. How wrong appearances could be. She'd imagined him then a much older man, at home by the fire with his pipe, working on his memoirs. The thought of it made her laugh aloud, she must remember to tell him.

There were footsteps now as she wrestled the gate and in the distance a figure approached. Tall and erect, as it had been then, moving silently towards her. She edged to the side as she had before, there was not much room to negotiate. One false step and either of them could step backwards into the river.

The figure advanced at a steady pace, glancing neither to left nor right, the face concealed by some kind of a hood, pulled forward against the cold. Clearly a local who knew his stuff; winters like this were the arctic kind. She stood there, politely waiting to greet the stranger. Good evening, she'd say and might offer her hand. They were very friendly, the people round here, and after tomorrow she would not see them again.

But the figure passed her without a glance and she fancied she felt an increasing chill. She took one swift look inside the hood then reeled back in disbelieving shock. Her heart was thumping so hard, she thought it might stop. For within the hood was no face at all, nothing but a swirl of empty mist.

She leaned on the gate to steady herself and when she finally raised her head, the figure, to her relief, was no longer in sight. John Endecott repenting his sin or Violet on her nocturnal patrol? Erin was only thankful she'd never know.

After a pause she pulled out her phone.

'Please come and fetch me,' she said.